MICHELANGELO'S GHOST

**The Jaya Jones Treasure Hunt Mystery Series
by Gigi Pandian**

<u>Novels</u>

ARTIFACT (#1)
PIRATE VISHNU (#2)
QUICKSAND (#3)
MICHELANGELO'S GHOST (#4)

<u>Novellas</u>

FOOL'S GOLD (prequel to ARTIFACT)
(in OTHER PEOPLE'S BAGGAGE)

QUICKSAND (#3)

"Charming characters, a hint of romantic conflict, and just the right amount of danger will garner more fans for this cozy series."
– *Publishers Weekly*

"*Quicksand* has all the ingredients I love—intrigue, witty banter, and a twisty mystery that hopscotches across France!"
– Sara Rosett,
Author of the Ellie Avery Mystery Series

"With a world-class puzzle to solve and riveting plot twists to unravel, *Quicksand* had me on the edge of my seat for the entire book...Don't miss one of the best new mystery series around!"
– Kate Carlisle,
New York Times Bestselling Author of the Bibliophile Mysteries

"A joy-filled ride of suspenseful action, elaborate scams, and witty dialogue. The villains are as wily as the heroes, and every twist is intelligent and unexpected, ensuring that this is a novel that will delight lovers of history, romance, and elaborate capers."
– *Kings River Life Magazine*

PIRATE VISHNU (#2)

"Forget about Indiana Jones. Jaya Jones is swinging into action, using both her mind and wits to solve a mystery...Readers will be ensnared by this entertaining tale."
– *RT Book Reviews* (four stars)

"Pandian's second entry sets a playful tone yet provides enough twists to keep mystery buffs engaged, too. The author streamlines an intricate plot....[and] brings a dynamic freshness to her cozy."
– *Library Journal*

"A delicious tall tale about a treasure map, magicians, musicians, mysterious ancestors, and a few bad men."

— *Mystery Scene Magazine*

"Move over Vicky Bliss and Joan Wilder, historian Jaya Jones is here to stay! Mysterious maps, legendary pirates, and hidden treasure—Jaya's latest quest is a whirlwind of adventure."

— Chantelle Aimée Osman,
The Sirens of Suspense

"*Pirate Vishnu* is fast-paced and fascinating as Jaya's investigation leads her this time to India and back to her own family's secrets."

—Susan C. Shea,
Author of the Dani O'Rourke mysteries

ARTIFACT (#1)

"Pandian's new series may well captivate a generation of readers, combining the suspenseful, mysterious and romantic. Four stars."

— *RT Book Reviews*

"If Indiana Jones had a sister, it would definitely be historian Jaya Jones."

— *Suspense Magazine*

"Witty, clever, and twisty... Do you like Agatha Christie? Elizabeth Peters? Then you're going to love Gigi Pandian."

— Aaron Elkins,
Edgar Award-Winning Author of the Gideon Oliver Mysteries

"Fans of Elizabeth Peters will adore following along with Jaya Jones and a cast of quirky characters as they pursue a fabled treasure."

—Juliet Blackwell,
New York Times Bestselling Author of the Art Lover's Mysteries
(written as Hailey Lind)

MICHELANGELO'S GHOST

A JAYA JONES TREASURE HUNT MYSTERY

GIGI PANDIAN

HENERY PRESS

MICHELANGELO'S GHOST
A Jaya Jones Treasure Hunt Mystery
Part of the Henery Press Mystery Collection

First Edition | October 2016

Henery Press
www.henerypress.com

Copyright © 2016 by Gigi Pandian
Cover art by Stephanie Chontos

Trade Paperback ISBN-13: 978-1-63511-069-2
Digital epub ISBN-13: 978-1-63511-070-8
Kindle ISBN-13: 978-1-63511-071-5
Hardcover Paperback ISBN-13: 978-1-63511-072-2

Printed in the United States of America

To my parents,
for dragging me around the world.

ACKNOWLEDGMENTS

I couldn't ask for a better editorial team than Kendel Lynn, Rachel Jackson, and Erin George at Henery Press. My first novel *Artifact* was the twelfth book they'd ever published, and *Michelangelo's Ghost* is number 114. It's been a wonderful journey to grow as an author along with such a supportive, creative, and fun small press.

Thanks to early readers Stacy Allen, Nancy Adams, Emberly Nesbitt, Sue Parman, Brian Selfon, and Diane Vallere, who pointed out the glaring blind spots I couldn't see in early drafts of *Michelangelo's Ghost*. Local writing pals Mysti Berry, Juliet Blackwell, Michelle Gonzalez, Lisa Hughey, and Emberly Nesbitt saved me from my tendency to procrastinate. If not for them, I'd still be doing laundry instead of typing "the end."

My parents were instrumental, as always. My dad made sure I got the India connections right, and true to her word of being up for helping with anything, my mom spent Mother's Day helping proofread the book—that's motherly dedication!

Words can't adequately express how thankful I am for James, who not only puts up with the long hours I spend writing but also encourages me to spin these tales. And most importantly, now that it's been nearly five years since I survived breast cancer, he makes sure I remember to seize the day.

And special thanks to author Linda Lappin, who lives not far from Bomarzo. Linda welcomed me to her home in a medieval Italian village and helped make sure I didn't slaughter the Italian language in these pages. Any mistakes are my own.

CHAPTER 1

What makes something a treasure?

Is it an object's monetary value? Is it rarity? Beauty? Romantic association? Sentimental attachment? Artistic integrity?

Or perhaps a treasure is something lost and then found. A sense of discovery. A buried object hidden from sight. A puzzle that screams to be solved. The thrill of the hunt. The difficulty in locating it. Maybe it's the person to whom it once belonged. Or anything that once belonged to a pirate.

The people who write to me all had different ideas about what a treasure is. There were a lot of them. That's why I was drowning.

I held a six-inch gargoyle statue in my hands. Its left wing was chipped, making me wonder if the injury was deliberate as it was in depictions of Ganesha, the elephant deity with a broken left tusk. I examined the broken wing, then set the gargoyle on my crowded desk. Finding space required tossing three empty coffee cups into the trash and eking out a few inches between a dozen other trinkets people had sent. The plastic leprechaun was weirding me out, so I turned him away from me.

This gargoyle figurine wasn't a treasure. It wasn't even a clue leading to one. The plaster replica was a small gift from a woman who hoped I'd help her find a missing set of family heirlooms. I opened my laptop and began composing an email to gently point out that a private investigator would be much more useful to her than a historian.

"Building a menagerie of misfit good luck charms?" A

handsome green-eyed man with dark brown skin grinned at me from my office doorway.

"Fish!" I jumped up and gave my brother Mahilan a hug. Even in my high heels, I had to stand on tiptoe to hug him properly. Mahilan was three years older than me, over a foot taller, and had skin several shades darker than mine. Most strikingly, his light green eyes stood out in contrast to my dark brown ones. We were opposites but at the same time unquestionably related. "I wasn't expecting you for a couple of days."

"I especially like the gargoyle. He's got more personality than the others."

"It's the chipped wing that gives him added character."

Hundreds of people had written to me since I helped find a long-lost treasure from India and return it to its homeland. An eager journalist misquoted me, reporting that I'd accept queries about treasures. The misquote spread across the internet, but my corrected quote didn't catch fire.

I shouldn't admit that I took a greater interest in many of the treasure seekers than in sending them polite thank-you notes. I've always maintained I'm not *that kind of historian*. You know the type. Those who seek out far-fetched treasures for fame and glory. One of my old professors, Lilith Vine, had fallen into that trap. It had ruined her career.

But I opened the emails and the physical letters. Every one of them. Sometimes it took me a while to get to them, but I did. I put in the work for the same reason I created an inviting office for my students, complete with comfy chairs and chocolate. If people were interested in history and valued my opinion, how could I not act respectfully in return?

"Please don't tell me I've been so immersed in replying to treasure seekers that I've been sitting at this desk for two days straight," I said. "Although it would explain why I'm so hungry."

Mahilan laughed and gave me another hug. "I've missed you, JJ. San Francisco is too far from LA. Can't you find a teaching job down south?"

"I've got a good life here." I mostly believed it. Nobody's life is perfect, right? "I'm finishing this last set of replies before teaching a class later this morning, but I could meet for lunch—"

"I'm not really here."

"You're not?"

"Our flight arrived an hour ago. Ava forgot a few things so she wanted to stop by the store before we head to Napa for two days of wine tasting and fine dining. I dropped her off at the mall and thought I'd swing by to see you before picking her up."

"Napa? Are you sure that's a good idea? There's a fire raging near there."

"We checked. It's not near where we're staying. You're still up for lunch in two days when we're back, right? I want to be sure you have a chance to meet Ava."

"How can I refuse that invitation? You never let me meet your girlfriends."

"That's not true."

"It's so true."

"Really?"

I nodded. "To be fair, it's probably because you have a new one every two weeks."

"Hmm. I'm going to remain silent so as not to incriminate myself. Anyway, I can't believe you kept that tabla-playing Ganesha statue after Lane broke your heart. Though the craftsmanship is superb. It's from Kochi?"

I nodded mutely as my gaze leapt to the statue in the corner of my office. I hated lying to my brother. It was one thing to keep him out of the loop when all he'd do was worry, but to actively lie to him was a choice he'd perceive as the ultimate betrayal. When I was a kid, Mahilan had been more of a father to me than our dad. We'd been through a lot together, and we didn't keep secrets from each other.

But at the same time, it wasn't safe for anyone to know Lane Peters and I were in a long-distance relationship. I could be putting my brother in danger if I told him the truth. I never meant to find myself dating a man who'd been an art thief before turning his life around, but we can't help who we fall for. Lane and I had tried to stay apart, but it hadn't stuck. So here I was, lying to the people closest to me.

"Since you're hungry," Mahilan continued, thankfully ignorant of the tension that had crept into my body language, "let me buy you your favorite croissant sandwich. You like it with egg, honey, and peanut butter, right?"

"You're nearly the only person who says it without cringing."

"Years of practice."

"Give me one minute," I said. "And then I'm all yours." I sat down at my laptop to finish a three-quarters-written email to the treasure hunter who'd sent the gargoyle. If I didn't do it then, it wouldn't get done. I was at least three weeks behind already. It wasn't my real job, so it was my last priority. I did a quick scan of the other unread treasure-related messages in my inbox, hoping I'd made at least a dent that morning. Good. I was only two weeks behind now. Then an involuntary gasp escaped my lips.

"What's the matter?" Mahilan looked up from his cell phone.

"A ghost," I whispered. "A ghost from the past."

CHAPTER 2

That afternoon, I drove to my old professor's home. Dr. Lilith Vine lived at Sea Ranch, a two-and-a-half-hour drive north of San Francisco, not far from the private university where she now taught.

When a person you believe you've wronged gets in touch with you after years of silence, you grab your keys and go.

I slowed and shifted gears in my roadster on the winding coastal road, glancing in the rearview mirror as I did so. I frowned. Was that the same black jeep that had been behind me since I'd left San Francisco on the Golden Gate Bridge? Even if it was, taking the 101 freeway to Highway 1 was the easiest way to get from San Francisco to coastal northern California. Just because an old professor had something important to tell me in person didn't mean someone was following me. I was overly sensitive because a colleague had once followed me across southwest India while trying to scoop my discovery. I pushed the thought from my mind and focused on the winding asphalt and scenic ocean view—and on Lilith Vine's strange invitation.

Lilith hadn't included details in her email. She wasn't any more forthcoming when I called her, saying it was easier to explain in person. I wondered what ill-conceived idea she'd latched onto this time, though it also crossed my mind that the invitation might be more about reconciling than convincing me of the merits of the farfetched research she'd unearthed. All I could do on the drive was wonder. She'd been civil but curt on the phone, simply inviting me to her house, where she promised to show me something I'd find worth my time. That's why I found myself speeding up the coast after teaching my last class of the day.

The northern California coast was both similar to and the opposite of the beaches I remembered from Goa, India. The Goan coast was filled with seemingly endless sand and lush greenery, whereas jagged cliffs and surly fog covered the northern California coastline. With the drought, the hills to the east looked like brittle haystacks that had been haphazardly strewn about. But both settings had inspired my childhood imagination with their views of the sea. My heart beat faster each time I caught a glimpse of the precarious rocky cliffs along the edge of the twisting coastal highway. I was almost disappointed when I arrived at Lilith's house.

I parked the car and sat looking at the ocean for a few minutes before getting out. What was I doing here? I'd made my decision years ago, when I chose a different path.

A crisp wind blew my bob of black hair around my face as I rang the doorbell next to a farmhouse-style oversized front door. A few seconds later, the door eased open. Gray hair flowed down Lilith's back, tapering just above the folded waistband of her purple yoga pants. Her hair was the same as I remembered it, though her body was thinner with frailty rather than good health. She leaned on an intricately carved cane with a Chinese dragon handle.

"I take it you found the house easily," Lilith said. "Since you're early."

I'd left San Francisco when I said I would, but I'd never been good at sticking to speed limits.

"You're much shorter than I remember," she continued as she ushered me inside and closed the door behind me. "Your personality is far bigger than your body."

"Is that a compliment?"

"Do you need one? You seem to be doing quite well without me. Is that why you took your time getting back to me? It's rather urgent, you know."

"No, I don't know," I said, trying to keep the impatience out of my voice. It was a defensive reaction, I knew, because I'd always felt bad about how we left things. "You didn't tell me anything in the email or on the phone."

"In a few minutes, you'll see why it had to be in person."

I took a deep breath and looked around the high-ceilinged living room. Like many professors, Lilith had filled her house with books. Not like the organized bookshelves you see in movies, but tattered paperbacks and pristine hardbound books sharing the same shelf, next to piles of books on the floor that didn't fit onto the crammed bookshelves. The stone mantel above an ornamental fireplace was lined with framed photographs of her as a younger woman in various locations across the world, most of which included a handsome dark-haired man with a charming lopsided smile.

"I was sorry to hear about your husband," I said softly.

"I got your condolence card. I wasn't expecting that. Not after I ignored you for so long. I've followed your career proudly though." Her lips were dry and devoid of color, but warmth radiated from her smile. For the first time since I'd arrived, I felt that she was glad she'd invited me. She motioned for me to take a seat on a wicker couch and poured me a glass of water from a carafe resting on a mango wood side table adorned with carvings of elephants.

"It's good to see you, Lilith."

"If you'd written back to me sooner—"

"I had to change my email address and phone number after amateur treasure hunters across the world got them. I only read emails that come into my old inbox when I have extra time."

"So it *was* your colleague who pressured you into calling me," Lilith said as she handed me the water. She didn't pour a glass for herself, but lifted a clay coffee mug to her lips. The ice cubes that clinked and the glassy look in her eyes told me she hadn't given up old habits.

"My colleague?"

"He didn't prod you into calling me?"

"Who are you talking about?"

"What was the fellow's name? Krishnan. That was it. Naveen Krishnan."

I groaned. "Naveen?" After such a relaxing drive, the name of my backstabbing colleague was the last thing I wanted to hear.

"His bio was listed next to yours on the history department's website. Unlike yours, his had a link to his email address and phone number. I called him and told him how important it was for me to reach you. He was quite attentive."

I groaned. "I'm sure he was."

"What's that supposed to mean?"

"Naveen Krishnan and I don't collaborate well." Whatever important information Lilith was about to tell me, my rival already knew.

I steadied my breathing. I was getting ahead of myself. I didn't even know what Lilith thought so important that she got in touch after all these years.

Lilith barked a laugh. "Don't worry. I haven't told anyone else about what I'm telling you. Don't you know me well enough to know that? I simply told him it was important I reach you." She lifted the mug to her lips and took a long sip. The look of relief on her face confirmed my suspicions that it was stronger than water.

"What exactly is it that you're telling me?"

"I've done it," she said. "I've found something big. Something that will redeem my reputation. I know you all think I've been chasing the ghost of that first discovery in my twenties, but I'm not crazy, Jaya. I'm not. This time, the ghost is real."

CHAPTER 3

My expectations shrank to a speck smaller than the tip of my stilettos. I'd heard Lilith's claims before.

Seven years ago, Lilith Vine had been a professor at the university where I was a first-year graduate student. She'd been granted tenure based on a notable discovery in Sri Lanka that she'd made while she was a PhD student. Following a clue in the novel of an early 19th century British soldier who fought in the Kandyan Wars, Lilith discovered an ancient religious text that had been preserved in a small temple.

It was clever research for a young historian studying religious history. She used fiction as a primary source for her historical research, realizing that much of what's recorded as fiction is based in fact. The combination of diligent research and creativity had led her to the connection nobody else had drawn.

That early success had gone to her head. She wanted to capture the fleeting feelings granted by fame and prestige. Instead of focusing on her work, she flitted from one project to the next, publishing fantastical ideas with nothing to back up her assertions. Because a reference in a pulpy novel had led her to a real-life discovery, she gave too much weight to potential facts in fiction. The more she struck out, the more she drank. She'd once been a draw for the university, but soon became a laughingstock. She was giving historians a bad name—and they noticed.

Even though tenure meant she couldn't be fired, she was given the least desirable teaching assignments and was shunned by her colleagues, making her life miserable. Lilith didn't have many options. She'd burned all of her bridges except one. She got an offer from a small university in northern California, and she wanted me to follow her there, offering to be my advisor in her new position.

A big part of me was drawn to Lilith. Her passion for her work was contagious. I had chosen my graduate program in part because of Lilith's interest in early trade routes across South Asia. That's why I said yes—before thinking better of it and reneging.

It was that false hope I'd given her that made me feel guilty. It's one thing to respectfully decline an offer. It's another to give someone hope before ripping it away from them. When other professors came to me and told me I'd be throwing away my career by following her, I listened to them. I picked the responsible, safe path. I chose to believe what everyone else told me: Lilith Vine was a crackpot.

It was the right decision to stay and work with Professor Stefano Gopal, but at the same time I'd wondered if Lilith had been unfairly judged. And I'd wondered what I might miss out on by choosing the safe road.

Looking at Lilith's earnest, drawn face, I asked myself the same questions yet again.

She picked up a leather-bound book. The dimensions were slightly larger than modern letter-size paper, and the cover was faded and dusty. There was no title, so I wondered if it was a ledger or diary. Whatever it was, it was old. The tremor in Lilith's hand as she held it up was barely perceptible. I wouldn't have noticed it if it hadn't visibly annoyed her.

"This," she said, waving the book in her hand, "is a sketchbook from 16th century Italy."

"You're studying art history now?" It was a perfect example of why she couldn't be trusted.

She waved off my question. "What do you know about Renaissance Italy?"

"About as much as a college freshman. Which is why I don't pretend to study it."

"Don't be so narrow-minded, Jaya. Art and religion are inexorably linked. I thought you had an imagination. That you were different. That's why I thought we'd make such a great team."

I kept my mouth shut.

"All right," Lilith said with a sigh. "The least you can do is humor me by hearing me out before you leave."

"I didn't say anything."

"You didn't have to. The look on your face. It's how they all look at me."

I realized I'd been sitting with my arms crossed stiffly across my chest. I relaxed the tense posture. "I didn't mean to—"

"I don't care what you meant. Just listen." She paused and took another swig. "I've discovered the missing artwork of a man who was a protégé of Michelangelo."

"*The* Michelangelo? The Sistine Chapel? *David?*"

"The one and only. Lazzaro Allegri was an artist hailed as a genius who might have rivaled the master—until he disappeared."

She sat back and waited for my reaction. Was I supposed to be intrigued by the fact that an artist had "disappeared"? It was the 16th century. Poor Lazzaro probably ate a tainted piece of meat or fell out of a window.

"I'm not a Renaissance historian," I said. "I'm flattered you thought of me after all this time, I really am, but why exactly did you bring me here today?"

"I found out where Lazzaro Allegri went when he disappeared. The artist abandoned his patronages in Italy. He went to India."

In spite of my better judgment, she now had my full attention. So much so that I nearly kicked over a stack of books piled next to the couch.

"Michelangelo's protégé," Lilith continued, "who applied Renaissance painting techniques to Indian subjects over five hundred years ago. This is a magnificent treasure, Jaya. Do you realize the significance?"

"It would be a big deal," I agreed. "My research on trade between Europe and India didn't delve much into art, but my advisor Stefano Gopal had been interested in the lack of artistic collaboration even when other aspects of culture melded.

"That's an understatement. This is bigger than anything I've seen discovered in my career."

More importantly, unlike many of Lilith's "discoveries," this was something I could believe truly existed. A missing connection in history that Stefano and others had always assumed existed but never been able to prove. "A Renaissance master who worked under Michelangelo," I said, "who created paintings that bridged Europe and Asia."

"For the second time in my life," Lilith said, raising her glass toward the thick wooden beams of her sloping ceiling, "I've found the truth that nobody else knew how to find. I need your help to prove it."

I looked into her desperate eyes. What had I gotten myself into by coming here today?

CHAPTER 4

"This sounds enticing," I said, and I meant it. Stefano Gopal would have been salivating if he'd been there with me. "But I don't know anything about Italy. I've never even been there. Surely there's someone better equipped to prove the paintings' value and validate your work. Professor Gopal wouldn't steal your work, if that's what you're worried about."

"I don't trust that man," Lilith said. The sudden coldness in her voice made me shiver. "You are *not* to tell him what I'm about to tell you. Do you understand?"

I imagined her rapping my knuckles with her cane if I were to disagree. "I won't say anything."

"Besides," she said with a wave of her hand and a smile on her face, "even if I trusted him, he's not who I need. You are. You're someone who knows about European trade with India in the 1500s, when Lazzaro Allegri lived. But of much more importance to me is that you're a historian with an imagination. That's why I wanted to take you with me when I moved universities. I wasn't wrong about you. Your discoveries have proven me right."

My insides twisted. I was betraying her all over again by giving her hope today, then letting her down. "I can't help you, Lilith. I wish I could, but I'm really not the right—"

"Tell me, what's your guess as to how an Italian nobleman found his way to India?"

"Are you distracting me or testing me?"

"Maybe a little of both."

I closed my eyes and remembered Lilith as she was when she was leading my first-year seminar. "What are the dates?"

"1528 to 1550. Lazzaro Allegri was in India for more than two decades before returning to Italy."

"He returned? I thought you said—"

"I'll get to the reason why in a moment. But first..." She let her unfinished sentence dangle in the air and motioned for me to answer her question.

I thought through the possibilities. "He could have been a missionary. A lot of Catholics went to India around that time. More were Portuguese, but I think there were some Italians. But I doubt that's what happened in Lazzaro's case. You said he was a painter. Italian artists and architects were in high demand. Or the marble trade could have put him in touch with Indian patrons. Many sultans at the time were great patrons of the arts."

"I knew it was right of me to contact you. You let your imagination guide you. Most historians would have refused to answer that question before doing more research."

"My imagination fails me now," I said. "If you've found Lazzaro's lost paintings, why get in touch with me? If you want someone who can help you figure out how to safely get them into the right hands, I know someone who'd be good to talk with. Two people, actually."

"Let me show you something. Be a dear and bring me that banker's box from the side table."

I obliged as Lilith continued talking.

"Lazzaro combined the Italian religious iconography common in Renaissance paintings with Indian people and settings," she said. "He sent only two of his numerous paintings home, but in a country and time when popes were a combination of royalty, rulers, and rock stars, you can imagine how they were received."

"Not well." All of Lilith's furniture looked either fragile or antique, so I set the cardboard box on the red and gold Persian rug at her feet.

"His paintings were considered blasphemous at the time. Ideas were changing in Italy, but it was still early in the Mannerist movement, and papal circles weren't yet as accepting of pagan icons. That came later. That's why he realized he had to hide the rest."

"As I told you, I don't know much about Italian history. I don't see why you need me to help examine the paintings."

"That's the problem, Jaya. I've only found proof of their existence."

"Wait, you're saying you didn't locate the paintings?"

"Not yet. That's why I need you and that imagination of yours."

I thought about the first "treasure" I'd discovered. A lost treasure from Mughal India that I found through a local legend from the Highlands of Scotland. Even though the riches were from the era of my historical expertise, my existing knowledge wasn't enough to find the solution. Teasing fact from fiction, much as Lilith had done years before me, was the key.

"I think you'd better start at the beginning," I said.

Lilith smiled and nodded. She knew she'd captured my imagination. "This spring, I was reading a paper by Wilson Meeks. You know the name?"

"I read a book of his on trade routes. Well-researched, but difficult to get through. It was great bedtime reading, because it put me to sleep."

"My sentiments exactly. An excellent researcher, a lackluster storyteller. But I noticed something interesting in this paper. It included an excerpt of a letter Italian nobleman Felix Rossi had written to a friend in 1570. He was complaining about the recent death of his blasphemous cousin—"

"Lazzaro Allegri."

"Indeed. The nobleman's wife was Lazzaro Allegri's niece. The letter's author, Rossi, considered Lazzaro's paintings of India abominations and wanted to gain favor with the Pope. But his wife valued her family's history. A footnote in Wilson's paper led me to the rest of the letters. Rossi's wife insisted on saving her uncle's artwork, rather than destroying it as other members of the family wanted. You see what that means."

"Lazzaro Allegri's masterpieces were saved."

"They're out there, Jaya. Waiting for us to find them. Don't you see? He was misunderstood—just like I am. Like both of us."

"You'd think the Michelangelo connection would have made up for the perceived blasphemy. Michelangelo was one of the artists who was appreciated during his lifetime, right?"

Lilith cleared her throat. "Their connection wasn't well-known."

"Oh?"

"You know how set in their ways scholars can be." She spoke tersely, the frustration rolling off her tongue. "Because Michelangelo was known to be difficult to work with, most Renaissance scholars dismissed evidence that Lazzaro was his protégé."

"Right." I studied Lilith's pursed lips. This was exactly the type of false conclusion she'd drawn countless times that had wrecked her career. "How exactly did you make the connection?"

"I'm not wrong about this, Jaya."

"And why the urgency?" I asked. "You said this was urgent and you wished I'd called you sooner, but all this happened almost five hundred years ago."

"You don't know about Wilson?"

"He hardly seems the type to steal your idea."

"I wish it were that simple. Wilson Meeks had a bad heart. He suffered several heart attacks in recent years, and his health was deteriorating more rapidly this year. Once you and I did more digging, I thought we might have more questions for him about his research."

A smile touched my lips. "You mean since he cites a hundred references in a ten-page paper, he's a walking encyclopedia."

"Quite. Unfortunately, we no longer have that option. He's dead."

My mouth fell open. "What happened?"

"Weren't you listening? He had a bad heart."

"I'm sorry to hear it. And I'm sorry I didn't get your email sooner. But even if I had, and we'd set out together in search of Lazzaro's paintings, what could Wilson have told you? You said yourself this lead was just a footnote to his work. It's not the most important question."

Lilith's glassy eyes sparkled. "I think I know where your mind is going, and you're absolutely right. Tell me what you think the real question is."

"What makes you think Lazzaro's paintings are a treasure that's been safeguarded for four and a half centuries?"

"That, my dear Jaya, is why I brought you here today." Lilith leaned forward and tapped her cane on the lid of the box. "Open the box."

CHAPTER 5

Lilith's box sat on the passenger seat of my roadster. With what I'd seen inside, I felt like I should pull the seatbelt across it. In the scheme of history, the contents of that box were much more valuable than my own life.

I couldn't quite believe Lilith had entrusted me with her discovery, but she'd insisted. She told me she'd traveled to Italy to find Lazzaro's treasure over spring break, but hadn't been able to put the last pieces of the puzzle together. She'd come home without the paintings, but with the clues needed to find them. Which she'd entrusted to me. Based on how difficult the trip through rural Italy had been, she knew her body was too frail to try again. In spite of her reticence to share her findings with others, the time had come. She was passing the torch to me.

The question was: Did I want it?

"All I ask is that you give me some of the credit for putting the pieces together," she said before seeing me out. "You're the only one I trust to not steal my ideas for yourself—and to see this through."

"I can't promise anything," I'd said. But after what I'd seen in the box...

Before starting the car, there was a phone call I had to make. I wished I could have called Stefano as well, but I needed to respect Lilith's wishes.

My finger hovered over my phone for a few moments. I cared more about Lane Peters than I ever meant to, but he inspired mixed feelings in me. His influence played out in unexpected ways. Earlier in the year, on a trip to the Louvre in Paris, I'd learned something unexpected about myself. Henry North, a man who was blackmailing me, made an offhand comment that I was enjoying the thrill of being part of an art heist. As much as I wanted to deny it, North was more right than he knew.

I wasn't a criminal, nor did I have any intention of becoming one. But doing whatever it took to uncover precious knowledge lost to history, especially when it was a cross-cultural connection never previously known? That was a different question. And the answer that desperately wanted to roll off my tongue was that it was damn tempting to chase a lead, regardless of where it took me.

It was late afternoon in San Francisco, meaning it was a decent hour of the morning in Portugal. I tapped the screen of my phone. The sound of ringing echoed through the car.

Lane had gone to Lisbon to help a friend set up a new museum. He'd been taking on a lot of jobs like that lately. I understood his reasons, up to a point. He couldn't return to his graduate program, and therefore he couldn't get a teaching job like mine. He was also paranoid that someone from his past would try to destroy him. "Paranoid" was probably the wrong word, since there was a rational basis for his worry. Even if North kept his end of the bargain, there were others who might wish him harm.

Lane had never hurt anyone, he'd only stolen things from exceedingly wealthy people, and he'd made up for his misdeeds many times over. Surely there was some way to set things right that didn't involve going to jail or running forever. It wasn't easy to see the solution though. That's why we'd had a fight the last time we'd spoken. Yet all I could think about was the joy I'd see in his eyes if he could be a part of bringing an important piece of lost history to light. Finds like this were how he atoned for his past sins.

The ringing stopped. The call had gone to voicemail. I asked Lane to call me back no matter the time. Frustrated that I'd failed to reach him, I drove off with a sharp screech of tires that offended two long-beaked birds that squawked at me as they flew away.

I was supposed to play a set of tabla and sitar music with Sanjay at the Tandoori Palace that night. I hit a snarl of rush hour traffic and realized I wouldn't make it back to San Francisco in time, so I called to let him know.

"You worry too much, Jaya," he said. "I'll be fine. The sitar stands alone."

Normally I'd agree. Not in Sanjay's case. My best friend didn't realize he was one of this hemisphere's worst sitar players, or that Raj turned his sitar microphone down and my tabla mic up. Raj hired professional musicians for the larger weekend crowds at the Indian restaurant. Sanjay and I played there for fun when we were free on weeknights.

When I reached San Francisco, I squeezed the roadster into a semi-legal parking spot—all right, a mostly illegal parking spot—on a precariously steep hill next to Buena Vista Park. The box wasn't too heavy, so I didn't mind walking the three blocks to my apartment. My grumbling stomach was the bigger concern. Lilith had offered me several beverage choices, but she only had stale Girl Scout cookies to offer for sustenance.

Before climbing the steps to my attic apartment I picked up a bowl of Bi Bim Bop—sizzling sesame-roasted rice with beef, vegetables, egg, and plenty of hot sauce—at one of my favorite Korean restaurants in the Haight Ashbury neighborhood near the Victorian.

I kicked off my heels inside the door and stood at the sink as I drank two glasses of water. Sitting down at the round kitchen table that overlooked the entire studio apartment, I ate my steaming dinner as I contemplated what I should do. My next day at the university would be a long one, since there were only two weeks left in the semester. But I couldn't resist the lure of the box from Lilith. I cleared my coffee table, took a deep breath as I glanced at the historical maps tacked to my wall, and opened the box.

The contents should have been in a museum or research library, but here they were in my sloped-ceiling four-hundred-square-foot studio apartment built illegally into the attic of a crumbling yet colorful Victorian house. In addition to Lilith's notes were three original documents.

The three surviving sketchbooks of Lazzaro Allegri.

Lilith had discovered Lazzaro Allegri's 16th-century sketchbooks in the attic of one of his descendants in the ancestral home in the province of Viterbo, Italy.

Though I wasn't an artist or an art historian, Lazzaro Allegri's talent leapt from the pages into my world half a millennia after he'd touched them. I lost track of the hours as I slowly turned the pages, immersed in the details that brought the images to life. Deftly rendered crosshatching showed the life-like muscles of both humble farmers and brave men in battle, and the use of chalk-smudged shadows brought out the power of the mythological creatures that hovered above the mortals. The style of the sketches looked similar to that of Michelangelo. I could see why Lilith wanted to believe there was a connection between Lazzaro and the famous artist.

But that's not what fascinated me most. It was the subjects of the sketches. The setting wasn't Italy. The subjects weren't Italians. The majority of the sketches were of Indian landscapes and people dressed in late-medieval Indian clothing. The opulent style of dress and the heroic battlefield scenes suggested something more: Indian royalty. Did Lazzaro have a royal patron?

Alongside the masterful drawings were notes that Lilith had translated into English. There was no mention of his patron, but something even more compelling. A hidden art studio where Lazzaro's sketches had been realized as paintings. That's what Lilith was searching for.

CHAPTER 6

The next morning, I scowled at my phone. Lane hadn't returned my call.

I was surprised I'd managed to sleep. In my dreams, lightning bolts splashed vibrant color onto black and white landscapes in India and Italy. The settings were vivid, but the people were faceless. Who had lured Lazzaro Allegri from Italy? And why did Lilith believe Lazzaro had a connection to Michelangelo? Neither question was answered in the sketchbooks or in Lilith's notes. Those questions would be at the top of my list when I spoke with Lilith later that day.

Though the sketchbooks contained a few snippets of text, they were mainly filled with hauntingly beautiful drawings of the people of India, plus a smaller number of eerie sketches of Italian settings. Lilith's notes from an interview she had with the present-day Allegri family indicated they didn't know the details of their ancestor, since they thought of him as a blot on their noble past. That's why the sketchbooks had been relegated to the attic, forgotten for generations.

Before heading to campus, I went for a run in Golden Gate Park. With my headphones on, I ran to bhangra beats that carried me past the Japanese Tea Garden, conservatory of flowers, and grove of redwood trees. I passed families on their way to the Cal Academy of Sciences, art students heading to the De Young Museum, and bicyclists enjoying the car-free paths.

Bhangra music combined traditional Punjabi music with

Western pop, a modern example of what's gone on for millennia through human migration. Different cultures sharing and borrowing from each other. Unfortunately, all too often that convergence had turned from sharing to stealing, when powerful men decided it was more lucrative to conquer and subjugate. British trade with India began with mutual benefits, including respect and intermarriage, but turned to war and eventually the rule of the entire country by the British Raj.

On my way home, I picked up a croissant sandwich and a triple-shot Americano with three sugars at Coffee to the People, a café down the street from my apartment. Ever since my first trip to France that spring, croissants hadn't tasted quite as good at home. But the tattooed staff at Coffee to the People no longer raised a pierced eyebrow at me when I asked for my usual topping—egg with honey and peanut butter—which almost made up for the disparity.

I got to the university a few minutes before my office hours started. No time to visit the library, but time to look up Lazzaro Allegri online. A single paragraph had been repeated on multiple online encyclopedias, acknowledging him as a minor Renaissance painter from a noble family from Bomarzo, Italy, a town most famous for its sculpture garden known as the Park of Monsters. The short history didn't include Lilith's assertion that Lazzaro had been Michelangelo's protégé.

I'd do some digging at the library, but I wasn't hopeful. Lazzaro hadn't been deemed important enough to history to merit more than a poorly cited paragraph. If Lilith was right, that was about to change.

I thought about the period of time in which Lazzaro had been in India. 1528 to 1550. The first two Mughal emperors had ruled during that time, but the sketches in Lazzaro's notebooks didn't look like either of them.

A knock on my office door brought me from the 16th century back to the present. A frazzled undergraduate stood in the doorway. It was nearly time for spring semester finals, so I was holding extended office hours. I'd scheduled appointments with more than a dozen students, but there were several more hopeful ones waiting in the hallway when it was time for me to wrap up office hours and grab a late lunch.

Of course I stayed. In spite of their tendency to procrastinate, I loved my students. They were far more important than an artist who'd been dead for centuries.

My students' questions kept me occupied longer than I realized. It was late afternoon by the time I saw the last one who needed help. The blinking light on the phone told me I'd missed a call from Lilith. In her message she said she was going out and asked me to call her back the following afternoon. I squeezed the phone with frustration. I'd have to wait another day to get answers.

If I hurried, at least I'd have time to stop briefly at the library before it was time to head to the Tandoori Palace. I wanted to find Tamarind, the university librarian who was my dear friend and confidante, but she wasn't working when I got there. I left for the restaurant, hoping I'd have time to eat something before our first set of music. Whenever Sanjay and I arrived before the dinner rush, the restaurant's head chef, Juan, insisted on cooking us whatever we wanted. If the kitchen was already bustling, we could feast on whatever extras were already cooked.

My stomach rumbled as I stepped into the fragrant kitchen. I was starving after skipping lunch. The scents of garlic, fennel seed, and toasted coconut made my mouth water.

"Anything new this week?" I asked.

Juan handed me the secret menu. I never knew what would be on it, because a new version was printed every few days or weeks, depending on the seasonal vegetables available. Diners had to know to ask for it. It contained dishes with a higher decibel of spices than most Americans could stomach. For people who grew up in India, however, spicy food was a given, so most dishes at Indian restaurants in America proved disappointing. Nearly everyone who requested the Tandoori Palace secret menu was originally from India or had lived there for longer than a two-week holiday.

"How spicy is the red snapper coconut curry?"

Juan grinned. "Off the charts. You'll love it."

Sanjay stuck his head into the kitchen. His bowler hat still sat on his head, and he carried an old-fashioned suitcase in one hand and a sitar case in the other. He looked like he was ready for a 1960s train trip with the Beatles.

"Saag Paneer and Chicken Tikka Masala, Sanjay?" Juan asked.

"Thanks. Extra mild would be great."

Juan winked at me, then got back to work with the cook who was chopping onions while Sanjay and I retreated into the break room.

"What's with the miniature steamer trunk suitcase?" I asked.

Sanjay tossed his hat onto a coat hook on the other side of the room. The weighted hat for his stage magic act fell perfectly on the hook, complete with a theatrical twirl. "Can't you guess?"

"New illusion?"

"Even better." He unlatched the one-foot square case, which I saw now was only faux antique, and showed me what rested inside.

"A replica of a severed hand holding a pen? I didn't think your act was so macabre."

Sanjay clicked his tongue. "It's a replica of the Houdini Automaton."

I stared at him blankly.

"It recreates Houdini's signature."

I wasn't sure if I was distracted by Lazzaro Allegri's treasure or if Sanjay was being particularly obtuse.

"You know what an automaton is." My best friend spoke slowly as if he were addressing a small child. "Sébastien loves to build them."

"I understand the concept of a mechanical device that's an early form of robot, but a wax hand that channels Houdini?"

"It's plastic. The gears form cursive letters: They're a forgery of Houdini's signature that a magician made long after his death. I still need to get a Houdini dummy to go with the pieces I've got here, but it's still pretty cool, isn't it?"

I picked up the creepy hand. "Sorry I couldn't make it last night. I had the weirdest day. An old professor got in touch and—"

"Not a problem. I might have to bail later this week myself. There's a chance I'll have to go to the theater."

"I thought your summer season shows weren't starting for a couple of weeks."

"With the fires, they're evacuating some areas. If the fire gets anywhere near the winery theater, I'll disassemble some of the illusions and store them in my loft. Truly, you don't see how cool this is? The Hindi Houdini collecting Houdini memorabilia."

"It's disturbing when you refer to yourself in the third person, Sanjay."

Juan brought us our respective spicy and bland dinners and we focused on eating for the few minutes we had before performing. When we were nearly through, Raj popped his head into the break room. "Children! The diners are waiting."

Most patrons didn't know we had a schedule, let alone know we'd be providing background music at all. But we obliged. I slipped off my heels and carried my tabla case to the corner stage.

Sanjay and I had a great rhythm together, in spite of the questionable sounds that emanated from his sitar. Although, was it my imagination or was he getting better? Sanjay had been my best friend since the day I moved to San Francisco. That was two years ago, but I felt like I'd known him my entire life. There was a brief moment when I'd wondered if we might become more than friends, but life hadn't played out that way.

I changed the pace of my tabla beats to keep pace with Sanjay's sitar riff. It was a tough instrument to master, and it was only a hobby for Sanjay to blow off steam when he wasn't performing stage magic to sold-out crowds an hour north of San Francisco in northern California wine country. I smiled to myself as I watched Sanjay's lips part, deep in concentration. He felt my gaze and looked up at me. I don't know why, but I was suddenly embarrassed. I looked away, out at the tables.

One of the diners had requested the secret menu. He was a

man sitting alone with his back to me, but I could see he wasn't a native of India. At least that was a decent guess. He was blond. I wondered if he'd get a shock when his food arrived, or if he knew what he was in for with the super-spicy order. As he spoke to the waiter, I caught a glimpse of his profile.

My right hand slipped off the tabla, causing the tapping rhythm of the raga to come to a halt. Nobody noticed except for Sanjay and the man sitting alone.

His true profile was concealed behind a false nose and most likely something placed in his mouth to give his angular cheeks a rounder shape.

But I'd know him anywhere.

Lane Peters wasn't in Lisbon. He was ten feet away from me at the Tandoori Palace.

CHAPTER 7

As my hand slipped off the tabla, Lane turned toward me. When our eyes met, I could have sworn I ceased drumming, but when I came to my senses a moment later I realized I'd been playing by rote.

Sanjay had met Lane, but he didn't give the man with new features a second glance.

Lane's eyes smiled at me through thick horn-rimmed glasses, and he mouthed the word "sorry" to me.

His eyes stayed locked on mine, and I felt as if he was looking through me. Sanjay knew everything about me—all the outward facts about my life. But Lane was the one who saw through my defenses. Lane was the one who understood what it was like to be so close to fitting in but always be an outsider, without even a country to truly call our own. Lane had never lived in any single country for more than a few years, attending the American schools in whatever country his father's business took him to. Sanjay was born and raised in the affluent Silicon Valley, and had only left California for magic act tours and vacations. My own life was a mix of the two.

Miraculously, I got through the set, during which Lane ate every bite of his spicy secret menu selection. The twenty-minute set wasn't long enough for me to figure out how I was going to explain Lane's disguise, or even his presence, to Sanjay, who didn't know about Lane's past as a thief. All Sanjay knew, or thought he knew, was that I'd had a short relationship with a guy who lived abroad, but the strain of a long-distance relationship had broken us up. It wasn't that far from the truth.

As soon as we wrapped up our improvised raga, I hopped from the stage and maneuvered through the narrow aisles between tables on my way to Lane, never taking my eyes off of him. I feared if I did, he'd disappear into the puff of smoke from the sizzling prawns a waitress carried past his table. My old waitressing instincts kicked in and got me through the obstacle course of tables, servers, and diners in less than five seconds.

I didn't take time to grab my shoes, which should have tipped off Sanjay that something was up, but I needn't have worried about him noticing. He headed for two giggling twenty-somethings who I assumed were some of his groupies. Sanjay was a good-looking guy and a charismatic performer. The Hindi Houdini Heartbreakers were a group of fans, mostly but not entirely women, who adored Sanjay's magic persona, The Hindi Houdini. After one of them discovered he played music at the Tandoori Palace a couple of nights a week, she posted it on their listserv. Ever since then, his fans would periodically show up at the restaurant. Sanjay got a kick out of it, enjoying the fluttering eyelashes during our breaks.

A disguise can hide many things, but even with colored contact lenses, the eyes don't lie. My insides melted as I reached Lane's table and saw the look in his.

"Sorry it took me so long to get here, Jones," he said softly.

With Sanjay distracted, I grabbed Lane's hand and pulled him into the break room, where I locked the door behind us. In close proximity, I breathed in the faint scent of sandalwood and the comfort of being with someone I knew so well and who kept me just off-balance enough to be exciting.

I pressed my back against the break-room door. Lane stood only inches from me. His face was no longer that of a stranger. He'd removed whatever it was that had subtly shifted the shape of his cheeks. His face and hair were now his own, but his dirty blonde hair was shorter than before and no longer fell over his eyes.

"You could have simply called me back," I whispered.

"Isn't this better?"

"Much."

He pulled me to him and drew me into a kiss. Since I wasn't in my heels, I had to stand on my tiptoes, and even then, he lifted me off my feet. If it hadn't been for the lingering spiciness on his tongue, I would have completely lost track of where we were. When I pulled back and he set me down, his glasses were askew.

"How long is your break?" he asked, straightening his glasses.

"Not long enough. And Sanjay is going to recognize you now. Especially if you're with me."

"He didn't seem to be paying attention to you when you two were onstage. Only that poor sitar he was massacring. You, on the other hand..."

"Are you *jealous*?"

Lane looked away from me, toward the locked door. "I didn't realize you two played for tips. I know second-year professors don't make enough to live comfortably in San Francisco, but if you'd told me that finder's fee didn't work out, I'd have—"

"It came through. The jar is there because some diners insist on tipping us. The money we collect goes to a homeless shelter."

Lane squeezed my hand before taking a step toward the door. "I'll be sure to leave a big tip on my way out."

"Wait, you're leaving?"

"I'll see you back at your apartment when you're done here."

"Do you need the key? Never mind. Of course you don't."

I woke up the next morning to the scent of strong coffee and cinnamon.

Lane sat at my kitchen table, the materials from Lilith's box spread out in front of him. Since the apartment was a studio, I could see him from the bed. I pulled on a robe and joined him.

The argument we'd had before he left for Lisbon was the same one we always had. He said he was protecting me by being so cautious. Because of bad choices he'd made when he was young, he'd never be free from looking over his shoulder. I saw his point that he didn't want to pull me down along with him, but what if I was willing to take the risk?

Morning light streamed through my kitchen window onto his disheveled hair. I didn't want to resume the argument.

"It's incredible, isn't it?" I said instead. I already knew his answer. I could see the fire in his eyes as he pored over the sketches. He had an intimate knowledge of art history. He'd tried to get his life on track by getting a PhD in the field, which is how I'd met him.

He threaded his fingers through mine and pulled his eyes from the drawings to my face. "The woman in front of me is even more incredible," he said. "I wish our lives were different, you know. I wish we could be free to show the world."

"I do too. And I wish Lazzaro Allegri hadn't been forced to hide the subjects of his art."

Lane let go of my hand. "The drawings in these parchment sketchbooks are like nothing I've seen before. The method is so similar to Michelangelo, but using techniques he must have learned in India. It's different from the representative style of Indian art from the same period, making it truly a fusion of artistic styles I didn't think existed at the time. And on top of that, the mix of Indian subjects and European mythology—" He tapped his finger on the most jarring sketch.

"The monster," I whispered. I hadn't meant it to come out as a whisper, but the unnerving figure that faded into the crackled page demanded reverence. "The monster that guards Lazzaro's hidden art studio."

CHAPTER 8

"Our monster," Lane said, "is a drawing of a twenty-foot stone carving that exists in Italy's Park of Monsters."

I shivered and pulled the robe tighter around me. "I know. I've already looked through Lazzaro's sketchbooks and my old professor's notes, which included her photographs of the park. But that doesn't make the monster any less creepy. A Renaissance-era garden with huge grotesque stone sculptures that look like the setting for a horror movie. Lost to the ages until it was rediscovered by Salvador Dalí in the late 1930s."

"Dalí helping discover such a macabre garden is perfect, isn't it? *Parco dei Mostri* inspired one of his paintings." He spoke the park's Italian name with a perfect Italian accent. His ability to pick up languages was one of the reasons Lane was so good at blending in wherever he went.

"Unsurprising. The uber-creepy garden isn't far from the Allegri home where Lazzaro lived after he returned from India. Lilith Vine thinks Lazzaro's masterpieces are connected to this Park of Monsters. She thinks his hidden art studio was located near one of the giant carved monsters."

"Lilith Vine?"

"Weren't you listening last night when I told you about my strange meeting with my former professor? She's the one who bought these sketchbooks because they point to Lazzaro's paintings that she's convinced are hidden in a secret art studio."

"Actually, you didn't get very far before we got...distracted. Why don't you start at the beginning?"

I tucked a messy lock of thick black hair behind my ear and thought about where to begin. "Lilith is a historian who threw her career away because she couldn't accept that she wouldn't achieve the same level of fame she had with an early success. She felt betrayed when I didn't follow her to a different university, and I don't blame her. But she got in touch because she thinks I can help her find the lost paintings of Lazzaro Allegri, the promising artist who was misunderstood and ostracized, much like herself."

"Ostracized for throwing away a promising career in Italy and painting in India instead?"

I nodded. "Lilith thinks he was Michelangelo's protégé before he left for India. He wrote only sparing notes in these sketchbooks, so I don't yet know who his Indian patron was, or if he really had a connection to Michelangelo. The only thing his notes make clear was that he had an art studio hidden in the Park of Monsters."

"Why there and not in his own home?"

"When he returned from India, he found himself unwelcomed by his family because he wanted to use Renaissance techniques to paint Indian subjects, not the Catholic depictions his contemporaries were creating. Letters from his cousin indicate his family didn't cast him out, but they wouldn't support his art either. A couple of his early works of art ended up in a museum, so we know he turned his sketches into paintings. Lazzaro Allegri's descendants still live in the ancestral home. That's where they found his sketchbooks, which they sold to Lilith for a hefty price. They had no knowledge of the location of his art studio though."

"Lilith's theory makes sense," I continued. "The Park of Monsters was built by Lazzaro's contemporary Pier Francesco Orsini, who went by the nickname of Vicino and lived not far from the Allegris. Vicino was an Italian nobleman who was a bit of an outcast within his family as well. It's easy to imagine why, as two black sheep in their respectable families, Vicino would let Lazzaro use his larger grounds for his studio. I have to wonder if there was a bit of a mentor relationship as well, because Lazzaro was old enough to be Vicino's father and had already traveled to India when they met."

I paused and looked for the sketch of a stone sea monster. "Lazzaro's notes indicate the art studio grotto is near the Park of Monsters sea monster statue named Proteus, or possibly another sculpture symbolically connected to water, but the grounds were so overgrown that Lilith wasn't able to find it. The park fell into disrepair after Vicino's death, so the studio was lost to the forest. But here's the cool part. You already mentioned Dalí being part of the group that rediscovered it in the thirties. But in the 1950s, a businessman saw an opportunity to create an attraction for Italian families. He did the initial work for us, clearing out much of the grounds. It's only been partly renovated, and much of it is still overgrown forest, so it makes perfect sense why Lazzaro's paintings haven't yet been discovered. Whatever secrets Vicino Orsini knew of his gardens, and whatever treasures hidden inside by Lazzaro Allegri, were swallowed up by the woodlands of Italy. For nearly five centuries, the trees have held Lazzaro's art captive."

I stopped my monologue and eyed Lane. "Why are you giving me that goofy lopsided smile?"

"You're even more beautiful when you get immersed in a story. You haven't even gotten yourself a cup of coffee or come up for air."

"Stop trying to distract me. You see why I have to go to Italy."

Lane murmured noncommittally as he stood up and fixed me a cup of coffee.

"What are you mumbling about?" I asked, accepting the mug. Lane had sweetened it not exactly the way I did, but this was even better. A hint of cinnamon accompanied the sugar.

"I hate to burst your bubble, Jones."

"I know these sketchbooks don't say exactly where to find Lazzaro's paintings. That's the whole reason Lilith came to me. She thought she'd identified where at the Park of Monsters Lazzaro's secret art studio was located, but she couldn't find it. But with what you and I can bring to the table—"

"That's not what I mean." He twirled a pencil between his graceful fingers. "Something is missing."

"Obviously something is missing," I snapped. "Lazzaro's missing Renaissance-style paintings of an Indian royal court." I calmed myself by savoring another sip of the exquisite coffee. I'd missed Lane's coffee-making skills, among his other talents.

"Step back and take a look at what Lilith gave you," he said.

"Exactly—look at everything she gave me. There's a treasure hidden somewhere in here."

"I hate to say it, but I think North was right."

"What's that supposed to mean?"

"You want the thrill of the adventure. You haven't stepped back to look at this for what it really is. That's why you're letting people get in touch with you about things like this—"

"What are you talking about? I didn't ask for people to contact me. I'm simply being courteous to people in dealing with this reality. And I called you because I thought this was something you would love. You want to give back to the world, and this is your specialty. You could help bring to light Renaissance paintings of India from a man who very well may have been Michelangelo's protégé. This would be a huge find. I thought it would be exactly the type of thing that would entice you."

"You're right," Lane said. "If there was anything to find."

I stared across the table at him.

The edges of Lane's eyes crinkled behind his glasses as he smiled at me. "God, I do love how passionately you throw yourself into everything you do. But in your excitement at this idea, you skipped a step. Why do we believe there are any paintings worth recovering?"

"I thought the same thing at first. But letters show that his niece prevented his studio from being destroyed, even though he was unpopular."

"That's not what I mean. I didn't ask why you think the paintings exist. I asked why you think there are any paintings *worth recovering*."

"Because of...Well, because—" I stopped myself.

Lane ran his hand through my hair, not seeming to notice how ratty it was. "I'm sorry I have to be the voice of reason, Jones. But even if we find Lazzaro Allegri's hidden grotto studio, and even if his alleged masterpieces are there, there's no chance the paintings survived."

"But the studio is there. Forgotten by generations. Hidden by an overgrown forest."

"I don't doubt that. That's the problem. You're looking for the grotto where he worked in secrecy. This wasn't an art studio inside the family's mansion. We're talking about a cave in the forest where he could paint in peace, away from his judgmental family. Five centuries exposed to the elements. There's no way paintings survived that. If you find them, there will be nothing left but dust."

CHAPTER 9

Lane made plans to return to Portugal later that day. I wasn't sure if he was using the passport issued in his true name—Lancelot Caravaggio Peters—and I didn't want to ask.

"It's right here, in Lazzaro's notes," I said, looking at Lilith's translations yet again as Lane got dressed. "He says his paintings will survive."

"That claim doesn't make him a magician, Jaya." Lane finished buttoning his shirt and joined me at the kitchen table. "He's been dead for nearly five hundred years. He could have had a big ego and assumed history would remember him, or that his cousin would see to it that his artwork made its way into a museum."

"What if it's saying something more? He wouldn't have died without making sure his paintings would be protected. Maybe if I take you to meet Lilith, she can help you get over your reservations. We're supposed to talk on the phone this afternoon, but we could drive up to see her in person. You can catch a later flight."

"That's a bad idea. Who are you going to tell her I am? You know I wish I didn't have to go, but—"

"I know," I growled. "You think it's safer for both of us. But what about a fulfilling life? We take risks the moment we walk outside, regardless of our pasts."

Lane studied my face but didn't speak.

"We don't have to worry about North," I continued. "Or—"

"It's not just them." He spoke slowly and deliberately, as if he were struggling with himself. "There's something else I should have told you. If I had, we could have avoided all of these stupid arguments."

"Then why didn't you?" I meant the words to sound sympathetic, but in my frustration I'm not sure I pulled it off.

He picked up a stray chopstick from the dish rack behind him and twirled it between his fingers. "I didn't want to burden you with knowledge of something that would worry you more."

"That's an even stupider reason than our arguments."

"It's about Mia."

"Oh." I felt a small pang of jealousy—all right, maybe it was a big one—when I thought about Mia. Or to be more precise, Amaia Veronique Alba, the most sophisticated name imaginable for an ex-girlfriend. She was his first love, and she'd died tragically. A lot to live up to.

"I didn't tell you what she did for a living or how she died."

"You did. You told me you two were in college together and she died in a car accident." My mouth went dry. "Are you saying that was a lie?"

"No. That's all true. But it's also not the whole story." He paused. The spinning chopstick became a blur. "Mia," he said, "was a thief."

"Oh." I didn't know why it hadn't occurred to me before.

"We were both putting ourselves through college with our extracurricular activities. But we weren't the same. For me, it was a game, getting back at people like my father who didn't need the toys they'd inherited. You know that. I thought, at first, that Mia was the same. But then—" He swore and broke the chopstick. "She got in over her head. And she died for her sins."

"Are you saying what I think you are?" I felt acid rising in my chest. I wished I hadn't had so many cups of coffee.

Lane swallowed hard. "They killed her, Jones."

I took the broken chopstick from his fingers and took his hands in mine. "I'm so sorry. Why didn't you tell me? You could have, you know."

"I was selfish. I didn't want to lose you. Part of me didn't want you to know just how dangerous knowing me could be."

"You thought I'd get scared off?"

"I should have let you go."

"You tried."

"And failed. I've been at war with myself, wanting to be with you but also wanting you safe. This middle ground hasn't been fair to either of us."

"What happened to her?"

"I never wanted to associate with thieves who were willing to use violence. That's why we split up. She didn't have the same reservations about the people she worked with. There was a museum heist that went wrong. Her partner killed a security guard. The next day, he took care of the only witness to the crime."

"Mia," I whispered. "She trusted the wrong man."

"She didn't know he was dangerous. But she should have guessed. Real life isn't like in the movies. There's no black and white distinction between gentleman thieves and gangsters. Well-intentioned people do what they need to do when things go wrong."

"Not all of them."

"No. But you can't be certain."

"Who—"

"You already know more than you should. I'm only telling you this now so you'll truly believe me about how risky it would be if we told people about us."

"You've never—" The words caught in my throat and I couldn't finish my question.

Lane pulled me close to him and rested his chin on my head. "No. Of course not. I never backed myself into a corner where it was my only option. But the fact that North found you through me showed me I can never truly escape my past. I'm so sorry, Jones. I completely understand if you never want to see me again after I get on that flight."

I wrapped my arms around him more tightly. "I don't think I'm ready to lose you."

"Then can't we just be here like this, enjoying the moments we can steal?"

I didn't seem able to form words. I needed to think. The fact that I was under time pressure didn't help. Lane was leaving soon, I had a class to teach at the university later that morning, then lunch plans with my brother.

Lane extricated himself from my arms and stood up from the table. A moment later he held up my running shoes. "Go. But make it a quick run. That way I can see you before I catch my flight."

"You don't make it easy for me to kick you out of my life, Mr. Mind-reader."

I ran through my neighborhood, not wanting to waste time getting to Golden Gate Park. It was early enough in the day that Haight Ashbury tourists weren't in full force, so there was room on the sidewalk. The locals were already off to work or safely ensconced in one of the dozens of cafés that dotted the history-filled neighborhood.

Lane was right. We had no future together. I didn't want to live my life in hiding. I couldn't see a solution. Either way, I lost.

I returned twenty minutes later drenched in sweat. I was back soon enough that Lane was still there. His smile didn't reach his eyes, so I knew he was having the same internal dilemma.

After I took a quick shower and was ready to leave for the university, he helped me put everything Lilith had given me back into the box. He kissed me goodbye on the doorstep, saying he wanted to finish cleaning my kitchen before he caught a cab to the airport.

As my tires screeched yet again, I knew I should have taken a longer run to work out my frustration. Lane was right that there was more danger than I wanted to know about.

I locked up the box of materials in my office file cabinet before teaching a graduate seminar. I was left with a little over half an hour until my lunch with Mahilan. It wouldn't take that long to drive to the restaurant. With plenty of time, I let myself succumb to the pull of Lazzaro Allegri's sketchbooks.

Despite Lane's point that the paintings couldn't have survived, I knew in my gut Lazzaro had left behind something worth finding. He'd given his soul to his work. He wouldn't have left it to be destroyed. He said so himself.

I unlocked my file cabinet and eased the notebooks carefully onto my desk. I could feel the life in the faded pages. Love had been poured into every sketch.

Twenty minutes until I was due at the restaurant.

I ran my fingers along the edges of the textured, gently crackling parchment pages that had breathed in the elements for centuries. As soon as Lilith and I were done following the sketchbook's clues to find Lazzaro's true treasure, the sketchbooks would go to a museum. I knew Lilith would agree with me. She'd paid the family thousands of Euros for these old notebooks after convincing them she was a scholar who only wanted to bring their ancestor's achievements to light.

Ten minutes until I was supposed to be at the restaurant.

I stacked the materials carefully into the banker's box and locked the box in the file cabinet. I was locking my office door when my cell phone buzzed.

I expected it was my punctual brother checking on me, but when I looked at the screen it wasn't his number. No number showed on the screen. Perhaps Mahilan's cell phone had fallen into a vat of wine while he and Ava were wine tasting and he was calling from the restaurant's blocked landline. I picked up. The only sound was a faint breathing.

"Hello?"

"The sketchbook." The words were slurred, but I could tell it was Lilith. I winced as I realized she was drunk. It wasn't even noon.

"I'm on my way to lunch right now. Thanks for calling me back, but I thought you'd be calling later—"

"Sketchbooks," she slurred again.

"Yes, I've had a chance to look at them." I talked as I hurried down the hall. "You're right, they're incredible. And I have a few questions. I'm on my way somewhere right now, but can I call you later this afternoon?"

"You must...know therefore...I'm sorry..."

I stopped walking so quickly my messenger bag slammed painfully into my hip. "Are you all right? Do you need me to call someone? Is anyone there with you?"

A rattling laugh, followed by a whisper. "No. Not alone..."

Oh no. "Who's there with you, Lilith? Is someone—"

"The ghost...Here with me...Should have known...couldn't escape...past."

"I'm calling 911." One thing was becoming abundantly clear. Lilith wasn't drunk. She was terrified. Was she having a heart attack? Or was there something more going on?

"Already called...for help...Come to...hospital." Her breathing was labored and her words more slurred than they had been a minute before.

"I'll be there."

"You need to know...You must know therefore..."

"I'm here." I held the phone between my shoulder and ear and fumbled with my car keys.

"You must know therefore...You must find..."

"Lilith?"

There was no answer.

CHAPTER 10

From the faculty parking lot, I spoke to the emergency operator.

I was worried both that Lilith hadn't been coherent enough to reach them, and that someone who wished her harm might still be there with her. I stayed on the line with the saintly operator until the paramedics arrived, then peeled out of the lot and headed north to Sea Ranch.

As I drove, I replayed Lilith's jumbled words in my mind. Was someone there with her? What had she been trying to tell me? What *must I therefore know*?

The buzz of my phone sounded from inside my messenger bag. I rummaged for it with one hand and groaned when I saw my brother's face on the screen.

"I'm so sorry, Fish," I said, putting him on speakerphone. "An old professor of mine has just been taken to the hospital, and I need to meet her there. I'm not going to make it to lunch."

"It's not Stefano, is it?"

"No, Lilith Vine."

A few seconds of silence followed before Mahilan spoke. "Are you nervous about meeting Ava?"

"What?"

"You've never mentioned being close to this Lilith Vine person before," Mahilan grumbled.

"It's not an excuse." I shifted gears and passed a tour bus on the approach to the Golden Gate Bridge. "Lilith is the professor I knew my first year of grad school. Remember the one who wanted me to follow her to her new university?"

"The crazy alcoholic flake who you felt guilty about for ages?"

"She's not crazy." Why was I so vigorously defending her? "She got in touch with me because she made a big discovery—a real one this time—and she needed my help. Two days ago she gave me a set of 16th-century sketchbooks of an Italian artist that point to a treasure of lost Renaissance paintings connected to India. But then just now..."

"You're breaking up, JJ. I didn't catch the last bit. What happened just now?"

"The connection is fine." My hands felt clammy on the steering wheel, and my mouth as dry as the brush of the coastal hills I was about to drive through. "I didn't finish my sentence."

What *had* happened just now?

I hadn't stopped to think about how big a discovery this truly could be. Lazzaro Allegri's lost masterpieces were interesting to me personally because of a possible new revelation about a cross-cultural influence between Europe and India. And the artwork was compelling to Lilith because it was an academic discovery that could redeem her reputation. I tried to focus on breathing. If the paintings truly existed, they'd be worth a fortune. It was all too believable that someone would threaten and hurt Lilith to get the sketchbooks that led to the paintings.

Lilith's words had been slurred, but it hadn't sounded like she was drunk. Had she been drugged? Had someone been trying to get the truth out of her? Had she told them she'd given the sketchbooks to me? My chest constricted. An SUV honked at me as I accidentally swerved.

"JJ?" my brother prompted. "Are you all right?"

"I'm driving on my way to the hospital. I should concentrate on the road."

"After you bring flowers to the hospital, you should join us for dinner. I'll call you later with details."

"Sounds good," I lied. I clicked off the phone and stared at the highway. What was so important that Lilith would call me while waiting for help to arrive?

* * *

I didn't know which hospital Lilith would be taken to, so once I reached the vicinity, I pulled over and began calling the regional hospitals. I found the right one on the second try. At the reception desk of the right hospital, I said I was Lilith's niece, assuming that was the only way I'd get to see her. Instead of being given the number of a hospital room, I was asked to wait a moment.

"You're Lilith Vine's niece?" a sad voice said from behind me.

I turned and saw a uniformed police officer.

"The thing is..." I began.

"You're not actually her niece, right?" the officer said. I wondered how long he'd been on the force. He didn't look older than my college students. His questioning brown eyes held the same intelligence as my brightest students.

"Not exactly. I care about her though," I added quickly, "and I thought that would be the only way to see her."

The officer took my name and led me away from the crowd of the reception area. "I'm sorry to tell you this, but she didn't make it."

"She didn't make it?" I repeated. He couldn't mean Lilith was dead. She was a force that couldn't be stopped. She'd survived malaria, a plane crash, and decades of faculty meetings. How could she be dead?

He shook his head and gave me a few moments to recover. "You want some water?"

"I'm fine." I couldn't seem to breathe, and my legs were shaking. I sat down, then stood back up. "Shouldn't you be asking me questions? Do you have the person who killed her—"

"Whoa. Say that again."

"You're a police officer. Doesn't that mean I'm right and somebody did this to her?"

"We get called in when there's an overdose. But it looks like she overdosed on legal narcotics. They pumped her stomach and found alcohol and Xanax." He reddened and swore.

"What?"

"I don't think I was supposed to tell you that."

"She was a functioning alcoholic. She had been for decades. She'd never overdo it."

He clenched his jaw and furrowed his brow, causing his young face to transform into that of a much older man. "I haven't been at this job for long, but the things I've seen." He sat down in a waiting room chair next to a table filled with wrinkled pop culture magazines. "People don't know each other as well as they think they do."

"I'm not psychoanalyzing her. I was on the phone with her when she was waiting for the ambulance. Something was wrong. She wasn't alone."

"She told you someone did this to her? Why didn't you say so?"

"I couldn't understand much of what she was saying," I admitted, "but she said someone was there and she was trying to tell me something important."

I told the detective about Lilith's research and how it could be worth killing over. He seemed genuinely interested, gave me his undivided attention, and jotted down a few notes.

"Well?" I said once I'd concluded.

"That's quite a story. I wish I'd had history teachers like you two."

"And the murder?" I said through gritted teeth.

"Oh, that. I didn't buy that part."

"But after everything I told you—"

He snapped his notebook shut. "You've told me the story of a lonely widow who achieved academic fame in her twenties, had been trying to recapture her former glory for forty years, and who self-medicated her depression with alcohol. A normally reserved woman who, when she was wasted and could barely think straight, reached out to the person giving her a last shot at a big discovery, thinking it was important to tell you the last thoughts on her research going through her mind. Tell me again what you heard her say?"

"She talked about someone being there with her—"

"A ghost. You said it was a ghost."

I scowled at him. "And that I needed to know something important."

"People often have epiphanies when they're dying. She could have felt like she was seeing her beloved husband you said died recently, and she wanted to urge you to carry on her research to make the discovery for her once she was gone. It's a tragedy, yes. But it's not murder."

The young officer made a decent case, but a niggling feeling tugged at me. I was missing something. Yes, it was a tragedy that Lilith's brilliance had been wasted by her inability to move beyond recapturing the rush of her early fame. But there was more to it.

In the hospital parking lot, I pulled my car keys from my messenger bag. There was nothing else I could do here. I'd taken off without thinking, and even though I didn't have classes to teach, I was most likely going to miss the entirety of that afternoon's office hours. I called the department secretary and asked if she could put a sign on my door that I was rescheduling.

The long drive gave me a chance to calm down. Was it possible I was creating intrigue where there was none? Was I following in Lilith's footsteps? Did I want danger, fame, and glory, instead of rigorous research, fact checking, and the security of a cozy office I'd have for decades?

My doubts dissipated as soon as I walked into my office. This was where I belonged. In my office I could always trust that I was safe, secure, and damn good at what I did. I closed the door and unlocked my file cabinet.

When I opened the lid of the box, my breath caught. The contents had been moved. While I was on my way to see Lilith Vine, someone had rifled through Lazzaro Allegri's sketchbooks.

CHAPTER 11

"You're sure?" Tamarind asked, her strong hands on my shoulders. "You're absolutely certain someone went through the box since you looked at it earlier today?"

"Positive." I scrunched and unscrunched my toes in my shoes and tried to focus on breathing. It wasn't working. My heart thudded in my chest. Someone had violated my office. In my not-very-well-organized life, my office was a beacon. I was finally finding my footing there.

Once I'd seen that someone had broken into my office and file cabinet, I called Sanjay. As a stage magician he knew a thing or three hundred about locks, so I thought he could check to see if someone had picked them. He didn't answer his phone, so I called one of my other close friends, who also happened to be one of the smartest people I knew. She worked a few hundred feet from my office and arrived within five minutes of my calling.

Tamarind wrinkled her nose as she examined the opened box. "How can you tell? Seriously, it's a bunch of papers and old notebooks."

"I'm sure the contents aren't how I left them. I'm sure I left the burgundy notebook on top. And now it's on the bottom. But I'm the only one with a key to both my office and the file cabinet."

"You look way more freaked out than I'd expect over hypothetical academic espionage."

"This is a big deal." I may have shouted the words. It was a good thing we were such good friends. In addition to being almost a foot taller than my five feet, Tamarind Ortega was big-boned and strong. She got her job as a librarian at the university because of her brains, but her ability to deal with San Francisco's more colorful characters who made their way into the library was a bonus. We became close friends when she helped me with a research project that turned out to be much bigger than the confines of the library.

"Uptight much?"

"I haven't told you the whole story." I sank down into my squeaking desk chair and looked from the maps that adorned my office walls to the menagerie of gifts on the corner of my desk to the solid door I always locked. "I think the person who broke in here just murdered a woman. Lilith Vine, a history professor, died of an overdose this afternoon. I think—" My voice broke. "I think they coerced her into telling them who had these documents. Me." I was glad I hadn't had time to eat lunch. I felt queasy.

"Shut. Up. Did you call the police?"

"Not about this burglary, but I talked to the police about Lilith. They didn't believe me."

I gave Tamarind a quick rundown of the importance of Lazzaro Allegri's Renaissance-style paintings of Indian royalty.

Tamarind crossed her arms, drummed her black-lacquered nails on her biceps, and surveyed my office. "Why didn't the burglar actually *burglarize* anything? These sketchbooks must be worth a small fortune."

"But the paintings are worth a big one. The burglar probably photographed the pages."

"Why not take the notebooks *and* the paintings you think they lead to?"

"Presumably they didn't want me to notice anything had been moved."

"Hmm," Tamarind said. "I'll be back in a sec. Don't go anywhere."

I paced the narrow office, wishing I could call Lane and tell him what was going on. But I knew he'd try to talk me out of going to Italy. That was especially clear after the conversation we'd had that morning. He could be stupidly noble, like his namesake. Was this how things were destined to be? Lying to protect each other?

My relationship with Lane wasn't easy to explain even to myself, because how do you have a proper relationship with someone who's a phantom? My soul was wrenched from me whenever he left. Not because I wasn't content on my own, but because I didn't know when—or if—we'd see each other again. This was no way to live.

Tamarind's reappearance startled me from my thoughts. I hated that I couldn't take her into my confidence about Lane. Besides Sanjay, she was my closest friend in San Francisco.

Tamarind's bright blue hair framed a scowling face. "You look like you've seen a ghost," she said.

"I suppose I have. The ghost of adventures past."

Tamarind opened her pierced lips wide. "You're not actually serious, are you? A ghost? I knew there must be a reason your office is always so cold!"

I pointed up at the air vent. "I can't control the AC. That's why I always keep a sweater in the desk drawer. No ghost. I was speaking figuratively."

"Oh." Tamarind pouted.

"Where did you disappear to?"

"I thought there might be security cameras in your building like there are at the library. No such luck."

"I wish I knew how to tell if a lock had been jimmied," I said.

"Look at you with burglar lingo. But what would that tell you? You're already sure someone looked through your stuff."

"I'm sure. Well, 99 percent sure. I wouldn't mind some proof."

Tamarind grinned and cracked her knuckles. "Stand aside, Jaya." She crouched in front of the file cabinet, cocked her head, and squinted her kohl-lined eyes.

I started to speak, but she held up a finger to shush me.

"Uh-huh," she said. "Just as I suspected."

"You can tell someone forced the lock?"

"No. I suspected I had *no* idea how to tell if a lock had been forced open, and now my suspicions are confirmed."

I sighed. "What if we use my magnifying glass?"

She shook her head. "What's that going to tell us? Only that it's not a virgin lock, which we already knew."

A familiar voice floated down the hallway. I poked my head out the door and saw Naveen Krishnan walking with a student to his office a few doors down from mine. I shut my door and leaned against it.

"Naveen," I said. "He wouldn't think twice about looking through something I'd locked up." Naveen and I had been hired in the history department two years ago, and we weren't sure that both of us would get tenure. Our approaches and specialties were different, but we could both teach intro world history, Asian history, and Indian history courses. If you'd asked me about Naveen last year, I'd have dismissed him as an unprincipled climber. But he'd been the one to save me in an uncomfortable situation that would have cost me my teaching position.

"I thought you two were friends now."

"Not quite. No. I think he helped clear my name because he truly believed it was wrong to beat me in such an unfair way."

"Like a twisted moral code," Tamarind offered.

"Naveen has his own moral code, for sure. But now I'm wondering if he wanted me around for another reason: to steal my research."

"You think he's that Machiavellian?"

"He's certainly smart enough to think through a long-game plan like that. And he knew a once-distinguished professor wanted urgently to meet with me to talk about important research." I shook my head and gripped the edge of the desk, shaking the menagerie of miniature sculptures. "But I can't see him killing Lilith."

"Yeah, it doesn't seem like his style." Tamarind shrugged. Much less of a reaction from her than I expected.

"You're more freaked out by the idea of a ghost than a murderer?" I asked.

"It doesn't sound like a murder, Jaya. She had an addiction. I know too many people who've struggled with that and lost. And she was obsessed with this research. Of course she'd ramble about it while dying."

"You think I'm crazy?"

"I didn't say that. But be realistic. Naveen is a snoop. Not a killer. This office break-in has to be his doing. He belongs here on this floor, so he can hang out outside your office without anyone noticing anything is up."

"That's a good point."

"You want me to scare some sense into Naveen?" Tamarind flexed her not-unimpressive biceps, visible under the sheer swerves of the wispy black blouse she was wearing over a black bustier.

"You didn't let me finish. It's a good point, but it's wrong. You didn't hear Lilith on the phone. Someone did this to her."

The words hung in the air for a few moments before my phone buzzed.

"Why is there a picture of Hrithik Roshan blinking on your phone?" Tamarind asked.

"That's not Hrithik Roshan. That's my brother."

"Shut. Up," Tamarind said. "*That's* your brother?"

Mahilan had darker skin than the Bollywood movie star Tamarind had mistaken him for, but she wasn't wrong about his movie-star good looks. He knew he was gorgeous, and although he used it to his advantage, my older brother hadn't let it go to his head. Well, not completely. He was a lawyer, and at thirty-three, he was a partner at a law firm in Los Angeles. He was a commanding and charismatic figure, so although I'd never seen him in court, I had no doubt he was as successful as his suits suggested. Some people have accused Mahilan of being a playboy or a player, but the simple truth was that he had always fallen in love easily.

"Hi, Fish," I said, picking up the call. I was about to tell him I couldn't make it to dinner, but he sounded so excited I couldn't refuse. "You have a time and place for me to meet you?" I said instead. I scribbled down what he told me.

"Fish?" Tamarind asked after I hung up the phone. "You call that gorgeous creature *Fish?*"

"First, that's my brother we're talking about."

"Point taken. But Fish?"

"I used to abbreviate his name Mahilan to Mahi. He hated it, so I doubled it. Mahi Mahi. Like the fish."

"Cute. Just like your brother."

I stopped by my apartment to freshen up before dinner and give myself a few minutes to think clearly in the security of my sanctuary.

I unlocked the apartment door and saw that true to his word, Lane had cleaned the kitchen, including throwing out the moldy items in the fridge and restocking it with snacks I could eat without lighting a burner. He hadn't touched the piles of research I'd left strewn about. He knew the way my mind worked and how I liked to have my notes spread out.

The kitchen table was now free from dirty dishes, but something had been added. A three-inch intricately carved figurine of a raven. It was immediately apparent that this wasn't a trinket like the gifts in my office. This was an original carving, made of marble. The bottom had the signature of an artist. The raven sat on top of an unsigned note in Lane's handwriting.

The Raven of Lisbon, to watch over you while I can't.

A quick search for the significance of the Raven of Lisbon told me why he'd picked out this particular piece. Legend held that ravens had fiercely protected the remains of a saint on his way home to Lisbon. The raven was now the symbol of the city. They symbolized protection on a journey.

Damn him. Just when I thought I'd made up my mind and was ready to end things, Lane had to go and do the most thoughtful thing.

CHAPTER 12

It felt more surreal than a Salvador Dalí painting that Lilith Vine had died like this. The woman who wanted me to be her protégé. Deluded, scattered, alcoholic. But at the same time, she was brilliant, passionate, and genuine.

Lilith hadn't wanted me to talk to the professor she felt had been part of my betrayal, but now that she was gone, my old advisor Stefano Gopal was my best hope for finishing what Lilith had started. I sent him an email asking for help, trying to stress the importance of my request while not seeming crazy. I don't know what compelled me to make the suggestion I did, or if I pulled off not sounding foolish, but before I could censor myself, I hit send.

I drove to the Cliff House to meet Mahilan and Ava for dinner. My brother had picked out the tried and true San Francisco institution. It was awful timing, but life doesn't wait for convenient moments. I doubted Mahilan would still be dating Ava in a month, but it was important to him that I meet her, so I went.

The sky was hazy. Wind must have pushed the smoke from the nearby forest fires across the Golden Gate. Though it wasn't yet the official fire season, the California drought had brought fires early this year.

Stepping into the restaurant's bar, I spotted my brother immediately. And despite the fact I hadn't even seen a picture of her, I also spotted Ava.

My brother had a type: powerful women. Some of them were whip-smart and gregarious, some pushy and assertive, and some calmly commanding. But none of the few I'd met had been completely unreadable. Ava was different. I couldn't tell if she was upset that I'd ruined what she was hoping would be a romantic dinner alone with my brother, or if her personality was always frosty.

"I'm glad you could join us for dinner," she said as she gave me a crushing handshake that left me feeling like I was being embraced by a clamp of icicles. "I'm so sorry to hear your friend is in the hospital. I hope she's okay." In her high heels, Ava was over six feet tall. Even though I only reached five feet in socks, I didn't normally feel like people were looking down their noses at me. Ava was the exception.

"Let's not talk about her tonight," I said, standing up straighter in my quite inadequate three-inch heels.

"Jaya loves being mysterious," Mahilan said.

Ava appraised me as I appraised her. I couldn't place her accent. It was almost American, but her inflections suggested she was European. Probably well-educated and well-traveled, which explained Mahilan's attraction. Not to mention the fact that her stylish pixie-cut black hair framed a face that could have adorned fashion magazines. Mahilan had told me she was close to his age, in her mid-thirties, and had a thirteen-year-old son who was in boarding school because Ava traveled so much for work.

"I don't mean to be mysterious," I said. "I simply didn't want to be a downer this evening. She passed away at the hospital."

"JJ." Mahilan gave me a hug. "I'm so sorry."

"I hadn't seen her in years until this week, then memories came back to me when I saw her. I don't think I'm ready to talk about it yet." More than memories, a double-sided fear that would completely ruin dinner if I explained it. Fear over a murderer nobody believed was real. And even if I were wrong about that— which I wasn't—I was gripped with a more personal fear: Was I becoming Lilith Vine? As much as I wanted the stability of academia, I craved the rush of finding lost knowledge, wherever it took me.

A hostess led us to a table with a view of the ocean. We spent the next few minutes appreciating the dramatic vista while we looked over the menu. By telling them Lilith had died, even though I hadn't shared my suspicion of murder, I feared I'd spoiled dinner before it began.

Ava eyed my red messenger bag, which I supposed was a faux pas at an upscale restaurant. Especially since it was even bulkier than usual. Carefully tucked inside were Lazzaro Allegri's three sketchbooks. There was no way those were leaving my sight. I tucked the bag under the table and wound the strap around my ankle.

I'd missed lunch, so I was ravenous. I felt like a clod shoveling food into my mouth next to the graceful Ava.

"You going to see Dad while you're up here?" I asked.

Mahilan shook his head. "He's staying with a friend on a commune in the middle of nowhere this month. Teaching sitar to the retreat attendees in exchange for room and board and yoga classes. Typical." He sighed, looking like a disappointed father rather than the other way around. "So what's the deal with this India-Italy Renaissance connection?"

I gave a start. I'd forgotten I'd mentioned Lazzaro Allegri when we spoke, before I realized Lilith had been murdered. I was glad he brought up Italy though, because talking about the Renaissance ended up giving us something to discuss during what otherwise would have been an awkward dinner. Everyone loves Italy, so we all had something to add.

"A Renaissance painter who spent some time in Italy may have painted portraits of an Indian court," I explained, "which would be a connection nobody's seen before."

"The Renaissance isn't all it's cracked up to be," Ava said.

Mahilan set his fork down. "You're joking."

"They were simply 'rediscovering' classical work. And treating it like it was the center of the universe. Zen monasteries in Japan were doing a lot more radical painting at the time. I don't know much about Indian art, but I bet they were having their own Renaissance that never got a catchy name."

"Renaissance artists raised their stature from that of laborers to real craftsmen," Mahilan said. "And the art, it speaks for itself."

"Wasn't a lot of their art financed by the Mafia?" I asked.

"The Medici weren't exactly Mafia," Mahilan said.

"Don't forget the corrupt popes," Ava added. She was growing on me already.

"Enough about art," Mahilan said. "Italy has some terrific ghost stories too."

Ava laughed. "I was certain you were going to say wine. That's why we were talking about going on a real vacation there."

"That too." Mahilan grinned and took a sip of his wine. "I remember the stories more though, because Italians are both dramatic and superstitious. A great combination for producing memorable ghost stories."

As the sun sank beneath the horizon and we ate bountiful plates of seafood, Mahilan told us two ghost stories—neither of which he remembered the ending to.

"If you'll excuse me," Ava said after the waiter cleared our plates. "It's time for me to call Carey. I'll be back in a few minutes. Will you order me a coffee?" She ran her hands across Mahilan's shoulders as she left the table.

With a mischievous smile on his face, Mahilan watched her walk away, then leaned over to me. "You do remember why I know so much about Italy and the Renaissance, don't you?"

"How could I forget? You said Renaissance art history classes were a fantastic way to meet women."

"You don't forget anything, do you, JJ?"

"So who's Carey?"

"Her son. She calls him every night at the time when he's waking up in the morning in Switzerland. She sends him a care package nearly every day. Or at the very least, a postcard. That way he knows how much she loves him, even though she can't be there with him. She wishes she didn't have to be apart from him, but as a single mom she has to make a good living, and her job working with multinational corporations has her on the road a lot."

I revised my initial impression of Ava. "She was standoffish because I invaded what was supposed to be a rare romantic dinner for the two of you, wasn't she?"

"Yeah, sorry about that. I really wanted to spend time with you, and have you meet Ava."

"She's Swiss?"

"Oh, you mean because her son is in boarding school there? No, she's a mutt, like us." Mahilan grinned. "It's one of the reasons we hit it off so well. She's half Basque and half Japanese. She grew up in Spain before going to school in England and the U.S. We all have a lot in common. I know you two are going to be great friends."

"Way to put the pressure on, Fish."

Mahilan caught the waiter's eye and ordered Ava's requested coffee, along with a dessert she hadn't.

Mahilan squeezed Ava's hand as she sat back down. He had a look on his face that reminded me of how happy he'd been when he'd started a dog-walking business in middle school. Mahilan had always loved animals, but our father wouldn't let us have pets. Though my brother was a ruthless lawyer in court and a powerful man in life in general, when he spent time with animals he melted. Just like he was melting in the presence of Ava.

Ava caught me looking between the two of them and smiled. "So," she said, extricating her hands from Mahilan's and resting her elbows on the edge of the table. "Is there a man in your life, Jaya?"

"No, I've only been in San Francisco for—"

"It's been nearly two years, Jaya," Mahilan cut in with a straight face. "Haven't you led Sanjay on for long enough? It's obvious you two love each other."

"Of course we love each other," I said. "He's my best friend. We wouldn't be very good best friends if we didn't love each other." I felt heat rising in my cheeks and hoped I wasn't visibly blushing. Ava watched me with amused interest, and it looked like she was going to say something, but I was saved by the waiter delivering our coffees and a chocolate torte with three spoons.

"You take him for granted, JJ," Mahilan said. "I hope you realize that before it's too late."

"I'm a great best friend."

"There's something you should know about my sister," Mahilan said to Ava. "She's brilliant, but clueless."

I said goodbye to Mahilan and Ava in the cliff-side parking lot overlooking the Pacific Ocean. A crescent-shaped sliver of the moon hung above us, with wisps of fog breaking up a cloudless night.

Mahilan gave me a warm hug, and Ava shook my hand. But unlike the cold and formal handshake that had greeted me three hours before, this one was warm and friendly. She clasped my hand in both of hers.

"I'm so glad this worked out to meet you," she said.

"Me too. Keep Fish out of trouble."

My phone buzzed. I'd missed three text messages from Sanjay, asking me to call him. This couldn't be good.

I waved goodbye to Mahilan and Ava, and called Sanjay back as I watched them drive out of the parking lot.

"Sanjay, sorry I missed you. I've had the strangest day."

"It's gone, Jaya," he said "It's all gone. All of my magic props. All of them. Gone."

I stared out at the black ocean. "You were burglarized too?"

"It was the Napa Valley fire. The wind changed. The flames got too close to the theater. I wanted to go inside to save my things, but the fire department wasn't letting anyone through. The fire got out of control. My theater burned down."

CHAPTER 13

I looked up at the hazy night sky, realizing the ashes from nearby fires were mixing with the fog.

"You're okay?" I asked. "You and your crew weren't hurt?" What would I do if anything happened to Sanjay?

"We're fine," Sanjay said. "One firefighter was hospitalized, but he's okay. But Jaya, the whole street burned."

"I'm so sorry," I whispered. I'd never heard Sanjay sound so defeated.

"What am I supposed to do? Wait. You said something a minute ago. You asked if I was robbed *too*. You were robbed?"

"No, sorry. I wasn't robbed."

"Are you lying to me?"

"Of course not," I said. "It wasn't an actually robbery. It's more complicated—"

"The Hindi Houdini sees all. His magic sees through all falsehoods."

"Do the Hindi Houdini Heartbreakers love it when you speak about yourself in the third person?"

"Yeah, they kinda do." He laughed for a second, then stopped mid-chortle. "Don't change the subject."

"You're the one who was interrupting me! Nothing was stolen."

"That sounds like misdirection to me. You were mugged but nothing was taken? I always thought that neighborhood of yours was trouble."

"Someone was inside my office spying on my research. It's a big deal because—"

"Oh, is that all? Okay, good. That uptight colleague of yours isn't a threat. I can go back to complaining. I had all of my new illusions there. I've been preparing for a new act for the summer season, so I'd moved nearly everything from my loft up to the theater. We've been monitoring the fires, and it was supposed to be safe. I didn't know the winds could change so quickly. By the time I'd driven up, the area was already cordoned off. What am I supposed to do now?"

"Are you home? Do you want me to come over?"

"You're not too busy? You weren't answering your phone."

"I'll be right there."

It was probably for the best that Sanjay had cut me off and not given me a chance to tell him about Lilith. In spite of his steadfastness, he'd always had an immaturity that made him seem much younger.

I stopped in the Mission to pick up tamales on my way over to Sanjay's loft in San Francisco's SoMa neighborhood. Sanjay was on the phone when I arrived, so he waved me inside before retreating to his office. I walked past his framed collection of classic magic show posters, underneath the gargoyle perched above the archway leading to the kitchen, and unpacked the food on the marble counter.

"Insurance rep," he said when he joined me a minute later. He was dressed in sweatpants and a t-shirt. Not a good sign. Sanjay performed in a tuxedo, and his casual clothing wasn't too many steps down from formal wear.

"Is everything okay?"

"Nothing is okay."

I guessed it was one of those days.

"I'm covered monetarily," he continued, "but who cares? Those illusions were years of work."

"You could recreate them—"

"And perform where? That winery was the perfect venue for

me. It let me avoid the Vegas scene but still charge high ticket prices. I'd carved out my own unique niche in the world of magic. Oh, are those tamales from the Tamale Lady?"

"What else?"

He scooped me into a hug, squeezing me so tightly he lifted me off the black and white checkered kitchen floor. "Thanks for coming over," he said into my hair. I felt more comforted and alive in his arms than I should have. The few seconds in which I thought he might have been hurt had been harrowing. More than I could take on this awful day.

Sanjay poured more whiskey than was wise into two tumblers. Sitting on bar stools around the kitchen island of his loft, I drank too many glasses without realizing what I was doing. No, that wasn't true. I knew exactly what I was doing. I was trying to distract myself from the knowledge that Lilith Vine had been murdered and I was in possession of her Renaissance sketchbooks.

I helped myself to another tamale and made a mental note to go for an extra long run the next day. Though the way my head was spinning from the liquor, I doubted I'd remember. What had I been thinking a moment before?

"Maybe it's time for a change," Sanjay said as he polished off the last tamale. "I can wallow or I can take steps to make my life better. What are you doing this summer? Want to go on a road trip? See Americana? Route 66. Goblin Valley. Jackalopes."

Before I realized what I was saying, the words "I'm going to Italy" popped out of my mouth. Followed by a hiccup. How many drinks had Sanjay poured us?

"Since when?"

"It just came up." I hiccupped again. "A research project is leading me to Bomarzo's Park of Monsters. It's a Renaissance sculpture garden filled with giant stone beasts: There's a dragon, a sphinx, an ogre, and other mythological creatures." What had Lilith wanted to tell me about those monsters right before she died? "Sanjay, there's more I should tell you about what happened—"

"Is it like the gardens at Hellbrunn Palace?"

My spinning head tried to focus. "That doesn't sound like a very Italian name."

"It's not. It's a palace near Salzburg, Germany that has hydraulic lever sculptures. They're still functioning, so when I was on tour in Europe a few years ago I made a detour to visit. You'd get a kick out of them. They're called 'water jokes' because unsuspecting guests are sprayed with water from hidden holes in the stones."

"Sounds rather immature."

Sanjay was laughing so hard he didn't hear my comment.

I was in no shape to drive home. I grabbed his spare sleeping bag and tossed it on the couch. I checked my email before going to sleep. Stefano had written me back.

You sound like a spy, my dear Jaya. 7:15 a.m. in front of the northern-most café outside security in the International Terminal at LAX? And not to tell anyone I'm coming? You have my curiosity piqued, as usual. It's a date.

CHAPTER 14

The next morning, I let myself out of Sanjay's loft before dawn to catch a six a.m. flight from SFO to LAX.

While I waited to board, my sleep-deprived brain decided it would be a good idea to do an internet search for something I'd been trying to avoid. Lane hadn't wanted to tell me more about Mia's death. But he'd given me enough information to look it up. I knew it was a museum theft that had taken place when Lane was in college and that a guard was killed. I didn't know the location, but luckily most art thefts didn't lead to murder, so there weren't many choices.

A chill swept over me when I found what had to be the theft in question. Instead of photos of the dead guard, the press had instead opted for something I presumed they thought would be less grisly. But the effect was the opposite. The sight of a blood-splattered calling card sent my imagination into overdrive.

It was a letterpress business card, elegant for its simplicity, with a set of symbols: ^V^. The card had been left at the scene of dozens of unsolved art thefts at museums and private homes. Two thieves, the article stated, had killed a security guard. After that incident, the thief who used the calling card had kept a lower profile and never again used his calling card.

Lane was right. I wished I hadn't looked for more details. I didn't want to know.

After the hour-long flight touched down, I made my way to the international terminal. It wasn't easy to identify the northern-most café outside security, but Stefano Gopal was hard to miss. He stood taller than most men, and his full head of thick white hair made him seem even taller. The white hair stood out in high contrast to his brown skin.

I spotted him standing at a high coffee counter, a child-size paper cup of espresso in his hand as he scanned the crowd through thick glasses. He didn't see me until I was a foot in front of him.

"I feel like I'm in a spy movie," he said with a grin, after kissing both my cheeks. Like my brother's new girlfriend, Stefano spoke with a mostly American accent mixed with an unidentifiable hint of something else. I knew his history, so this was an accent I could place: a combination of Indian and Italian that had mostly washed away after he came to the United States at sixteen. Nearly sixty years had gone by, but there would always be some things we couldn't forget from our pasts.

"It's almost time for finals," he continued, "but I couldn't pass up your invitation."

"Are you finally going to retire this year?"

"Why would I do a silly thing like that?" Deep lines covered his face, more numerous than the last time I'd seen him.

"You've been threatening to since I first met you nearly a decade ago."

He swatted away the comment like a mosquito. "Can you imagine me if I retired? I'd wither away. They'd find my skeleton sitting upright at my home office desk. My students keep me young."

"You've still got us, even when we're no longer your students."

"That I do. Now what have you dragged an old man out of bed for?"

On the flight, through the fog of a hangover, I'd thought about what would be best to tell Dr. Stefano Gopal, the history professor who'd served as my advisor in graduate school after I turned down the offer to follow Lilith. He'd seen promise in me when I wasn't sure it was there myself and helped make me into the scholar I became. He was someone I trusted without reservation. But there was no sense in worrying him about a burglary and possible murder. Nobody had followed me to Los Angeles. I'd booked the flight at midnight and boarded less than six hours later.

I also wasn't sure how he'd respond to the name Lilith Vine. I thought I'd let the evidence speak for itself to get his unbiased opinion. I unwrapped Lazzaro Allegri's sketchbooks, which I'd wrapped in scarves and a plastic bag.

"We have two hours," I said. "I have a class to teach at one o'clock, so I'm on a ten-thirty flight back to San Francisco."

"Let's get to it."

Stefano's face paled as I flipped open the first sketchbook. "*Ada-kadavulae*, Jaya." He flipped the scarf wrapping back on top of the notebook. "My God, what have you done?" He looked furtively around. "I was joking when I said we were in a spy movie. But you—we—these—" His protruding Adam's apple bobbled in his long neck as he swallowed hard.

"I didn't steal these, Stefano. They were purchased from an old Italian family who found them in an attic. They'll go to a museum as soon as I'm done with them." I wondered, now that Lilith was dead, if that were true. Had she bought them legitimately as she'd told me? And she hadn't actually given them to me, just left them with me.

"Good."

"How could you think that I would—?"

"Nothing you do surprises me." Stefano wiped his brow with a tiny napkin from the coffee counter. "Do you remember what I said when you defended your thesis?"

"How could I forget? You said I got inside the minds of the figures in the British East India Company like narrative non-fiction that's being adapted as a screenplay for a big-budget movie. I believe you also added that you were worried I'd give one of the other members of the committee a heart attack, since you were certain he hadn't read anything so exciting since reading Ian Fleming's James Bond novels as a young man."

He chuckled. "That imagination of yours. You bring history to life."

"And that makes you think I'd steal from a museum?" It was truer than he knew, but I wasn't going to tell him that.

"Why don't we get back to this notebook," he said. "Who's the artist?"

"I'd like your opinion from what you see, before I tell you more."

"I'm not an art historian, as you very well know."

"I do. You're the one who taught me the importance of specializing to attain deeper knowledge. That's why I think you'll spot clues in these sketches that you, as someone who studies cross-cultural historical influences on India, will see. I've said too much already. Take a look and tell me what you see."

"The student has become the teacher." Stefano chuckled as he pulled protective gloves from his jacket pocket to turn the pages.

He jotted down notes in his own notebook as he squinted at the sketchbook. He nodded and gasped at regular intervals, occasionally muttering a few words. I caught "a late-medieval kingdom," "not Hindustani classical art," and "sultanate." I watched him while he worked, though I doubted he noticed me or any of the thousands of people hurrying past us.

"Double espresso," he said, not looking up. "Two sugars. And seltzer water."

I obliged, and got myself the same. Stefano wriggled his nose at the soggy paper cup and the plastic bottle of fizzy water. After sixty years, he still missed the way Italians served coffee.

Twenty minutes later, he tucked his pencil into his jacket pocket and met my gaze with fire in his eyes. "I thought, at first, that this was the artwork of a late-medieval kingdom Indian artist who traveled to Italy and learned their techniques and mythology, but these notes...This was an *Italian*." His lips trembled. "It's not Michelangelo, is it?"

"No, but you're close. Very close."

He nodded slowly, the excitement in his eyes growing. "These are sketches of Bomarzo's *Parco dei Mostri*. The Park of Monsters, sometimes referred to as the Sacred Wood." He pronounced the village name not as I'd been imagining, but as *Bomartzo*, adding a T sound to the word, like the pronunciation of pizza.

"You know it?"

"I know it well. Most people outside Italy haven't heard of it, but in Italy it's a big draw for families. With these mythological stone creatures, it's a cross between an amusement park and peaceful gardens. Something for the whole family. I visited several times as a child. That's why my mind leapt to Michelangelo."

"What do you mean?"

Stefano adjusted his thick glasses. "You don't know?"

"Know what?"

"Michelangelo is said to have been the artist who designed the Park of Monsters."

CHAPTER 15

"Are you sure that's not just a local legend that Michelangelo designed the Park of Monsters?" I crossed my arms. "Wasn't your mom a storyteller who embellished everything? My research didn't come up with anything that indicated—"

"In your email," Stefano said, "you said you'd only come into possession of this information a couple of days ago. You couldn't possibly have visited Bomarzo in person. What has your research entailed?"

I mumbled an answer.

"What was that?"

"You're right," I said. "I've only had time to do online research so far."

Stefano shook his finger at me. "You know what a mistake that is."

"It's worse. Much of what I found was conflicting. And after looking at these beautiful drawings, looking at amateur photographs felt like blasphemy."

"What do you think you learned about Bomarzo and its Park of Monsters?"

"In 1552, or thereabouts, nobleman Pier Francesco 'Vicino' Orsini had recently returned from being a prisoner of war in one of the Italian Wars raging across Europe. He envisioned a garden that would shock people's sensibilities, rather than please them with beauty, so he transformed the heavily forested hunting grounds of Bomarzo into a labyrinthine garden of mythological creatures.

Nobody can agree on Vicino's motivation for designing the garden. Was it a tribute to his late wife, or the effort of a man broken by war trying to make sense of religion and the world, or simply an attempt to outdo other noblemen? At the time, it was dubbed a Villa of Wonders and drew visitors including the pope. But Vicino's family never approved. Shortly after his death, his Park of Monsters was overrun by the forests surrounding it. In most of the articles I unearthed, which were few and far between, Vicino's Mannerist sculpture garden was attributed to architect Pirro Ligorio—not Michelangelo."

"Not bad. Pirro worked with Michelangelo on other projects, and according to some art historians, the craftsmanship of many of the beasts suggests Michelangelo's hand more than Pirro's." Stefano shrugged. "Art historians never agree on anything."

"So nobody knows the real architect of the gardens?"

"Only theories."

"What else do you see in the sketchbooks?"

"These sketches of Bahadur Shah of Gujarat's court—"

I gasped. "You know who these figures are?"

"Of course." Stefano blinked at me. "Isn't that why you wanted me to see them?"

"I wanted you to be part of this."

He smiled and patted my hand. "*Grazie.* I'm not one hundred percent certain, of course, since I'm no art historian. But the timing fits."

"A royal court," I murmured. "Lazzaro was lured to India by a royal patron."

"You didn't guess as much, based on the clothing portrayed?"

"I suspected, but the timing also fits with the first and second Mughal emperors, which is where my mind went. But that didn't make sense, because Babur and Humayun weren't patrons of the arts. That didn't come until generations later with Akbar. If he went to India with the patronage of the Sultan of Gujarat, he stayed on after Bahadur Shah's reign." I thought about my original answer to Lilith's question about what would have drawn an Italian to India.

Many European missionaries fell in love with India and stayed on, adopting local customs. It would have made him even more of an outcast when he returned home.

"I would need to do more research to be sure, but Bahadur Shah was a great patron of the arts, long before the Mughals were. He supported Hindustani classical music and art."

"Before he was killed by the Portuguese. They were fighting at the time, explaining these battle scenes. The Sultan wouldn't have trusted any Portuguese men, but an Italian—"

"Very good," Stefano said. "What I'm confused about, though, is that these are all preliminary sketches, as if he's preparing to turn these into more finished pieces of art. The Italian text accompanying some of these illustrations bears this out. The artist's notes describe his studio, and it sounds like he's describing his own private grotto in the forest."

"That's right."

"I didn't think you read Italian. You've had time to get this translated already?"

"The person I got this from translated it."

"The person? No name?"

"I'll get to that. Finish telling me what you gleaned from his notes."

He chuckled again. "All right. In this notebook, many of the sketches of sculptures resemble the famous Renaissance garden. The artist used his own style, so these drawings are distorted. Even so, I recognize many of the carvings: Venus, the Sphynx, Neptune, and Neptune's sea-monster son Proteus. Plus one of the most striking stone carvings: Orcus, a king of the Underworld. The open mouth of the stone beast is a full-size door that people can walk through." He slapped his hands together and grinned gleefully. "Here, his notes on the page with the Orcus sketches say how his artwork will be saved in his studio. He describes the grotto he used as his art studio, and goes on to say it was located there at the sculpture. This is exciting! Why are you frowning, Jaya?"

"Orcus wasn't the sculpture Lilith Vine thought his notes

pointed to. Are you sure you don't mean Proteus?" Was Stefano's childhood association with the gardens clouding his judgment?

"Lilith Vine?" Stefano's glasses slipped down his nose. "That woman is the unnamed person who gave these to you?"

"I didn't want to bias your opinion by leading with that information."

"You're right. It would have made me take these less seriously." He tossed his glasses onto the table and rubbed his eyes. "How did she find it? Did she throw enough darts at the wall that she finally hit another bullseye by accident?"

"Lilith spotted a reference to a master artist's 'blasphemous artwork of heathens' in India in one of Wilson Meeks' papers. To Wilson, it was merely a footnote in a paper on Italian trade in the 16th century. But to Lilith, it suggested Renaissance paintings deemed blasphemous had been saved by the family from destruction—but hidden from public view. The artist's name is Lazzaro Allegri, as you can make out in his signature in these sketchbooks. He was a painter who Lilith thought might have been a protégé of Michelangelo, before leaving the Florentine art scene of Renaissance Italy when he was enticed to go to India—"

"By Bahadur Shah. This is brilliant, Jaya. I can hardly believe Lilith Vine is the one who made the connection."

"Lilith didn't make the royal patronage connection. She was focusing on finding Lazzaro's paintings."

"Lilith is searching for these paintings in his studio?"

"She visited the Park of Monsters but couldn't find it, even though she knows it's connected to one of the statues symbolizing water."

"Water," Stefano murmured. "That's why she formed her theory? If you'd come to me earlier, I could have saved you both some trouble. Lilith isn't fluent in Italian."

"She speaks Italian. I've heard her."

"She's proficient. Not fluent. There's a difference. True fluency includes nuance."

As I knew all too well. Translation was a messy process. It was all too easy to get it wrong. What misled Lilith had misled many people before her. Language had evolved between locations and over time, such as Latin becoming Italian, and countless regional dialects referred to as "Italian." The same was true of English. Even though many of the British East India Company documents I'd consulted were written in English, it would be inaccurate to read a 16ᵗʰ century document as if it were a 21ˢᵗ century one.

"In this sketchbook," Stefano said, "he does write of water. But Lilith misinterpreted the reference."

"*Acqua* seems like a pretty basic word to get wrong."

"*Mi trovate quando diluvia* is what your artist Lazzaro wrote. He used *diluvia*, a word used to describe a biblical flood, so the phrase could be translated as 'You'll find me when it's flooding.' Proteus is a sea monster rising from the grass as if out of a fierce sea. I bet that's why Lilith believes it's the clue, even though the note wasn't next to his sketch of Proteus. Yet notes about Lazzaro's art studio and artwork are next to the Orcus drawings. Why write the notes about his art studio on that page, if it wasn't connected?"

"It's the last page of the sketchbook," I said. "He probably ran out of space. Orcus, the Ogre king, is from the Underworld. From Hell. Of course Lilith would dismiss the proximity of the note and drawing, because I can't see how the Underworld is related to either water or flooding—"

"It's not," Stefano said, "unless you're both fluent in Italian and know the park."

I gaped at Stefano.

"*Mi trovate quando diluvia*," he repeated. "As any native Italian speaker knows, 'diluviare' doesn't simply refer to the water that accumulates during a flood, it actually refers to the exceedingly heavy rainfall that causes the flood. Lazzaro Allegri's note more accurately states: 'You will find me when it is pouring rain.' Orcus is not only the drawing where the artist chose to write his notes, but it's the only creature at the Park of Monsters where you can walk inside to get out of the rain. Inside the Orcus is a sheltered stone room."

The swirl of travelers around us turned into a blur as I stared at my wise old advisor, and the hum of voices disappeared as the sound of my own heartbeat filled my ears.

"Lilith didn't ask the right people for help," I whispered. "She's been searching for his treasure in the wrong place."

CHAPTER 16

"You sound as if you're helping her," Stefano said with a frown.

"I'm afraid it's more than that. Lilith died this week." I didn't want to worry Stefano, so I left it at that. "I'm the one who's picking up the search."

The hunt was calling to me. But it was also calling to an unknown person who was dangerous. I now knew where to find Lazzaro Allegri's paintings. The person who drugged Lilith to get information out of her knew I had the notebooks. Did they also know where to find Lazzaro's treasure?

"Be careful, Jaya." The earlier amusement on Stefano's face had vanished. "Beautiful things have a way of arousing passions in people."

It was time for me to catch my flight, but I promised to keep Stefano posted about what I found.

Now all I had to do was stay ahead of Lilith Vine's killer, find the paintings of Lazzaro Allegri's that linked Renaissance Italy and late-medieval India's royal court in Gujarat, and pray the paintings had survived the test of time. Oh, and survive finals week at the university.

Outwitting a killer wasn't my biggest fear, I realized. It was making sure I didn't become Lilith Vine. After the childhood Mahilan and I had experienced, I wanted stability. Reliability. Didn't I?

I accepted a bag of trail mix from the flight attendant, and immediately crushed it in my hand. It was better than screaming on the short commuter flight from Los Angeles to San Francisco. The man wearing an expensive tailored suit in the seat next to me gave me a sharp glance. I faked a smile, which seemed to convince him I wasn't a danger to anything besides peanuts and pretzels. He forgot about me and returned to reading his tablet.

I looked out the oval window and thought about why this discovery might be worth killing over.

Bahadur Shah, the sultan of Gujarat, lured an Italian master painter to his 16th-century court, while the more famous Mughals were just getting started.

Lazzaro Allegri created Renaissance paintings of Indian royalty, linking Renaissance Italy to India nearly five centuries ago, long before art historians had recorded such a connection.

And if that wasn't enough, Michelangelo had a possible hand in designing the Park of Monsters sculpture garden where Lazzaro had created his masterpieces.

I reduced the bag of trail mix to dust, then hid the evidence of my frustration in the seat pocket in front of me.

Lilith Vine had been drugged to coax her into revealing that I had Lazzaro Allegri's sketchbooks. The valuable sketchbooks that rested at my feet underneath the seat in front of me.

I was certain someone had killed Lilith, but the more I thought about it, the more I doubted they'd actually intended to kill her. They left before she died, leaving her with time to call both an ambulance and me. The killer might not have known how much alcohol she routinely drank, so they didn't know the pills would cause her to overdose. She was a functional alcoholic, so it wasn't easy to spot.

It seemed likely the killer wasn't an expert or they would have used a better truth serum, not simply anxiety medication that would put her into a relaxed state. Unless there were even more drugs in her system that a future tox screen would turn up. Pumping her stomach at the hospital would only have revealed the most obvious drugs. Perhaps she'd even taken the Xanax herself. I really didn't know much of anything.

I gripped the armrest of the plane, causing another furtive glance from my seat mate. I ignored him.

Who was the ghost Lilith had mentioned? Had the accidental killer disguised himself so in her hazy state she believed it was a ghost? And what had Lilith wanted me to know? What "must I therefore know"?

I had thought she was having trouble finishing her sentence, but maybe she was trying to tell me I knew more than I thought I did. Lilith had said she was sorry. Which could have been an apology for lying to me—or for giving me up by telling the killer I had the sketchbooks.

Because the killer hadn't taken the sketchbooks when they had a chance, I could make an educated guess that they weren't after the money such a find could be worth, but wanted the sketchbooks to lead them to the paintings. They already had what they needed, so I didn't need to worry about the sketchbooks at my feet. Right?

Due to heavy fog, the plane circled SFO for twenty minutes before being cleared to land. When we touched down and I turned my phone on, a missed call from my brother blinked on the screen. I listened to the message, which was, unfortunately, in Hindi. Neither of us spoke fluent Hindi, but for the past year Mahilan had been trying to get better at his, so he liked to practice whenever he could.

"I've got a surprise for you, JJ," he said when I called him back on the way to my car.

"How do you know I didn't understand your message and already know the surprise?"

"I've given up on you by now."

"Then why did you leave the message in Hindi?"

"I'm an optimistic pessimist."

I laughed, and the release of tension felt wonderful.

"You've been bugging me that I haven't taken a 'real' vacation in ages," Mahilan said. "I'm finally going to do it. I just finished a big case, which is why Ava and I were able to come up for that wine country getaway. I've got so much vacation time banked that Ava and I decided to go to Italy."

"Your reminiscences of Renaissance art history classes got you interested in Italy again? That's great. Where are you two going?"

"Wherever you are."

"Sorry, I don't think I caught that."

"It's such an interesting challenge you've got. Finding the lost masterpieces of an Italian who traveled to India during the Renaissance. Ava and I can experience Italy and help you at the same time."

I stared at the phone and swore under my breath. How could I head this off? "I'm going really soon, just as soon as finals wrap up this coming week. And don't you two want to take a romantic vacation on your own?"

"We're both Type A overachievers, JJ. Can you imagine me lying on a beach?"

"I can, actually. As long as you had your phone tethered to your hand."

"Touché."

"Truly, Fish, I'd love to take a vacation with you, but this isn't really a vacation." I reached my car and climbed inside.

"I understand. It'll be a working vacation. You can put me to work."

"That's not exactly what I meant." I locked the car doors and looked out at the parking lot. Was my assumption correct that there was no reason for someone to come after me for the sketchbooks? I pushed my messenger bag out of sight under the glove compartment. "There's more to this than I've told you. The professor, Lilith Vine, who brought me the information..."

"The one who passed away?"

"Right. I think her death might not have been an accident. I mean, I believe it was an accidental overdose, but not by her own hand. Someone broke into my office to look at the sketchbooks I told you about after they visited Lilith and drugged her so she'd tell them where Lazzaro Allegri's sketchbooks were. They wanted information, but she accidentally overdosed."

Mahilan swore. "Where are you? The police station?"

"No, the police don't believe me. Hello? Are you still there, Fish?"

"Tell me," he said in his cross-examination voice, "exactly what happened."

I told him what I'd worked out on the flight.

"There doesn't seem to be enough evidence," he said when I'd concluded, "to irrefutably prove what happened."

"This isn't a court of law. I don't need to prove beyond a reasonable doubt who searched my office and killed Lilith—"

"You're missing my point, JJ. There's no proof that anyone besides Lilith had a hand in her death, nor is there proof that anyone searched your office."

"Didn't you hear what I saw with my own eyes in my office?"

"Eyewitness testimony is the least accurate type of evidence. It's a problem in court, because jurors give it more weight than they should. We firmly believe what we think we saw, but our eyes deceive us."

"I'm not wrong about this."

"I understand you believe someone moved the valuable notebooks in your office, but your eyes could have deceived you. As for Lilith, she had an addiction. You'd lost touch with her. You don't know what else she was taking. Lots of people accidentally overdose, and they say crazy things before they lose consciousness."

I sank down into the seat of the car, more deflated than ever. "I thought you, of all people, would believe me."

"I don't disbelieve you."

"You were easier to understand when you were speaking Hindi."

"Even though there's no hard evidence to support your claims, I'm concerned about what you've told me. And it's all the more reason for us to come with you to Italy. What kind of big brother would I be if I didn't protect my little sister?"

I felt a lump in my throat. "Really? You still want to come with me after everything I told you?"

"I'm going to tell you something, because you and I promised to never keep secrets from each other. But don't go acting all weird on me, okay? You promise?"

"Now you've got me worried. You don't have a terminal disease or something, do you? One that's making you seize the day?"

"Honestly, I don't know where your imagination came from. No. I'm perfectly healthy. It's just...I want you to get to know Ava better. I think she might be...I mean, someday..."

My brother was not usually one to get tongue-tied. "Are you saying you're going to propose to her?"

"No! I mean, not now. Maybe not ever. It's just..." A long sigh sounded over the phone. "She might be the one, Jaya."

CHAPTER 17

One week later, a driver with a sleek black town car picked us up at the Leonardo da Vinci airport in Rome. Mahilan had arranged for the luxury.

Our flight had arrived in the morning, and it was a two-hour drive to the villa Mahilan had booked. He'd insisted I stay in a suite with him and Ava, instead of the *pensione* that was more in my price range. With the luxurious presidential suite, we'd have our own separate space but also be able to spend time together.

I was exhausted from making it through finals week, helping students and grading papers, so I'd slept on the flight. Now I was fully awake. While Ava rested her head on Mahilan's shoulder in the town car, I sat in front with the friendly driver. After only a few minutes on the road, Mahilan and I turned to each other and burst into laughter.

"What am I missing?" Ava asked.

"It's just like India," I said.

"Nobody picks a lane," Mahilan explained. "Drivers hover between lanes, always looking for a better way to get where they're going."

"The difference here is that they're speeding rather than inching along in traffic," I said.

"And no rickshaws—but just as many scooters."

We cut through Rome and headed to Bomarzo on Via Salaria, the old salt road, which gave way to a larger highway. Medieval walled villages were perched on hilltops overlooking canyons, vineyards, and in the modern world, the Autostrade highways.

Within two minutes of leaving the highway, it was as if we had entered another world. With the freeway hidden by an overgrowth of trees, and hilly vineyards dotted with stone houses in front of us, I saw no evidence it was the 21st century.

The driver stroked his goatee and frowned as we made a sharp turn onto an even smaller road. I followed his gaze. Along the side of the road was the first blot on the landscape I'd seen on our drive. A group of abandoned stone buildings covered in moss and ivy might have looked like picturesque ruins except for the fact that graffiti covered them. To my architecturally untrained eye, the crumbling construction appeared similar to the houses and churches in the medieval villages we'd passed, but the other buildings hadn't been deserted. As the driver continued on the rural road that wound around the ruins, we passed what was once the entrance. A crooked wooden sign read *Castello del Fantasma.*

"Castle of the ghost?" Ava said. "That's a cool name for a winery. Too bad it went out of business."

I noticed, then, that the silhouetted shape of a wine bottle had been etched onto the sign. I was surprised to see half a dozen tiny cars in the gravel parking lot. I reminded myself that the cars weren't actually tiny for Italy. I'd only just landed, so I was still in my American mindset, where the classic roadster I'd inherited was considered a small car.

The town car jerked as we continued onto a steep section of the road. I twisted around to get a better look at the parking lot. A hand-painted sign rested on the ground next to the stone archway of the one building with a proper door. The sign simply read: *Bar.* I smiled and turned back to the steep narrow road the driver was expertly navigating. I had no idea what would happen if another car came along from the other direction. Gravel scraped against the undercarriage of the car as the road crested and revealed what would be my home base in Italy.

The villa near Bomarzo that Mahilan had booked wasn't

simply a self-contained resort. It was its own medieval walled village. I knew from the promotional materials he'd shown me that it was located on an isolated hilltop overlooking a forest punctuated by vineyards, twenty private cottages and suites placed around a central main street with the reception area, two restaurants, a bar, a spa, a gym, and even a one-room art gallery. But that description didn't prepare me for the splendor of a true medieval village.

Two staff members showed us around the grounds, pointing out the hidden paths, flower gardens, and outdoor sculptures that were replicas of famous Renaissance works of art. Subtle placards in both Italian and English noted that the unhewn stone walls were made with materials from nearby quarries, all of the art in the gallery was by local artists, and most of the food in the restaurants was grown onsite.

It made sense to stick together, but I wasn't entirely happy about being in such close proximity to the lovebirds. The suite had two bedrooms, each with a private bathroom, plus a shared sitting room in the middle. It wasn't just Mahilan's love life that was going better than my own. During finals week at home, Tamarind had helped me with further research, but half the time she gushed about Miles, my poet neighbor she was now dating.

I wished yet again that I could have told Lane what I was doing. I was perilously close to calling or emailing him, but I knew he'd believe I was in danger and try to talk me out of it.

In the common room, I fixed myself a sugary espresso from the in-room espresso maker. The walls were so thick that even though the windows were large, not as much natural light fell into the room as I expected. I took my coffee and phone to the window overlooking the vineyards and hopped up to sit inside the two-foot-thick stone windowsill. I brought my knees up to my chin and looked at the photograph on my phone: the raven Lane had given me. My protector.

"Oh, Lane," I whispered.

"Did you say something?" Ava asked.

I nearly dropped the phone and spilled my coffee. "I didn't

hear you come in." I climbed down from the window nook. "I thought you two were taking a nap."

"I'm here to collect you for lunch. Your brother is famished."

Mahilan, Ava, and I sat down to a late lunch on a courtyard overlooking the valley with the vineyard.

The three of us shared a bottle of Rosato wine and sopped up fresh bread with olive oil and vinegar while we waited for our food. Mahilan pulled his phone from his pocket to snap a picture of me devouring a fat slice of bread while Ava cheered me on, but Ava blushed and covered her face, saying she must look awful from jet lag.

I stuck out my tongue and made a face. "Now I look far sillier than you, Ava. And that photo better not end up on social media, Fish."

"Cousin Connor is going to love that photo," Mahilan said with a wicked grin, as he took a close-up of my face.

"You're friends with Connor?" I asked. "Of course you are. You get along with everyone. He's not exactly your cousin, you know." I tried to grab his phone to delete the photo but gave up. The formal waiter looked horrified when he appeared at the table with our *antipasto* and the three of us broke down in a fit of laughter.

"What's that?" Mahilan asked, pointing his fork at my plate.

"*Carciofo romanesco*. The artichoke of Rome. Fried, in this case." I took a bite of the warm and crispy artichoke. The olive oil and garlic brought out the nutty flavor, and the preparation made it melt in my mouth.

"I didn't see that on the menu."

"You were too busy making eyes at Ava when he told us the specials."

"When in Rome," Ava said, raising her glass.

Mahilan scowled at us, then promptly forgot about being upset as soon as he took a bite of his own appetizer. He closed his eyes as he savored his *Arancini*, rice balls stuffed with mozzarella.

Without realizing it had happened, I was beginning to relax. Could this be becoming a real vacation? A working vacation in which I'd look into Lilith's last wishes and help art history scholars locate a lost set of Renaissance paintings linked to India, but a vacation nonetheless. Nobody suspicious had appeared, after all. Had my imagination gone too far, as Lilith's often had?

"The Park of Monsters is open for another couple of hours," I said. "Do you two want to come with me?"

Mahilan eyed me as if I'd grown a second head. "We're not scheduled to visit until tomorrow."

"We could do both, you know. It's only something like six Euros for the entry fee."

"I don't care about the money. Even though it does sound rather irresponsible to pay for such a brief visit."

"Is he always like this?" Ava asked, laughing and sticking out her tongue at Mahilan.

"Our schedule," a reddening Mahilan said, "has us relaxing this afternoon to get over jet lag."

It was my turn to be horrified. "We're in Italy. *Italy*, Fish. You're going to stay inside the villa instead of exploring?"

"We each have our own ways of combatting jet lag. I, for one, scheduled a massage."

"I'm going to check out the outdoor yoga class happening soon," Ava said. "Have fun at the monster park."

I wanted to go on a run to make sure I slept well that night. In the meantime, since the Park of Monsters was only open for another couple of hours, I decided to do that first.

The villa was about ten kilometers from Bomarzo's Park of Monsters, farther than I wanted to run. I phoned the front desk and asked the concierge to call me a taxi.

"Where are the *bambini*?" a portly diver asked me when he arrived at the reception area ten minutes later. He wore a jovial smile and bobbled back and forth as if he were bouncing invisible babies on his knees.

"It's just me."

"No family?" He swung his hands through the air.

"What am I missing?" I had no idea what his gesture had meant. "Do I need a kid to get inside the park?"

He grinned at me. "*No, signora.* But you'll see. *Scusi. Un momento.*" He stepped aside and answered his buzzing cell phone, leaving me inside the reception area.

"Has everything met with your satisfaction so far?" the elderly concierge asked.

"It's so perfect that your villa has already made me forget this is a research trip. *Grazie.*"

"*Prego,*" he said, acknowledging my thanks.

"What's the history of this place?" I asked. "I didn't see it in the pamphlet inside the suite."

He pretended to cough to cover a laugh. "Most of our guests wish to know of local wines and the menus of our restaurants. Not local history."

"But you know the history?"

"*Un poco.* This hilltop village is over nine hundred years old. Fifty years ago, the residents began to leave. This was when the winery at the bottom of the hill closed. Only twenty years ago did the villa buy the property."

"I'm surprised they didn't buy the abandoned winery too."

"You said you are here to visit the *Parco dei Mostri*?"

"That's right."

"You will enjoy the Sacred Wood, *signora.* Most visitors to our local gardens have not traveled as far as you, but I have always thought it should be more of a destination for all people who wish to understand the unique opulence of Renaissance gardens."

"I'm hoping to explore more of the area on foot as well."

He pushed a map across the desk and circled our location and that of the Park of Monsters.

"Are there good paths to go running?" I asked.

"*Sì.*" He traced a few small roads for me. "But stick to these paths," he added. With wrinkled fingers, he tapped the map with vigor.

I couldn't imagine the roads around here being too crowded. "Are the other roads private property?"

His eyes flitted around the reception area, avoiding mine. He straightened an already perfectly neat stack of papers on the high counter. He hadn't appeared to be a nervous man until that moment. He nodded, as if he'd made a decision and whisked a thick black marker from underneath the counter. With the marker, he crossed out an area of the countryside not far from the running paths he'd marked.

"What's there?" I asked. I squinted at the map, trying to make out what he'd crossed out. "A quarry? Or a private section of the nature reserve?"

"That, *signora*, is an area where you must never, ever go."

"Why not?"

"Ah! Your driver has returned. I wish you a wonderful visit to our *Parco dei Mostri*." The concierge pressed the map into my hands and lowered his voice. "Please do heed my words, *signora*. We have much to offer visitors, but there is nothing but death in those woods."

CHAPTER 18

After the unsettling encounter, I asked the taxi driver about that area of the map the concierge had blocked out.

"Superstitious old man," he said dismissively. But his carefree smile had been replaced with a tight-lipped one.

"Superstitious of what?"

"It does not matter, *signora*. Why spoil such a beautiful day?"

Twenty minutes later, after driving through a series of winding roads in the tiny Volkswagen that barely contained the driver's girth, I saw what he meant about kids being the heart of the park. Laughing children ran through the gardens, their parents in tow. The macabre Renaissance garden had become an amusement park for local families.

I picked up a map of the gardens and compared it to Lazzaro Allegri's sketches. My goal was to head straight to the Underworld Ogre from Lazzaro's notebook, but I didn't get far. I couldn't help stopping every few yards. Even crowded with people, the Renaissance garden's mysterious presence permeated the grounds.

Two kids ran circles around weathered gods of antiquity flanking the sphinxes that greeted visitors as they stepped through the castle-like stone arch to officially enter the gardens. The Latin inscription on the slab underneath the main sphinx had been translated for visitors. *He who does not visit this place with raised eyebrows and tight lips will fail to admire the seven wonders of the world.*

Past the sphinxes and gods, a startling sea monster appeared on the winding path. Framed by lush forest behind it, the stone figure emerged from the ground as if the earth were the sea. Its hungry mouth was lined with teeth, each one as large as my head. Only the top of the monster was visible, as if he was peeking above a crest of waves in the ocean. His wide eyes and flared nostrils suggested he was about to swallow an unwitting victim before plunging into the dark waters below.

The carving was so evocative that I found myself shivering as I remembered my own encounter plunging into the cold dark waters outside of Mont Saint-Michel in France. I tasted salty water on my tongue and felt the sand under my feet. Overcome with an intense desire to get away from the sea, I stumbled backward.

I couldn't even pretend to blame my inelegant retreat on my high heels, because I'd sensibly worn boots to explore the woodland park. The taste and physical sensation must have been my imagination. If there was any place on earth where it was forgivable to succumb to fanciful imaginings, this was the place.

I willed myself to pull my attention from the treacherous tides of Mont Saint-Michel to the stone monsters connected to Michelangelo's protégé. Which, I reminded myself, was a fanciful idea itself. Lilith had no evidence, at least none that she'd given to me before she died. And I had no evidence that another person had a hand in her death. What did I owe Lilith and her crazy ideas? She'd lured me to Italy as Bahadur Shah had lured Lazzaro to India.

I glared at the sea monster. It must have been Proteus, the carving Lilith's mistranslation had led her to believe was near Lazzaro's hidden art studio. My eyes followed the lines of stone, which morphed from sea creature to frothy waves. A globe and castle, also made of stone, were affixed to the monster's head. The pamphlet suggested the castle represented the Orsini family's power in the world. Even though Stefano had corrected me about the translation's more likely meaning, I thought it was worth checking out. Especially since I knew Lazzaro's paintings wouldn't simply be resting inside the shelter of the Orcus.

A low wooden fence kept visitors from stepping off the sanctioned path. Having recovered from my memories, I was about to hop the fence for a closer look at Proteus when I spotted two men in green shirts chastising a father and son. I didn't understand the Italian words they spoke, but the message was clear. People weren't supposed to climb on the statues. I'd have to come back later. With one last glance at the sea monster, I wasn't sure I was disappointed.

I continued along the path that coiled through the forest in unexpected loops. From a distance, the moss-covered stones tricked you into thinking they were natural formations. But as I stepped closer, their animated visages became clear. Descending farther into the labyrinthine park, the statues became more obvious. And more monstrous. I'm not sure I would have wanted to spend time with Vicino Orsini. If this was his idea of honoring his dead wife, I would have hated to see what he envisioned for his enemies.

A mother held her son so the boy could reach the "mouth of truth" of a Medusa-like creature with an open mouth. The boy shook his head furiously, refusing to put his hand inside. His sister marched past him and squealed with delight as she placed her hand in and out of the monster's mouth.

More men in green t-shirts walked the grounds, making sure nobody climbed on the stone carvings. The staff dressed and acted casually, but they did their jobs. One castigated a mother who was helping her daughters climb the trunk of an elephant. I watched them for a moment before realizing the elephant was eating a man.

One of the green-shirted men stood out from his fellows; unlike the others, this man wore a hat. But this was no ordinary hat, meant to shield one's face from the sun, and the man wasn't strolling casually down the path with the others. He was crouched behind a weather-worn wall of stones next to Neptune, the top of a black pirate hat peeking over the mossy stones.

As a family stopped and pointed at the giant figure, the man jumped up and raised his hands above his head and roared.

The father screamed, the wife laughed, and their two children clapped their hands in joy. The comedian proceeded to recite what sounded like an epic poem.

"*Bellisimo*," the laughing wife said, kissing her fingertips and flicking her hand in the air.

"Francesco!" snapped a young green-shirted man with perfectly tousled hair.

The joker removed the pirate hat from his head, and the two men entered a heated exchange in Italian. Unable to understand them, I moved on, reminding myself I wasn't there to absorb Italian culture, as fascinating as it was.

The map of the park showed that I'd almost reached Orcus, the Ogre of the Underworld. This was the creature from Lazzaro's notebook that, according to Stefano's translation, Lazzaro's studio was near. I hurried past a dragon who had a look of curious surprise on his face—and stopped short.

I'd reached the Ogre I was after. The king of the Underworld was nothing like the friendly dragon in his wake. Hollow black eyes wide with horror, beneath wild eyebrows shaped with rage, above an open mouth that served as a doorway. The door to the Underworld. The monster had no body. Instead, a set of stone steps led from the path up to the doorway mouth.

A stunning woman with black hair and eyes spoke to me in Italian, and I responded in my broken Italian that I didn't speak the language.

"Ah, *Americana*! We do not see Americans so much. You are of Italian lineage, no? I was saying if you do not like the look on L'Orco's face right now, you return later. His expression, it changes depending on the way the sunlight falls on him."

"Thank you for the tip. When do you like to visit?"

"The beginning of the day. This is the hour when he has the least power, as it is the longest distance from night. With my youngest *bambina*, it is not so easy to arrive early. Lucia! *Arresto!*" She left me and chased after a young child, her long hair billowing behind her.

Sleek green moss covered the Ogre's face. The carving had been built into an existing stone on the side of a small hill. It was at least three times as tall as me, and the mouth that served as a doorway was higher than six feet. Two stone teeth hung from the top. A Latin inscription was carved onto the top of the doorway mouth. It paraphrased a quote from Dante's Inferno: *Abandon all hope ye who enter here.*

Unlike most of the carvings at the park, visitors were encouraged to touch this one. With my heart thudding, I watched as a family posed with wide grins inside the mouth of the king of the Underworld. Could I be steps away from finding Lazzaro Allegri's hidden art studio?

Once the family climbed down the steps and continued on, I took their place. I walked through the mouth into darkness, expecting to find Hell.

Instead I found a picnic table.

I glanced around the ten-foot square dining room. That's what it was. A stone dining table and stone benches were built into the slab floor. I ran my hand along the stone walls, the table, and finally the floor. The sculpture was solid. There didn't seem to be any way to build a secret passageway into this stone beast.

I rested against the cool stone and took in the room as a whole. I doubted this room itself had once been Lazzaro's studio. Even in the 1500s, this ghoulish room had been open to the public. I reminded myself that Lazzaro's cryptic message, *mi trovate quando diluvia*, didn't state his studio was actually *attached to* the Ogre statue. It simply said we could find him there. It could be nearby.

I rushed back outside and examined my surroundings. Though Lazzaro's sketches had been skillful, he'd taken artistic license to make the creature's face more savage in his own interpretation. I circled the overgrown area. Narrowly, at first, before widening my radius and finding the large fountain Stefano had mentioned. The circular fountain with a winged Pegasus in the center was filled with moss, not water. And it was far from any formations that could disguise a sheltered cave.

This couldn't be right.

There was no hidden grotto anywhere near the Ogre. Stefano Gopal's translation was wrong too.

CHAPTER 19

How could Stefano have been wrong? Italian was his native tongue. But his native tongue in the 20th and 21st centuries. Not the 16th. And landscapes change over time. Had the layout been different in the 1500s? I didn't have Stefano's home number, so I called his office and left a message.

I bought every book on the Park of Monsters that was available in English at the gift shop, including a novel. I doubted a work of fiction would tell me anything useful in my quest, but couldn't resist its title, *Signatures in Stone*, and its description that the Park of Monsters was a pathway to enlightenment. Sitting at a picnic table near laughing children, I skimmed the books. These weren't academic tomes. These were books for tourists. Even the heftier books were conceptual studies on topics such as pagan iconography in the Renaissance, or comparing the Park of Monsters to other Renaissance gardens like the water jokes gardens in Germany that Sanjay had mentioned. None of these books contained original documents from the 1500s. Why would they? This was a tourist destination for Italians, not a research library. If I could find a local library or archives, that would be more useful. It would also be more useful if I spoke Italian.

I wasn't going to let myself get dejected so soon. I'd only been in Italy for a few hours. Jet lag was making me cranky. I needed to go on a run to snap out of it. I got a cab back to the villa and changed into my running gear.

I had over an hour of sunlight left. Plenty of time to fit in a good run and make it back to the villa. While I stretched, I examined the map the concierge had given to me earlier. There were several trails that would work. I tucked my phone, hotel key, and map into the pocket of my vest and set off through the countryside. I left my headphones off in order to get the full experience of my new surroundings.

Without music to focus on, I thought about the warning the concierge had given me. *There is nothing but death in those woods.* The driver hadn't wanted to talk about it either. Surely there wasn't a hidden danger like a serial killer at large or a pack of rabid boars that were endangering tourists. Because of the area of the map suggested as off limits, it was more likely to be a landslide that had killed someone. The region was rocky enough for that type of danger. We'd passed several quarries on our drive to the villa.

There was only one path down the villa's isolated little hill. The same small road we'd driven up. At the base of the hill I passed the abandoned *Castello del Fantasma* winery. Raucous laughter wafted out of the building with the bar. As I ran by, I spotted a young waiter I recognized from the villa talking animatedly with an older man with a weather-worn face.

Several miles later, I'd smelled the sweet scents of late spring flowers, seen the juxtaposition of medieval stone houses next to modern gas stations, and felt the warm Italian sun as I ran through pockets of sunshine between the lush green trees. Only too late did I realize that I shouldn't have cut through a vineyard to avoid a steep hill. The path I was now on didn't correspond to anything on my map.

I kept running until the dirt path met what I thought looked like a larger road up ahead. But it must have been a private road, because no signage was visible.

The sun hung low in the sky. As I stopped to stretch and think about what to do, I felt the chill from the sweat that coated my skin. I had my phone with me, so I could call my brother or the villa front desk and try to explain where I was.

A car approached. I tried to flag them down by waving both my hands, but the two women in the car simply waved back at me. How on earth did one signal that you needed help in Italian? As I typed that question into my phone, another vehicle approached on the road. This one was a baby blue moped. It stopped of its own accord, without me having to guess the best way to flag it down.

"*Ciao, Bella,*" the young man said, coming to a stop a few feet away from me. He continued speaking in rapid Italian.

"*Mi dispiace, non parlo italiano.*" I hoped I hadn't completely crucified my attempt to say I didn't speak Italian.

"*Americana?* I would not have guessed. I saw you at the Sacred Grove today, but did not hear you speak. You have Italian ancestry, no? You enjoyed our gardens?"

Even though he'd changed clothing, I recognized him now. He was one of the men who made sure people didn't ruin the stones. He couldn't have been out of his teens, but he'd been the one reprimanding the joker in the pirate hat. He ran a hand through the tousled hair that fell to his shoulders. It was a practiced gesture, one that I was sure made teenage girls swoon. The white shirt he'd changed into was a thick-collared dress shirt unbuttoned halfway down his chest on the warm night.

"I enjoyed it very much," I said. "You've just gotten off work?"

"*Sì.* I do not possess your beautiful legs, so I just have my moped to carry me home. You ran all this way?"

I laughed. "No. And I seem to be lost."

"Where are you trying to be?"

I showed him the villa on the map. He took off his helmet and handed it to me. "You are a long way from home, *mia Bella.* I will see you safely there."

I knew he was a member of the community with a job at the park, and I was confident I could fight off a teenaged kid if it came to that. I put on the helmet and climbed on the back of the moped.

Since the moped didn't go much faster than I ran, while we drove to the villa I learned he'd never been farther than Rome, and that he was seventeen and working at the Park of Monsters while saving money for college. He loved practicing his English, so he talked nonstop and welcomed my corrections.

"You know the history of the gardens?" I asked.

He shrugged. "Orsini," he said. "This is the family who built it. The man, Pirro? Pietro? I forget his name. He was crazy. This is all I know." Hopefully he wasn't going to be a history major when he got to college.

I asked him about the phrase *mi trovate quando diluvia* that Lilith and Stefano had translated differently.

"Pouring rain, *sì*," he confirmed. That meant Stefano's translation was right. It was Lazzaro himself who'd created a mystery. Was the deception deliberate or was I missing something?

My new friend Niccolò dropped me at the villa. He handed me a scrap of paper with his phone number.

"To practice my English," he added hastily when he saw my face, then grinned. "If you have extra time in Italia and desire to thank the man who helps you when you are lost."

I accepted his phone number and handed his helmet back to him. "Before you go, I wanted to ask you one last thing. What's with the area of my map that's been crossed out?"

His shoulders tensed as he looked at the map. He tried to play it off as a shrug, but his voice belied the forced nature of his carefree pose. "You go there?"

"No, but I'm curious—"

"*Mi dispiace.* It is later than I think."

"It'll only take a moment for you to tell me—"

"I am late to meet my sister. *Arrivederla, mia Bella.*"

I stared after Niccolò as his scooter kicked up dust on the gravel path leading out of the medieval village and back to the 21st century. Why was everyone wary of talking about that off-limits area? If it was dangerous, wouldn't they simply tell me so?

"JJ?"

I turned to see my brother, dressed impeccably in an off-white linen suit, walking toward me. Ava was at his side, her hand draped casually over his elbow. She wore a sleeveless summer dress in vibrant yellow with a high waist and long skirts that flowed to her ankles. They were a stunning couple.

"Your brother was worried," Ava said, "since you're late for dinner and didn't answer your phone."

"I must not have heard the phone with the noise of the moped."

"You were on a motorcycle?" Mahilan asked, dropping Ava's arm. "Really?"

"I'm fine, Fish."

"Do you know how many people are killed in motorcycle accidents each year?"

"I wore a helmet, and I doubt Niccolò drove faster than ten miles an hour."

"Niccolò?" Mahilan sputtered. "Who's Niccolò?"

"Didn't you grow up riding on scooters?" Ava asked.

"We did," I said. "Three or four of us on the same scooter. Fish has forgotten his roots."

"I think they make you surrender them when you pass the bar exam," Ava said.

"You two are hilarious," Mahilan said. "Seriously, JJ, take a proper taxi next time."

"Let me take a quick shower and I'll meet you for dinner. Order me whatever the special is."

Inside the cozy restaurant with waiters and sommeliers fussing over us, I was torn between enjoying the luxurious vacation that I never would have been able to afford if my brother wasn't treating me and examining my surroundings critically. I was trying to do both, and thus failing miserably at each. I couldn't completely unwind, yet I couldn't get a handle on what had happened to Lazzaro Allegri's lost masterpieces and who would have hurt Lilith to get that answer.

I meant to stay focused at the task at hand, but as soon as a plate of cocoa-rubbed beef was set down in front of me, I succumbed to decadence.

* * *

In the morning, I wished I hadn't been quite so decadent with the wine pairings that went with each course. I had an appointment with Enzo and Brunella Allegri, descendants of the family Lazzaro Allegri had belonged to. With contact information Lilith had provided, I'd emailed them from San Francisco while I was setting up the trip. Though they didn't know what they could tell me that would be helpful, they said they'd be happy to meet with me. I hoped they'd be more open to talking to me than the people I'd met so far. But it would probably be a good idea if I didn't begin with my question about the off-limits area.

I'd meant to ask Niccolò about finding a local library or archives I could visit that day too, but he'd left so abruptly after I asked him about the forbidden area of woods. I was due at the Allegris shortly, so I couldn't worry about that now.

Mahilan, Ava, and I had made plans to visit the Park of Monsters together in the afternoon after my appointment. The Allegris had invited me to their home, which from what I'd seen online looked more like a castle than a house.

"Mind if I tag along and do some sketches?" Ava asked over breakfast. "I read about their spectacular flower garden. I thought I'd make some drawings to send Carey."

"You two are abandoning me to finish breakfast alone?" Mahilan said.

I impulsively decided to call Lane. Since I was in Italy, there was no danger that he could talk me out of coming. He'd be angry, yes. But he'd get over it.

It wasn't only that I wanted to hear his voice. I also wanted to think through what was going on. Both Lilith and Stefano had been wrong about the location of Lazzaro's hidden art studio. Lane had seen the sketchbooks too. Had he seen something I'd missed?

I hoped to catch him, but even if I reached his voicemail, that would have been all right. What I got instead wasn't all right at all.

Lane's phone had been disconnected.

CHAPTER 20

"You sure you're okay?" Ava asked as she drove a bright orange Fiat Panda to the Allegris'. Mahilan had decided that since we were effectively in the middle of nowhere, and I couldn't be trusted not to hop on scooters with strange men, it would be best to rent a car.

"Jet lag," I said.

But all I could think about was why Lane's phone was disconnected. Had he taken Lilith's hypothesis more seriously than I'd realized and looked into it on his own, encountering the person who had hurt Lilith? Or was it his way of forcing me to make a clean break? Neither scenario was a welcome one.

"Where are you going?" I asked as Ava turned onto a road leading down into a valley.

"The GPS says to go this way. Why do you sound so anxious?"

"It's nothing," I said. "Never mind."

We were descending into the area I'd been warned away from.

Enzo and Brunella Allegri were younger than I expected from the formality of their correspondence. They must have been in their late thirties.

Brunella's voluptuous curves stood out in striking contrast to Enzo's small skeletal frame. Based on their appearances, I expected her handshake would be warm and friendly and his cold and hard. I was mistaken. Brunella's handshake was clammy and perfunctory, but Enzo's was warm and enthusiastic. He pumped my hand several times in greeting as I mentally kicked myself for jumping to conclusions.

"Come, come!" He waved Ava and me inside.

"Thanks for meeting with us," I said.

Brunella frowned. "I did not realize there would be two of you. I did not save enough *bomboloni*."

"I don't need anything," Ava said quickly. "Jaya is the scholar. I'm an amateur artist. You have such beautiful gardens, I was hoping to sketch them while the three of you talk."

"*Sì, sì,*" Enzo said. "The roses are not blooming yet, but the poppies are *magnifici*."

They spoke perfect English, but with Italian accents. Enzo's was strongest.

"Would you make tea, my love?" Enzo asked Brunella.

"It is nearly summer," she said. "Who needs tea?" Her bosom threatened to break out of her dress. It was a good thing she was wearing such expensive clothing or I was sure the seams would have given up.

"Cappuccinos, then. The day is young."

"I'm fine," I said.

Enzo sighed. "You are sure? How can we help you?" He motioned for me to sit anywhere.

A phone in the hallway rang as I sat down on an exquisite chair made in a classical style with ornate embroidery. It was the wrong choice. I'd been drawn to its decorative beauty suggestive of another century. I hadn't realized the lumpy chair was most likely an original.

"*Amore mio,*" Enzo said to Brunella. "*Telefono?*"

She replied in rapid Italian that I didn't follow, and Enzo went to answer the phone.

"You have a beautiful home," I said to Brunella. It was true, even though it was chilly inside despite the warm day. Between the stately furniture and sedate oil paintings of men and women who vaguely resembled Enzo, I felt as though I were in a museum.

Except for the newspaper that lay open on an antique side table next to a plate of donuts.

"*Grazie, signora.* If only it were not in the middle of the country. *Bomboloni?*" She gestured toward the platter of donuts.

"Thank you." I got up from my uncomfortable seat and helped myself to a round pastry with custard sticking out on top. One glance at the adjacent newspaper told me why it had been left out. The paper was open to the society pages. Included in the spread was a photo of Brunella and Enzo dressed in formalwear, smiling for the camera with two other people. The Roman Pantheon was visible in the background.

"*Mi dispiace.* I forget to put this away." Brunella reached so slowly for the newspaper that she appeared to be moving in slow motion. She was still fussing with the paper by the time I sat down in a more comfortable chair with my fried pastry.

Enzo came back into the room. "My apologies. How can we assist you?"

"As I mentioned when I got in touch, I'd love to know what you can tell me about your ancestor Lazzaro Allegri."

"I have heard many things about my family who came before me," Enzo said. "But one never knows what to believe. I fear I would be telling you only fiction."

"His father embellished everything," Brunella said. "He made it impossible to know what was true and what was a fairy tale."

"*Sì, sì,*" Enzo said. "You must speak with Francesco. He is the man who knows the history of these parts best."

I couldn't contain a smile. A local historian was worth his weight in gold. "Could you give me his contact information?"

"No."

"No?"

Brunella giggled and plopped down in the first chair I'd abandoned. "He does not mean to refuse you. We don't have his phone number. Do you know his surname, Enzo?"

He shook his head. "But I know where you can find him. Francesco works at the *Parco dei Mostri.*"

"Are you sure she should talk with him?" Brunella asked Enzo.

"Why not? He is full of historical information. Oh, you mean because—"

"*Sì.*"

"Because of what?" I asked, watching their animated expressions.

"No matter," Enzo said. "He is...*come si dice?* A character. Larger than life, I think you would say. You understand? If you visit, ask anyone for Francesco. They will know him."

"Thank you. I'm visiting the park this afternoon, so I'll be sure to ask for him. I also understand you met with an American Professor, Lilith Vine. She's how I found you."

"Ah!" Enzo said. "I wondered. But I think you must be as brilliant as you are *bella*, so no man can hide, eh?" He chuckled.

"Strange woman," Brunella said. "A very strange woman."

"She came to our home for dinner once," Enzo said. "She drank as if she is five men, not one woman."

"That's Lilith," I said.

"This is not the strange part," said Brunella. "She refused wine from our cellar! She wanted spirits—" Brunella shuddered, "—with 'mixers.'"

"I'm sorry to tell you she passed away," I said.

"Passed?" Brunella repeated, then reddened.

"I am most sorry to hear this," Enzo said.

"I'm carrying on her research."

"*Sì,*" Enzo said. "I'm sorry if you came all this way for what we can tell you, because we don't know much, as I tell you over email. I believe *Professoressa* Vine saw the ghosts of history where there were none. She believed in a figment of my ancestor's imagination."

"You could be right," I said. "I don't believe her theory about where to find Lazzaro Allegri's artwork was correct. But I'm hoping that even though you don't personally know more about your family history, there might be more documents."

"*Sì, sì,*" Enzo said. "Is a good idea. What else do you need?"

"You sold Lilith Vine some sketchbooks," I said.

"Lent," Enzo corrected. "She paid to borrow them. You have them to return?"

"Oh?" That answered one question. "I didn't realize that. But once I return home I can get the three notebooks back to you."

"Four," Brunella said.

"What?"

"Four books with the art inside," Brunella said. "*Quattro*. Not three. From the attic with the rest of Enzo's family junk."

Four. Not three.

That's what Lilith had tried to tell me on the phone. That there was a missing notebook. I misheard her slurred words and thought she'd said that I "must know therefore," but what she had been trying to say wasn't "therefore," but *there were four*.

What had happened to the fourth notebook?

CHAPTER 21

"You're certain?" I asked. "Four notebooks."

"*Sì, sì*," Enzo said.

"Yes," Brunella agreed. "Enzo made the copies. Where are they, *Tesoro*?"

Enzo scowled at the floor.

"I know you hate the attic," Brunella snapped. "But *Professoressa* Jones needs them. Must I do everything?" She stood and smoothed the wrinkles of her tight dress.

"Tito's machine was broken," Enzo said. "*Professoressa* Vine was trustworthy. She signed a receipt. There seemed no reason—"

Brunella cut in with sharp words directed at Enzo. She spoke in rapid Italian, so I didn't catch what she said, but by her tone she seemed to be admonishing him.

"*Sì, sì*," Enzo said, slinking backward and looking as if he were about to fade into the life-size painting on the wall. "I know if we lived in Rome as you wished we would be near a copy center. And good restaurants. And a beauty parlor. But then we would not have my ancestral home."

"It's a beautiful home," I said.

Brunella's eyes narrowed. "It is beautiful, yes. But if you had to spend the winter in these stone walls, you too would wish for an apartment in Roma."

I left the bickering Allegris and went in search of Ava. What had happened to the fourth sketchbook? Why had Lilith withheld that information from me?

I had a sinking feeling I knew the answer. *She wanted the credit.* I was a pawn. I could help her get close to Lazzaro's paintings, then with a key clue in that missing sketchbook, Lilith could sweep in and take the credit.

When she realized she was dying, she wanted to tell me. Unless...Could the Allegris be lying? Had they kept a fourth notebook they found in the attic? No, that made no sense. It would have been simple enough to not tell me about the fourth notebook. Lilith had known about it, but failed to tell me until she was dying. Most importantly, the Allegris had no motive to lie. Lazzaro's paintings were theirs. It would have been to their advantage for me or Lilith to find them.

Standing in front of the massive house, I saw no sign of Ava. As I walked through the gardens, I tried calling Lane again. His phone was still disconnected. I didn't like this at all.

The more I learned, the less I knew. I groaned. In my surprise at learning about a fourth sketchbook, I'd forgotten to ask them about the "dangerous" area on the map. I hurried back to the front door, but stopped myself before knocking when I heard their raised voices. I understood enough words to understand Brunella was still upset at Enzo about the missing notebook. I'd return the three notebooks Lilith had borrowed once I was home and could retrieve them, but unless I figured out what was going on, the fourth piece of history would be gone forever. I backed away from the door and went in search of Ava. I could ask this Francesco fellow about the area I'd been warned away from.

I wandered through the lush gardens that surrounded the castle-like house. These were different from those at the Park of Monsters. There were no sculptures here. This garden instead was made up of well-tended plants, most of which I didn't recognize. Flowers of every color of the rainbow bloomed on the grounds, all bracketed by evergreen trees that gave the land a cozy feeling.

I found Ava sketching some beautiful purple flowers growing

in window boxes in front of a house that looked like an in-law unit not far from the castle. This must have been where servants had lived in past centuries.

"Any luck finding out what you needed?" she asked.

"I'm not sure," I said. I looked over her shoulder at the charcoal sketch of the flowers. "You're very talented."

"It's nothing," she said, quickly flipping the notebook shut. "An artist isn't a practical occupation for a single mom."

"Everyone needs a hobby. I play tabla at an Indian restaurant two nights a week."

"Your brother told me about your drumming. I think for a while he was worried you'd work at a restaurant for the rest of your life."

"He told you how I waitressed for a few years between high school and college?"

"Since you graduated early, it makes sense as a life choice to me." Ava slipped her sketchbook into her purse and we walked down the path to where we'd parked the rental car.

"I bet you wouldn't say that to your son if he wanted to do the same thing."

"I suppose you're right." She laughed and looked out over the flowers. "I have no idea what Carey will become, but I know it'll be something great."

Sun poked through overhanging tree branches, sprinkling us with sunlight as Ava navigated the winding roads back to the villa. It was such a peaceful drive that when my phone rang, it startled us both. I extracted the phone from my messenger bag with a good feeling it was Lane calling to tell me he'd made a mistake by ending things without talking to me. My face fell when I saw it was the number for the villa.

"What's up, Fish?"

"I thought you would be back by now. It's nearly one o'clock. Should I wait for you for lunch?"

"We'll be back in a few minutes."

I clicked off the call and tossed the phone back into my bag.

"Who were you hoping for?" Ava asked.

"You noticed?"

"I consult with international businesses. It's part of my job to be good at reading people. It's a guy, isn't it? You were hoping it was your friend Sanjay who Mahilan mentioned?"

"There's a guy. Not Sanjay."

"No?"

"It's complicated."

"Isn't everything?" She looked wistfully at the gravel road. "You think I like being away from Carey so much? But we all have to make choices. I feel so lucky to have met Mahilan. I didn't expect what I felt—" She shook her head and maneuvered the SUV around a tight bend in the narrow road. Once the road straightened, she stole a glance at me. "You're worried. Why?"

"I care more about this guy than I want to. It's a long-distance relationship. If I can call it that. I don't even know if it's real, which is why I haven't told Mahilan. Please don't tell him what I'm telling you. I shouldn't even be saying anything, except I'm worried."

"I won't say anything. And I'm sure you don't need to worry."

"His phone is disconnected."

"For how long?"

I thought about it. "A day?"

She laughed. "I'm sure he forgot to pay his phone bill. He'll realize it soon enough." She was silent for a few moments before continuing. "You know, I wasn't sure what to think of you from your brother's description, but you're even more amazing than advertised. Which is saying a lot, because Mahilan adores you. I'm sure there's a perfectly innocent explanation about your boyfriend's phone."

Lane Peters was off the grid. There was no innocent explanation in sight.

CHAPTER 22

Back at the villa, I told Mahilan and Ava to go on to lunch without me, and to order me something rich and creamy. I knew I wouldn't enjoy a bite of lunch if I didn't first look into finding that fourth notebook.

Since Lilith's death wasn't being treated as a homicide, her house wouldn't be a crime scene. It wouldn't be difficult for someone who knew how to pick locks to gain entry to look around for the fourth notebook. Lilith had tried to tell me about it before she died. Surely that meant she wanted me to have it. Even though she'd only "borrowed" the notebooks.

"I'm sorry to wake you," I said when Sanjay answered the phone.

"You didn't wake me."

I looked at the time. One p.m. in Italy was only four a.m. in San Francisco. "Up all night practicing a new illusion again? I'm glad, because I really need your help. I need you to drive up the coast to Sea Ranch to—"

"I'm not in San Francisco."

"You're not?"

"I'm in France, staying with Sébastien."

"You are?"

"You heard about what's going on with him, right?"

"I feel terrible that his pneumonia is lingering. It's my fault he has it."

"It's not your fault, Jaya. He wanted to help you."

"What kind of person lets a ninety-year-old traipse across France on a treasure hunt?" Sébastien had insisted on helping, but I shouldn't have let him.

"Good point. You probably should have stopped him."

"Thanks for your support." I wished Sanjay had been there in person so I could have thrown something at him. "I'm pretty sure he's in better shape than I am. And he doesn't look a day over seventy."

"Not anymore."

I winced. "That bad?"

"He won't let anyone help him. He checked out of the hospital and was at home by himself."

"What about Jeeves?" I asked.

"His automaton butler doesn't *actually* do everything a real butler would do. Sometimes I wonder about you, Jaya. Anyway, since he won't accept in-home care, several young magician friends of his have been taking turns visiting him. Tempest was about to leave, so I flew out here to take her place."

"I thought you said he wouldn't let people visit to take care of him."

"He won't. But he'll impart his vast knowledge to the next generation. If the visit is about us, not him, he loves visitors."

The retired stage magician from Nantes, France defied expectations at every turn. He and his partner Christo headlined for a few very successful years before retiring to the French countryside. Sébastien had never enjoyed the spotlight. Building ingenious creations behind the scenes was his passion. He'd replicated many classic magic show devices, such as the famous chess-playing Turk and Jean Eugene Robert-Houdin's mechanical orange tree, and also created his own. For many years, he and Christo got their wish to live outside of the spotlight. But practicing stage magicians knew he was a fantastic resource, so they tracked him down. Sébastien became a magic consultant. Grudgingly at first, but by the time I'd met him he'd fully embraced the role of mentor.

"I hadn't offered to visit because of my Napa schedule of shows," Sanjay said. "But now that there's no more theater, I'm pitching in to look after him while he teaches me. Oh, Jaya, you've gotta see this. Look at the screen of your phone in two seconds."

"Sanjay, this is important. Um, Sanjay?"

He'd already gone to find whatever it was he wanted to send me. A second later, a photo text message popped up on my phone. It was Sanjay taking a selfie with Jeeves, Sébastien's wheelchair-bound automaton butler. The wheels allowed the robot Sébastien created with clock-making technology to maneuver through the house. I wasn't entirely sure how much Jeeves could do on his own, and Sébastien wouldn't tell me, preferring to keep up the mystique.

"Sanjay—"

"Hang on a sec."

I heard a woman's voice in the background. A woman?

Sanjay came back on the line. "Sorry about that. We're about to sit down to lunch. What was it you wanted?"

"Who was that?"

"Tempest is here."

"Oh."

"You there, Jaya?"

"Never mind." He couldn't help me from France. And should I really have expected him to, even if he was in San Francisco? "You're busy. Have fun with Sébastien and Tempest. Give my best to Sébastien."

"Á bientôt," Sanjay said without even attempting a French accent.

I hung up the phone. My brother was right. I took Sanjay for granted. I expected he'd always be there for me, regardless of when I called or what I asked of him.

I thought about dragging Tamarind into this, then realized how crazy I was being. *Like Lilith.* I couldn't expect a librarian, no matter how punk she claimed to be, to break into a house for me.

I had to get a grip. This was no way to treat friends. I didn't even have reason to believe the fourth sketchbook was in Lilith's home. It was entirely possible the person who'd drugged her for information was now in possession of Lazzaro's sketchbook with the key clue. They could have broken into my office to make sure I didn't have the information. That made much more sense. I had the background bits of information that needed to be put together.

I stared at the raven on the screen of my phone for several minutes. Was there anything else I could do? Stefano hadn't returned my call either. At least his number hadn't been disconnected. I still didn't like the situation one bit.

A missing boyfriend.

A dead professor.

And the trusted advisor I'd turned to for help was nowhere to be found.

CHAPTER 23

Even the smooth buttery risotto couldn't make me forget my troubles.

"I'll never understand," Mahilan said, "how the simplest ingredients make these amazing meals. Before you sat down, JJ, the chef came out and told us how this *fettuccine al burro* is made with only butter, parmesan, salt, pepper, and nutmeg. But it tastes like so much more. It's like magic."

"Fascinating," I mumbled.

Mahilan set down his utensils and shook my shoulders. "We're on vacation, JJ. Cheer up. I know it's a working vacation for you, but still."

"Let me show you how to eat pasta like a European," Ava said, placing her hands on Mahilan's. "An Italian would never twirl like that."

Neither of us joined her forced laugh.

"Your risotto is getting cold," Mahilan said.

"I'm not hungry."

"Are you still upset about—" Ava began.

"Lazzaro Allegri had another sketchbook," I cut in with a sharp look at her.

She mouthed *sorry* to me. I should never have opened up to her about Lane. But to be generous to my maybe-future sister-in-law, she didn't know why it was such a big deal for me to keep it a secret.

"I'm in a funk," I said, "because I learned that Brunella and Enzo Allegri lent Lilith four sketchbooks, not three."

"I thought you said she bought them," my brother said.

"There's that too." I pushed my risotto aside and went over my meeting with the Allegris.

"Most of the time," Mahilan said, "a missing item is simply a misplaced item. I can't tell you the number of times a lawyer has mislabeled a box. Depositions all look alike. She probably misplaced it and found it when cleaning up. You said her house was crammed full of books."

"You're forgetting she was killed over this research," I said.

"You think you know better than the police?"

I glared at my brother.

"Why don't we order dessert?" Ava suggested.

"The police," I said, "don't know as much as I do."

"What *do* you know, JJ?" The tenor was light, but it held a hint of the patronizing tone I remembered from when he used to lecture me before I found direction in my life. "I gave you the benefit of the doubt before we left, but nothing has happened here in Italy."

"I think your sister might be on to something," Ava said.

"You do?" Mahilan and I said at the same time.

"I don't know about the poor woman who was killed," Ava said, "but the missing paintings from Lazzaro Allegri make sense. All three of us are examples of the small unrecorded cross-pollinations that go on across the world. Lazzaro brought different cultural art forms together almost five hundred years ago. His work is out there. Somewhere. Being here in this place, with all this history, can't you feel it?"

Mahilan gave up. After espressos, he drove us to the Park of Monsters.

"I can see why this place is called the Sacred Wood," Ava said as we stepped through the archway that led to the sphinxes. "I should take Carey here over his summer vacation."

"This place is creepy," Mahilan said, turning up his collar as he eyed a two-faced statue that towered over him. "A statue of a giant ripping a man in half, a stone elephant strangling a man to death, the mouth of Hell. What kind of man built this place?"

"Vicino Orsini," I said. "A man nobody agrees about." Was he a madman or an artistic genius? I imagined art historians asked themselves that question about many artists.

I spotted a man in a green shirt and asked him if he knew Francesco. He didn't speak English, but recognized the name Francesco, and pointed me to a gray-haired man in a green shirt a ways down the path. It was the comedian from the day before. Now I understood what Enzo meant about him being a character.

I pulled Ava and Mahilan away from the leaning tower. Mahilan was trying to take her picture, but Ava was blushing and refusing. We approached Francesco. He was a mirror opposite of seventeen-year-old Niccolò. Once-black hair had turned almost completely white, he wasn't much taller than I was, and where the teenager had radiated open-ended friendliness, Francesco wore a guarded expression. I guessed Francesco to be in his seventies. We introduced ourselves and he shook our hands in turn, with a surprisingly firm grip from such weathered hands. As he listened to us speak, his cautious face brightened.

"You are talent scouts from America?" He spoke English with a thicker accent than Enzo and Brunella's. "You have heard of my performances?"

"Performances?" Ava asked.

"Oh." His face fell. "Not talent scouts."

"We heard you were the man to speak to if we wanted to learn the true history of this place," I said.

His face brightened again. "I have a break coming up in thirty minutes. You wish to meet me inside the cafeteria?"

We spent the next twenty minutes wandering from one stone creature to the next. Ava's favorite was the jolly dragon. Mahilan liked the Pegasus, perhaps the only statue in the whole park that couldn't have been described as creepy even by a child.

I climbed onto the edge of the fountain.

"What are you doing?" Mahilan hissed.

"Keep a lookout for me."

"Keep a lookout?"

"For anyone in a green shirt. I didn't look at this as carefully before as I should have."

Ava hopped up onto the wide edge next to me, but didn't stop there. She stepped onto the mossy floor of the empty fountain.

"I don't see anything," I said, joining her.

"Neither do I," Ava said. "I wonder if the moss is thick enough to hide anything beneath it."

"I thought of that, but this used to be a functioning fountain. Wouldn't it be a bad idea to have an art studio beneath running water?"

Mahilan nearly yanked my shoulder out of its socket as he pulled us from the fountain onto the path. It was time to make our way to the cafeteria anyway, and I hadn't seen anything that looked like it could lead to a hidden grotto. I didn't protest as Mahilan marched us to the cafeteria.

"How can you eat?" Ava asked.

"What?" Mahilan said. "This eggplant parmesan looks great."

"We had a three-course lunch two hours ago."

"We're on vacation."

"What do you think he was talking about when he mentioned his performances?" Ava asked.

"I saw him joking with some kids yesterday," I explained. "I think he'd like the Park of Monsters to be more like an interactive theme park, like how amusement parks at home have actors jump out and scare people around Halloween."

"This is certainly the place for it," Mahilan said.

"Here's Francesco." I waved him over to the corner of the cafeteria where we sat underneath a giant black and white poster showing the Park of Monsters in the 1950s. In the photograph, sheep grazed around the stone monstrosities.

"Hello, my friends," Francesco said with a warm grin.

"Can we get you anything?" Ava asked.

"*Grazie mille, signora.* You are too kind. But I have only *venti* minutes. What can I tell you?"

"My sister is a historian," Mahilan said. "We're here on vacation, but she can't resist learning the local history."

I wasn't sure if Mahilan was purposefully being misleading because he was secretly worried that I was right about the danger. Or perhaps not showing his hand was simply second nature for him after practicing law for several years.

"There is much history in these parts. You have come to the right man."

"Why won't anyone tell us why nobody goes into this section of the woods?" I asked, showing him my crumpled map.

"Has nobody told you?"

"You mean you know? And you'll tell us?"

He shook his head and chuckled. "If you really want to know, I will tell you. But...You must be certain you wish to hear it."

Mahilan rolled his eyes, but he was sitting next to Francesco and outside his field of view.

"We do," Ava said, giving Francesco a winning smile.

"It is the ghost," he said. "And if I tell you the story, *the ghost will know*. Then you, too, will hear her mournful wail."

CHAPTER 24

"You don't seriously believe—" Mahilan began.

"We'd love to hear the story," Ava said, smiling coyly. Was she flirting with the elderly actor?

Francesco turned from us and looked out the window to the lush greenery covering the hills and canyons that surrounded us. The vegetation was so thick that it was impossible to know what lay beneath the treetops.

"The history of my province of Viterbo is filled with tragedies. The Italians truly savor life because of our collective memories of the pain that came before us. Peasants died of starvation in spite of the rich land, wars called our men from their families, families fought for power and land."

Mahilan stirred restlessly. He looked as if he wanted to speed Francesco along, when our elderly companion whirled around from his contemplative view and met each of our eyes in turn.

"There is perhaps no greater tragedy than not knowing what happened to a loved one. This is why there is such power behind our ghost."

In spite of myself, my skin prickled.

"The story begins with noblewoman Marguerite Allegri."

"Allegri?"

"*Sì*. I do not know her maiden name. She married a son of the Allegri family who owned much of this region."

"Lazzaro?" I asked.

"No, *signora*. Lazzaro Allegri was a man of ill repute who never married. This would have been one of his many cousins.

Marguerite was a woman who loved her husband as passionately as only an Italian can do. Marguerite begged her husband not to go to war. We don't know if she had a vision of the future, or whether she simply loved Antonio too much to part with him. Especially under such dangerous circumstances. The danger was known, you understand. Vicino Orsini was held captive during the French-Spanish Wars for three years, before a ransom was negotiated to bring him home."

Francesco paused, shaking with emotion. "Marguerite pleaded with her husband not to go—and she was right. For seven years, she waited for her beloved Antonio to return. She received no word from him, yet she waited faithfully. She was a beautiful woman, with lush lips no man could resist, and seductive black hair that flowed beyond her full hips." Francesco pantomimed the shape of a voluptuous woman as he spoke. "She had a strong personality uncommon for many women of that time, and would not consider any of her multiple suitors. She waited. And she waited. Her silky hair turned brittle and gray. Her smooth skin shriveled. And her engaging manner dried up and blew away as if dust in the wind."

His lip quivered. "Excuse me. I must have some water."

Ava handed him her bottled water.

"*Grazie.*" He drank the water, gripping the bottle with a shaking hand. "Marguerite spent her fortune sending men to search for her husband. It was a rainy night almost seven years to the day that Antonio had departed when Marguerite received news of him. The messenger, soaked to the bone by the heavy rain, brought the remains of her beloved. That night, Marguerite's mournful wail was heard across the land. Nearly a skeleton herself after years of waiting for word of her husband, she took to her bed and died of pneumonia—or was it grief?—a few weeks later."

Heartache overcame me. Both for Marguerite and for myself. I didn't know what had become of Lane Peters. Would I ever learn what had happened to him? I groaned inwardly. I was falling prey to Francesco's theatrics. My thoughts weren't usually so melodramatic.

"The poor woman," Ava whispered. She held Mahilan's hand tightly in her own.

Francesco squinted at her. I believed he'd forgotten we were there. "The villagers learned of her death in a most unusual way. She had sent the servants away and refused to see anyone. Yet night after night, as the rains continued, the villagers heard her woeful cries. A small group went to her home to check on her."

"She was there alone?" Mahilan asked.

"Yes and no," Francesco said. "They found her body there, but she had been dead for many weeks."

I shivered.

"Then who—" Ava began.

Francesco's eyes locked on mine. "*Signora* Jaya understands what I'm saying."

"The ghost," I said. "The wail the villagers heard was believed to be her ghost."

"Not 'believed to be,'" Francesco said. "It *was* the ghost."

I unfolded the map I'd been given. "Francesco, is this where the ghost supposedly roams?"

Francesco squinted at the map and nodded.

My brother snatched it from my hands. "You have a ghost map, Jaya? Where did you get a ghost map?"

"Until a minute ago, I didn't know what I had. All I knew was that nobody wanted to talk about why I shouldn't go running there."

"Yes," Francesco said. "Is bad luck."

"What's a ghost going to do to her?" Mahilan asked.

Francesco balked. "You care for your sister, yes? Then you must not let her go there."

"I'm curious," Ava said. "Do people emerge from that section of the woods with white hair or something?"

"It is much worse, *signora*. The ghost has killed before."

"You're kidding," I said. "Right? You're a comedian. I saw you joking with the kids at the park."

"*Sì*, but I am not joking now. I tell you I am an actor. Many years ago, when I was a young man, a film crew came to film a movie inside the Park of Monsters. This was the 1960s, not long after the forest was cleared away for the park to reopen after centuries. There was still much to be discovered."

"Let me guess," my brother said. "A horror movie."

"You make fun," Francesco said. "But you should not. Yes, it was a horror movie. There was not much budget. American actors were the stars, but local men like me played small parts."

"Can we find it?" Ava asked. "What was it called?"

"Sadly, the film was never completed."

Mahilan shook his head. "They didn't get the proper permission from the owners of the park? Such a common problem. People never think to consult a lawyer until it's too late to—"

"This was not the problem," Francesco said. "The actor playing the lead in the film heard the ghost one night when it was raining. As a foreigner, he was intrigued. He went out looking for her."

"Where does one look for a ghost?" I asked.

"Between Orsini land and Allegri land. This same area on your map. Neither of the families wishes to claim it. Not with the ghost."

Mahilan rolled his eyes.

"He found her," Francesco said.

We all gasped. Even my brother.

"When the actor returned from the woods, he was bloodied. He did not tell us what had happened, but from that moment on, we could tell he was possessed. He began acting secretively and missing his scheduled shoots. A few days later, he could no longer contain the ghost. He began to have fits. His spasms became so great that he was unable to breathe. When he died in front of us, he had a frozen look of fear on his face unlike anything I have ever seen. It is something I will never forget."

Francesco wrapped his arms around his chest. He looked like he might be about to have a fit himself.

"That poor man," Ava whispered.

Francesco shook himself. "It was many years ago. But yes, it affected many of us. This is when the *Castello del Fantasma* winery closed. Even though it is not on the land where the ghost can be heard, nobody wished to offend the ghost who kills."

"That's why nobody will buy the ruins," I said.

Francesco chuckled. "The brave men who opened the bar do not pay rent. It means it is the cheapest place to buy *caffè* in the morning and *vino* in the evening."

"Why exactly does a ghost want to kill people?" Mahilan asked. He'd recovered from his captivation of a minute before, and a smirk now showed on his face.

"She is angry. Confused. She felt, more than anything, that she was betrayed. Antonio promised to return to her, yet he did not. He was killed by foreigners in a foreign land." Francesco's tortured eyes looked past us into a point on the horizon that I could have sworn was in another century.

We all followed his gaze in silence. He was one hell of a good actor. When he spoke of betrayal, I felt as if a knife was twisting in my own gut. Had Lane betrayed me? Was I doomed to go on with life not knowing what happened to him?

"It's a great story," I said, breaking the spell. "And you're a superb storyteller, Francesco. You tell it as if you were there. Not only in the 1960s, I mean, but in the 16th century when the ghost story came to be. Did you find this information in local archives?"

"There are no archives that I know of, *signora*."

"Then how—"

"I may not have been completely truthful with you, I must admit. I know so many details because I was there. It is the reason I wish to remain here in these gardens. You see, I am the reincarnation of Pier Francesco 'Vicino' Orsini."

CHAPTER 25

"You always find the crazy ones, Jaya," Mahilan said. It was an hour later and we were back at the villa, sitting on our suite's balcony. Mahilan poured us each a glass of a sweet wine made from Aleatico grapes, a necessary form of sustenance after our talk with Francesco.

"I thought he was a darling man," Ava said.

"I would have too," Mahilan said, "if his stories hadn't been so creepy." He gave her a kiss on the top of her head and handed her the glass of wine.

"To eccentric history buffs," I said, raising my glass, and clinking it with theirs. "It doesn't matter if he's crazy, you know. His belief that he's the famous Orsini who built the Park of Monsters is why he studied the local history that everyone else had forgotten. And now we're one step closer to finding Lazzaro's studio."

"We are?"

"It's a real connection between the Orsinis and the Allegris."

"A ghostly connection. Which doesn't seem very real."

"Have you no imagination? There's something going on here. *The rain.* It can't be a coincidence that Lazzaro's notes talk about finding him when it's raining, and this historical ghost story has to do with the rain."

"I hate to break it to you, JJ, but that's the very definition of a coincidence."

"If Francesco hadn't been dragged back to work by his

supervisor, I would have asked him more about Vicino. Maybe he knows something about Michelangelo too. I'm going to have another talk with him."

"Not alone," my sensible brother said. "Remember someone has already killed once."

"I thought you didn't believe me." I studied Mahilan's face to see if he was being serious. His lip wasn't curling as it did when he suppressed a smile, and there was no amused glimmer in his green eyes, so I determined that he was.

"Things keep getting weirder and weirder," Mahilan said. "I'm inclined to either believe you completely or dismiss everything outright. The only problem is I can't decide which to do."

"You don't seriously think Francesco could be the killer, do you? A frustrated actor who works in a quaint Italian village across the world from California?"

"Nobody spends time with that man alone," Mahilan said. "I mean *nobody*."

"I agree," I said.

"You do?"

"Don't look so surprised, Fish. I don't think any of us should go off on our own with suspects until we know more about what's going on. I'll go with Ava to see Francesco."

"Have you suddenly become a folklorist instead of a historian?" Mahilan asked. "I thought we were looking for Lazzaro's art studio that's supposedly hidden somewhere in these woods."

"Folklore is based on fact. He could be a great resource to point us in the right direction."

"Or lead us astray," Ava pointed out.

"The ghost story is just one example," I said. "It's not the embellished ghost story details I'm interested in. It's all the local history that's buried in there—true facts we can look up. Vicino Orsini created that macabre Renaissance garden. I haven't been able to figure out the exact dates of his birth, death, and when he was a prisoner of war. Nobody even knows with certainty the identity of the architect who realized Vicino's vision for these gardens. If I can pin down information that's been passed down locally, but not to Renaissance scholars or hobbyists posting on online encyclopedias, I can fill in the blanks about the creation of Vicino's garden, Michelangelo's possible involvement, and how they both knew Lazzaro Allegri. Someone had to know where Lazzaro's studio was hidden."

Mahilan's expression morphed from a skeptical scowl to an open grin. "You would have made a great lawyer, Jaya. The way your mind fills in the missing pieces."

"Right now it feels like it's all missing pieces. Even though Francesco didn't think a main set of town archives exist, I want to find a local library."

"With you being oh-so fluent in Italian?" he said.

I glared at my brother. "I'll get someone to translate. Ava, are you all right?"

"It's later than I realized, and I want to get something into the post for Carey today." She polished off her small glass of wine and stood up. "I think I'll make a sketch of Francesco. Maybe I'll turn it into the start of a comic strip with that ghost story. You two stay out here and enjoy the view. It's too bright to draw."

"She's a great mom," Mahilan said once Ava had closed the balcony door behind her.

I couldn't place the emotion in his voice. Pride? Happiness? Or could it be...

"You're in love with her," I said.

He didn't look at me, keeping his eyes on his fingers as he twirled the stem of his glass. He set the glass down and met my gaze. "You know me, JJ. I fall in love every other day."

"I know. But not like this. You really—"

"I know. Scary, right?" He added more wine to his glass. A lot more. Like the Italians, Mahilan knew how to live well. "I don't know what it is, JJ. I've never felt like this before. It's so real. So *raw*."

"That, Fish, is love."

We sat in silence for a few minutes. How could I pretend to

know what love was? My relationships had always been passionate, but was that love? Why did my insides feel so twisted up as I sat there?

The balcony door slid open and Ava stepped back outside. "What do you think of this?" She handed Mahilan a postcard-sized sheet of thick paper with a pen and ink drawing. Francesco's animated face had been captured in a few deft strokes of Ava's pen. In the background was the scene he'd described: a mournful woman standing atop a hill in the rain, looking out over an empty, winding path.

"It's beautiful," Mahilan said. "Just like the woman who drew it." He pulled her into his lap, leaving me feeling like a third wheel even though this trip to Italy had been my idea in the first place.

"What's the plan, you two?" Ava asked, extricating herself from Mahilan's arms.

"I'm going to do some more research into Bomarzo and Vicino Orsini, and if the facts support it, we need to go back to the Park of Monsters when there aren't people around."

"My thoughts exactly," Ava said.

"You mean right when it opens?" Mahilan asked.

Ava and I shared a look. "Not quite," she said.

"We need to go when it's closed," I added.

Mahilan crossed his arms and smirked. "How are we going to manage our own private viewing? I suppose you two are going to charm the owner like you did Francesco."

"It's not like there's an electric fence surrounding the park," I said. At least I hoped not.

Mahilan gaped at us. "Breaking in? You're seriously suggesting breaking and entering? In a foreign country?"

"There's no breaking," I said. "Simply taking a stroll after hours. Maybe a little bit of harmless fence-hopping."

"It's trespassing, at worst," Ava said.

"*Et tu*, Ava?" Mahilan said. "I give up. When do we break into this damn Park of Monsters?"

CHAPTER 26

We made plans to break into the park late that night, around eleven o'clock. I doubted it needed to be that late, except the villa's restaurant wasn't even open for dinner until eight, and Mahilan insisted on having a proper dinner. Which, since we were on vacation at a fancy Italian villa, meant a four-course dinner with wine pairings.

With four hours until dinner, Mahilan and Ava wanted to go look at nearby Etruscan ruins. I wanted to get some research done before we went back to the park, so I stayed in the suite with my laptop and internet connection.

"You're staying here with the door locked, right?" Mahilan said.

"Of course, Fish."

Half an hour into my research, I hadn't found any more than I had before I left San Francisco. The internet was the same in Italy as it was in the U.S., except for defaulting to Italian sites.

I'd promised Mahilan I wouldn't talk to anyone who could be dangerous. I agreed with him. So I called the flirtatious teenager who wanted to practice his English.

Niccolò had just gotten off work and said he would be delighted to drive me to a library. He warned me it was expected to rain that evening and suggested I bring a jacket and hat.

When Niccolò pulled up at the villa, I saw that he hadn't followed his own advice. He was dressed in the same half-buttoned style of shirt as he had been the day before. He tossed his movie-star hair as he stepped off his moped to greet me.

"*La biblioteca* will be closed now," he said, "but I know the librarian. I tell him we will bring him wine. He will meet us there to let us inside."

Fifteen minutes later, as the sun hung low over the vineyards, Niccolò and I pulled up in front of an ancient stone building. The baby blue scooter kicked up dust on the dirt clearing that served as a parking lot and road.

A tiny white-haired man stood in front of a door twice his height. He greeted Niccolò in rapid Italian and kissed his cheeks, then kissed my cheeks as I handed him two bottles of wine.

"He is from the south," Niccolò said, as if I needed an explanation. The enthusiastic kisser was introduced as Orazio Benedetti; *Signor* Benedetti, as Niccolò respectfully addressed the older man.

Jangling a set of skeleton keys, Orazio opened the heavy wooden door and let us inside.

I explained to Niccolò what I was after, and he translated for the librarian. As I expected, only a small fraction of the books in the library were in English. As I *hadn't* expected, the "small" library stretched on for what seemed like miles. Not all in one direction, but through winding staircases so narrow I could barely squeeze into them, leading up to a mezzanine and hidden rooms. Niccolò got to put his English skills to the test as he translated the volumes Orazio brought for me.

"This book, it says there are many ideas behind the Sacred Wood. This is another name for the *Parco dei Mostri*, yes? These ideas, they compete with each other. The historians are not sure why Vicino Orsini built his garden as he did." He frowned. "They did not teach us this at the park. They tell us he devoted the beautiful gardens to his departed wife. That the darkness was his grief, and the beauty was in honor of his wife. But this book says the great man did not truly love her."

"Lots of materials I read said he kept mistresses," I said.

Niccolò waved his hand dismissively. "This is not the same thing as not loving a woman. He is an Italian in the—" He broke off and counted on his fingers. "An Italian man in the 16th century. Of course he had mistresses."

"I'm not judging him. I'm more interested in information on what his gardens looked like when first constructed."

"No carvings have been destroyed," Niccolò said. "Some pieces are lost, like the nose, but they are all there."

"I mean the landscape."

He looked at me blankly.

I tried again. "The land. The forest. Streams that may have once existed but have now dried up."

"*Sì*, I will look for this."

Orazio found an early map of the Park of Monsters. Niccolò had been right. There were no streams to explain Lazzaro's note.

My musings were interrupted by a sudden exclamation from Orazio. He called out with a string of rapid Italian phrases and thrust his head over a precarious wrought-iron railing above us.

"What's he saying?" I asked Niccolò. "Did I hear *fotografia*? He found photographs?"

"Your *italiano* is *perfetto*. Soon you will have no use for me." He winked at me. "*Sì*, he says he found photographs."

They were black and white prints from the 1930s and '40s. Orazio chuckled and pointed at one that showed sheep grazing in front of outraged stone monsters.

"One last thing," I added. "I'd love to find any references to a ghost story about people who were contemporaries of Orsini."

"Contemporaries?"

"People who lived at the same time as Vicino Orsini." I didn't want to say the name Allegri for fear of biasing my research. I wanted to see if Orazio would independently find the same story that Francesco had told me.

"Ah. Contemporary." He spoke the word slowly as he typed it into a collection of English notes on his phone.

While Niccolò consulted with the librarian, I browsed through a row of beautiful books. Many of them looked like antiques. Lane would have loved this place.

"*Signora*," Niccolò said. "I believe it is our famous ghost story you speak of. *Signor* Benedetti found one of the original printings of this story." He held up a pamphlet-sized book, its leather cover faded and torn. "It is many centuries old. Orazio only trusts me with it because he knows me since I was a baby."

A zing of excitement hit me as I thought about the person who wrote the local legend for posterity, and the hands of people from so many generations that had held the book over the centuries.

"Someone has already told you the ghost story?" he asked hesitantly.

"Francesco."

Niccolò shook his head. "He should not have told you."

"You think I'll hear the woman's mournful wail now? And that as a foreigner, I'll be possessed to go in search of a murderous ghost, like the unfortunate actor? Surely you know that's a superstition, Niccolò. He was probably on LSD or some other drug. It was the sixties."

"You have not heard this, *mia Bella*. If you had, you would not think us foolish." His face was deathly serious.

"I'm sorry. I don't think you're silly." I hoped I hadn't offended him. I knew it was only a superstition, but when everyone around you believed something, it was difficult not to believe it too.

"I will read to you the story of Marguerite and Antonio Allegri?"

"Allegri," I whispered. "Yes, Niccolò. Please do."

It was true. The locally famous ghost story was about a relative of Lazzaro's. But what was Lazzaro Allegri's connection to Pier Francesco 'Vicino' Orsini, the creator of Bomarzo, where Lazzaro had hidden his paintings?

Niccolò's phone rang. He gestured animatedly with his hand that wasn't holding the phone as he spoke spiritedly and resentfully to the person on the other end of the line. My guess was that it was a family member.

"*Mi dispiace*," he said as he hung up. "I must bring my sister home. I will not be long. You stay with Orazio, yes?"

"Um, sure." I hoped he'd be back early enough that I'd beat Ava and my brother to the villa.

Niccolò put his hand on Orazio's shoulder and murmured something while Orazio nodded.

"*A dopo,*" Niccolò called out, twirling his hand as he descended the narrow staircase to get back to the front door of the library.

"*Un momento,*" Orazio said. He disappeared through a doorway that I would have sworn was a bookshelf and emerged less than a minute later with two wineglasses in one hand and an Italian/English dictionary in the other.

He popped the cork of one of the bottles of wine I'd brought, which he'd put in a miniature fridge to chill as soon as I'd arrived. Niccolò had been the one to pick out the white wine that was a blend of chardonnay and pinot grigio. The seventeen-year-old was the one who explained to me how the volcanic earth of the Lazio region was especially good to produce white wine, and who steered me away from the bottles of wine with the prettiest labels.

With Orazio's print dictionary and my phone translator, the old librarian and I learned we had a lot in common. He'd studied history in college, but wanted the security and community of staying close to home, even when many of his friends left for Rome or America.

He knew about the ghost story but didn't seem bothered by it. He was more interested in the people left behind. "Lazzaro Allegri," he said. "*Sì.* Friend of Vicino Orsini. *Eccentricissim.*" He paused and looked at his dictionary. "Eccentric men."

Orazio didn't know anything about a hidden art studio, but said the Allegri family had written Lazzaro out of the family bible, so he wasn't surprised. I wasn't either. I asked him what he knew about Michelangelo. He didn't think very highly of Michelangelo's personality. Like Francesco, he acted like he took it personally. Unlike Francesco, Orazio didn't think he'd lived through the Renaissance. He simply felt passionately about history.

"Michelangelo visit Bomarzo," Orazio said.

I nearly knocked over my glass of wine. "He did?"

He consulted his dictionary again.

"*Sì*. Visit is correct word. He visit short time, no live here."

I asked him if he'd heard that Michelangelo had designed the Park of Monsters, as Stefano had mentioned was one theory.

"No," Orazio said emphatically.

There went that idea.

When Niccolò returned an hour later, Orazio and I were sitting on the floor surrounded by historical photos of the region. The bottle of wine was nearly empty.

Niccolò grinned. "*Vino* makes for good friends, yes?"

Niccolò translated the short story as he read. I occasionally corrected his English, but it was quite good and didn't need much help. There was no date attributed to the legend, but this book had been printed in the 16th century, so the timing fit. It was the same tale that Francesco had told—except for the ending.

"I translate well?" he asked with a shy smile, after he wrapped up the chilling tale.

"It was perfect. There was only one thing you said incorrectly several times. You kept saying the ghost was the husband, not the wife."

"Husband is the man, yes?"

"That's right."

"I have read the story correctly. This book speaks of the husband who misses his wife while at war. Then he dies of grief when he returns home to find she has died."

"You mean it's the ghost of a *man*?"

"*Sì*. I always heard the story as being the ghost of a woman." He shrugged. "Maybe I remember it that way because I have always thought the ghost sounded like a woman."

"You've actually heard the ghost? This isn't just a story you believe?"

"We have all heard her. And when the rains begin, *signora*, she will find you too."

CHAPTER 27

Niccolò was silent as we drove back to the villa. I wasn't sure if he needed to concentrate in the darkness or if the ghost story had shaken him. The rain Niccolò predicted hadn't broken, but a cool summer wind blew around us, causing the small moped to veer precariously when bursts of wind snuck up on us.

Niccolò dropped me off a few minutes before I was due to meet Mahilan and Ava for dinner.

I knew, logically, that legends changed over time. Especially over five centuries. But there was something about the element of the story that had shifted that I couldn't let go of. The basics had remained the same, that a husband and wife who loved each other had been separated and searched for each other, learning of the other's death during a rainstorm and dying of grief, so their ghost would wail whenever it rained. But the story the present-day locals knew was about the ghost of a woman, whereas the much earlier version talked of the ghost of a man.

Two ghosts? That was all I needed. Even though I didn't believe in them.

Mahilan wouldn't hear of foregoing wine with dinner—we were on vacation, after all—but Ava and I convinced him the three of us should only share one bottle. We had to keep clear heads for what awaited us. I neglected to mention that I'd left the room and already had half a bottle without them.

As we ate braised oxtail and more fried Roman artichokes, they told me about the Etruscan ruins.

"Could I get some of the cocoa sauce I ate yesterday, for these artichokes?" I asked a waiter.

Mahilan laughed after the waiter left. "He recovered well, but he nearly lost it. Glad to see you back to your normal self."

"What am I missing?" Ava asked.

"You don't want to know about Jaya's eating habits," Mahilan said. "I'm sorry you didn't join us at the Etruscan ruins, JJ. You'd have loved the history. I hope you at least got up from your laptop to walk through the grounds."

"Well, about that, Fish..."

His jaw pulsed. "Seriously, JJ? You left the villa?"

"I didn't go anywhere alone. My friend Niccolò took me to the library." The waiter returned with a dish of chocolaty sauce. I dipped a bite of artichoke into the sauce, then let the combination melt in my mouth. I was right about how heavenly it was. I hoped it wouldn't give me a food coma before our nocturnal expedition.

Mahilan's nostrils flared and his face turned red. "You went out with a strange Italian man? You specifically promised—"

"That I wouldn't talk to anyone dangerous. I talked to a teenager who works at the Park of Monsters and an octogenarian librarian even shorter than I am. Neither one has anything to do with this."

"None of us," Mahilan fumed, "can say for sure who has anything to do with this."

"That ghost story Francesco told us does originate in the 1500s."

"A ghost story, JJ, is hardly important—"

"It's the same story?" Ava asked.

"That's the interesting thing. I think we might have two ghosts. Both Marguerite and Antonio Allegri. Everyone we've met believes it's her ghost haunting the hillside, but in the 1500s, it was Antonio who supposedly haunted these woods."

* * *

We arrived at the Park of Monsters after eleven o'clock. We could have been there sooner, but Ava and I had insisted we park the car a distance from the entrance and approach on foot.

"I can't believe I'm going along with this," Mahilan muttered as he stumbled over a rock on the road. "What two-headed monster have I created by bringing the two of you together?"

Ava laughed and wrapped her arm around Mahilan's elbow.

We fell silent as we reached the entrance. Instead of trying to break into the main entry gate, we circled the sprawling park until we saw a thick covering of trees that would obscure our hopping the fence. I tossed the rope ladder we'd made up to the top bars, climbed over, and pulled the ladder up and onto the other side of the wall.

Though we'd planned for the clandestine visit with black clothing, gloves, and flashlights, we hadn't done the type of reconnaissance Lane would have done if he'd been here with me. I hoped we were properly disguised in case there were video cameras.

We'd mapped out a path of stone structures that were likely candidates for a clue to Lazzaro's studio: the Ogre, Proteus, and Pegasus.

At night, I was especially struck by the fact that none of the sculptures looked quite like Lazzaro's sketches. I knew creative types had always used artistic license, but it makes the work of a historian much more difficult.

With clouds above, it was effectively a moonless night, so we were forced to use our flashlights. In the darkness, the harsh beams of light bouncing off the stone monoliths created an eerie sensation, as if we were slicing pinpricks of light through Dante's Inferno.

Since the garden was laid out on multiple levels, we had to watch for stone steps that appeared in unexpected places. In the forest that had overtaken the majority of the sculpture garden, we never would have found the creatures we sought without our maps.

Even though the gardens had been restored over fifty years ago after being lost to overgrowth for five centuries, nature still reigned supreme in this Sacred Wood.

"I don't understand what we're looking for," Mahilan whispered. "We already looked during the day."

"For anything we missed." I didn't bother lowering my voice. If anyone was looking for us, our flashlights gave us away much more than our voices. "You pulled me and Ava out of the fountain so quickly we never got a good look at that area, for one. We need to look more carefully for anything in the stones that could lead into a larger section hidden by overgrowth."

"Which nobody has found in all this time?"

"It's more common than you'd think," I said. "Archaeologists and historians wouldn't have jobs if we remembered our pasts. Remember this whole place was forgotten for over four centuries."

"Nearly five hundred years," Ava murmured. "You think we can find it?"

"With a stage magician for a best friend, you learn all about various ways secret passageways can be hidden and revealed."

"Doesn't Sanjay use high-tech gadgets for his illusions?" Mahilan asked. "Damn." His flashlight illuminated the dragon and he stumbled backward. To be fair to my brother, the grinning dragon didn't look nearly as good humored in the darkness.

I steered Mahilan back onto the path. "Sanjay was trained in the classic methods, and the basic concepts were the same. Hydraulics, basic engineering concepts that architects have known for millennia. Even with robotic technology, lots of people still build things the solid old-fashioned way. Sébastien has replicated many classic automata illusions, and his work is in high demand."

"Who's Sébastien?" Ava asked.

"A retired French stage magician to whom we are indebted for saving Jaya's life," Mahilan said.

"I take it that's a story for another day." Ava shone her light at a fork in the path.

"I'm afraid it is," I said. "I think we want to go this way. We cut across the path too soon. How did we get so turned around?"

"This place is a maze," Mahilan grumbled. He continued to do so as we hopped a low fence leading to one of the creatures we wanted to examine: Proteus.

I checked the rocky areas of land near the sea monster raising its head from the earth, and also the mouth of the carving itself, to make sure there weren't any moving pieces in the stone. Had the park's creator, Vicino Orsini, kept his fellow outcast Lazzaro in mind when constructing his sculpture garden? Or had the studio grotto been added later?

Vicino had built the park in the 1550s, shortly after Lazzaro returned from India. I didn't want to destroy anything, so I gingerly went over all of the points in the stone that I thought might give way as part of the original design.

"Nothing here." I sat down on the grass that served as the sea monster's ocean in front of its giant mouth.

"What was that?" Mahilan whipped his head around and squinted into the darkness. "A twig snapped. I swear I heard a twig snap. It's like something is stalking us."

"You didn't hear—" I began.

"I heard it too," Ava said. She clicked off her flashlight. "Turn off your flashlights."

I stood up and found my brother's hand.

We stood in darkness for several minutes, with no sound except our breathing.

My eyes adjusted to the near-black darkness, and I could make out shadows that I knew must be Mahilan and Ava. But without any detectable features, in this macabre park they looked more like faceless monsters.

"Shouldn't we—" Mahilan whispered.

"Shh." Ava and I both cut him off.

"But—"

"Look," Ava whispered. She raised her arm, pointing toward the hill above us.

I could make out the shadow of her arm well enough to see the spot she indicated. Then I wished my eyes hadn't yet adjusted. Because there, atop the mound above the sea of monsters, a translucent figure walked across the earth.

"It can't be," Mahilan said. "It's the ghost."

The apparition was still for a moment—then headed right for us.

CHAPTER 28

I watched, transfixed, as the shadow moved silently across the rocks. The ghostly figure was the shape of a person rather than an animal, but devoid of features.

"The ghost," Mahilan exclaimed unnecessarily.

I don't know how long I would have stood there if Mahilan hadn't grabbed my hand. He pulled Ava and me with him as he ran.

"We can move better on our own, Fish," I said.

"Then *move*," he hissed.

Though I was a runner, I wasn't ever a competitive one. I don't think I'd ever run faster than I did that night. Branches whipped against my face as I kept pace with Mahilan.

"We're going the wrong way," Ava whisper-shouted. I'm not sure if Mahilan heard her and ignored her, or if his ears were thudding as loudly with his heartbeat as mine were.

We caught our breath against a boulder that blocked our path. "What the hell was that?" Ava asked. "It didn't have a face."

"I don't want to know," Mahilan said. "All I want to know is how the hell to get out of this place."

"I told you we were running away from the entrance," Ava said.

Mahilan swore.

"I don't know where we are either now," I said. "It was all I could do to stay on the path and keep my eyes on you two."

"Let me get my flashlight," Mahilan said.

"No," Ava and I said at the same time. She put her hand on Mahilan's.

"Ghosts don't need the light from our flashlight to see us," he said.

"It wasn't a ghost," I said, sounding much more confident than I felt at that moment. I pulled several twigs from my hair.

"Then what the hell was it?"

"I don't know. But not a ghost."

"It was rigged by a *person*, of course," Ava said. "Am I the only one with my head screwed on straight? You're the one with the magician friends, Jaya. You of all people know it's possible to fake things like that."

"Why would someone go to the trouble?" I stretched as I spoke. We'd run quite a distance.

"For this damn treasure of Lazzaro Allegri's."

I shook my head, even though they could barely see me. "Your theory is that someone has been pretending to be a ghost—for *centuries*—getting each new generation to take their place, as they walk around scaring people who try to find Lazzaro's art studio? It doesn't make any sense."

"You're combining two facts that don't go together," Ava said. "First, you've got the ghost story. There are ghost stories that capture people's imaginations everywhere. I'm sure you've got some good ones in San Francisco. In this case, superstitious locals have a local ghost story that's been passed down for generations. I'm sure they all *believe* they've heard the ghost when they hear a wild animal cry out, since the story has made its way into their consciousness. This place is pretty rural, and Mahilan and I saw several animals while we were sightseeing today."

"I had a similar thought. Even the teenager I spoke to believes in the ghost."

"And second," Ava said, "you haven't kept your quest to find Lazzaro's paintings a secret. Any ambitious local could have heard about it, and be using the ghost story to frighten you off."

Ava had a point. "That's not a bad idea. But why? Only

someone with specialized knowledge would know what a valuable discovery this could be."

"Rich Americans are looking for a lost treasure in their backyard," Ava said. "Someone without pure intentions might think it was an opportunity to get their hands on whatever we're after, regardless of what it is, then figure out what to do with it later."

"I hate to interrupt this fascinating discussion between you two treasure-hunting BFFs," Mahilan said, "but don't you think we should get out of here? In addition to that *thing* out there, I just felt a raindrop on my nose."

"I did too," I said. "We might as well turn on the flashlights. Otherwise we'll get drenched and freeze to death out here."

This time it was Ava who put a hand on our arms to stop us. "I heard someone," she whispered. "Close."

Mahilan swore under his breath and felt for my hand. "My eyes have adjusted well enough. Let's keep moving."

"Where?" I whispered back. "I haven't yet figured out where we are. We passed the lions at some point, but they're in the middle, so that doesn't tell us anything."

"Anywhere that's not here. This twisting path has to lead somewhere."

Mahilan pulled us along what I'm pretty sure was a path, but I could barely make it out as rain began to fall more steadily. I stumbled. My brother steadied my arm.

"Is that you breathing in my ear, Ava?" Mahilan asked.

"Who else would it be?" she whispered. "If you really think it's a ghost out there, you wouldn't feel it breathing."

"I read somewhere that apparitions are known to make chilled breath occur," Mahilan said, "as well as scents."

"Are you joking, Fish?" I asked. "You only read articles like that so you can laugh at them."

"I follow the evidence, JJ. It's not my fault if that's where the evidence is pointing."

I rolled my eyes in the darkness, for no one's benefit but my own.

The rain was falling harder now. I heard thunder rumbling in the distance, and nearly slipped off the dirt path.

Next it was Ava who tripped. Mahilan let go of my hand to help her up.

"The ground is too uneven here," she said. "We should turn back."

"Let me take a look," Mahilan said. He had to raise his voice, because the rain had turned torrential. "I think it's safe enough to turn on this—"

I didn't hear the next word. All I could hear was the horrific sound of the earth giving way beneath my brother's feet.

CHAPTER 29

"No!" Ava screamed.

She lunged forward. I stretched out an arm to stop her. She was at least as fit as I was, and much taller, so I doubted I could have held her back if she wanted to get away. But in the fraction of a second my arm was on hers, it gave her time to reconsider an impulsive action.

With shaking hands, I turned on my flashlight. It took me three tries.

Even with the light I couldn't see too well through the rain, but what I saw was even worse than I'd imagined. We'd walked to the edge of a precipice.

"Mahilan," Ava called. "Can you hear me?"

No answer.

I shone my light over the edge. The pressure in my chest eased slightly as I saw it wasn't a deep cavern. Only about fifteen feet. But still enough to injure someone, or—I swallowed hard. I couldn't lose my head. I wasn't going to think about the alternative.

"Fish!" I shouted.

Ava dropped onto her stomach and inched her way toward the edge. "I don't think any more of this muddy earth is going to give way. I'm going down."

"What are you talking about?" I grabbed her arm. "We need to go around—"

"I can't lose him, Jaya. I can't." Her brown eyes shone like glowing embers in the beam of my flashlight. We stared at each other as furious raindrops pelted us.

"You think I can?"

A moan came from beneath us.

"I'm coming to get you," Ava called to him.

"We need to find—"

"Hold this," Ava said, pushing her small black backpack into my arms. It was heavier than it looked. In her hands she held a length of rope. She shone her flashlight through the rain. "That one. That tree is strong enough."

Ava tied the rope around the base of the tree, then stood back and examined it. "Know anything about knots?"

"Not really."

"Say a prayer, then."

Before I could stop her, Ava slid down the steep and muddy slope where Mahilan had fallen.

I was torn between following Ava's progress and making sure the knot was secured. I forced myself to stay with the knotted rope. I'm not sure exactly what I would have done if it had started to give way, but luckily I didn't have to do anything. After an eternity that was probably no more than three minutes, two mud-covered figures emerged.

Mahilan's chest heaved and he sprawled out on his back.

"Are you hurt?" I asked, rushing over to him.

"The only thing wounded is my pride. And maybe these leather shoes."

"What are you doing on the ground then?"

"Seemed the best way to let the rain wash all this mud off of me."

A bolt of lightning filled the sky with a burst of white light. He wasn't kidding about the mud. Ava leaned over and kissed his muddy nose.

"You guys," I said, shivering as another crash of thunder and lightning filled the sky. "I think we'd better find shelter."

Ava and I helped Mahilan up.

Ava held her backpack above a drenched map of the labyrinthine park, while I shone the flashlight between the map and our surroundings.

"We must have cut through this section," I said. "We're not far from the Ogre's hellmouth."

"Can you *please*, for the love of God, call it something else?" Mahilan said.

"Here." Ava pointed at a spot on the map not far away.

"I see it," I said. "You can lean on me, Fish."

"Lazzaro's monster?" Mahilan said. "That's what you two are talking about? I'll stay here. This is a nice spot."

"There's shelter inside its mouth," I said. "A full room that's out of the rain and lightning."

In spite of Mahilan's insistence that he was fine, he was limping. I put my arm around him as we made our way to the stone Ogre, its open mouth waiting for us.

We climbed the nine steps leading to the black hole of a mouth. The steps were slick with rain. In his discombobulated state, Mahilan slipped. He took both Ava and me down with him. It wasn't a hard fall, since the steps were shallow, but the backpack ripped and our rope ladder tumbled out.

"Don't lose that," Ava said. "We'd be trapped here all night."

"You take Fish. I'll get the ladder." I fumbled on the slippery steps until my hands felt the rough weave of the rope. I clutched the coarse material, then scrambled up the steps and into the stone room.

"Let me look at your ankle," Ava said, pushing Mahilan down onto the stone picnic bench.

"It's fine, really," he said. But he winced as Ava eased off his mud-caked shoe.

I stood at the edge of the doorway, underneath the two stone teeth, looking out at the pouring rain.

"Good," Ava said. "Let us know if our 'ghost' comes back."

Now that I was standing still, the chill from the rain was catching up with me.

"Your ankle isn't too bad," Ava said to Mahilan. "It might swell a little though. I'm going to put your shoe back on. You'll need it to walk out of here."

"We're walking out of here?" Mahilan asked. "Shouldn't we call for help?"

"And tell them what?" I said, sitting down next to my brother. "That we broke into a national park, were prodding antique statues to see if they led to a secret hiding place, and caused a landslide by not sticking to the proper paths? Do lawyers get disbarred for transgressions in foreign countries?"

Mahilan glared at me.

"You're the one who wanted to tag along with me," I pointed out.

"I thought," he said through clenched teeth, "that it would be a fun vacation."

"Look," Ava said, nodding her head out the Ogre's mouth. "The heavy rain seems to be passing. It's not quite twelve. We can be back in our cozy beds in time to get a good night's sleep. I'm sure everything will seem less crazy in the morning."

She was right that the heavy swath of rain was letting up. The wind was pushing the storm elsewhere. Another burst of lightning illuminated the sky outside, casting an eerie shadow on the floor inside the Ogre's mouth. But this time, the thunder was a few seconds away.

"It's as good an opening as any," I said. "I can barely hear the rain at all. Shall we?"

As Ava and I helped Mahilan up, the three of us froze at the same moment. The sound that pierced the air was unlike any I had ever heard before.

The ghostly, mournful wail of a woman cut through the silence and echoed through the Park of Monsters.

CHAPTER 30

Even ever-elegant Ava looked shaken. I can't say I was in better shape myself.

I knew there was no such thing as ghosts, but *that sound.* I'd never heard such a sorrowful howl in my life.

"We're leaving," Mahilan said. "Now."

Nobody objected.

The three of us half-walked and half-ran hand in hand back to the spot where we'd entered the park. Now that we'd oriented ourselves, had our flashlights on, and didn't have heavy rain blinding us, we made it out of the park in fifteen minutes and were back at the rental car in another ten. My foot ached as I ran, but I chalked it up to sisterly concern for Mahilan's fall.

I took the wheel of the car and locked us inside. Ava sat in the back with Mahilan and checked out his ankle again. I fiddled with the seat of the car, moving it up several inches so I could reach the pedals. Only then did I realize I'd lost one of my boots.

I'd been running on adrenaline, so I hadn't noticed that my boot had slipped off. I had no idea where it could be. I closed my eyes and steadied my breathing. There was nothing to be done about it now. It was an indistinct black boot, and I had my heels and sneakers at the villa. I told myself it was fine. But I couldn't help imagining the Ogre laughing at me.

"You two are still going to deny that was a ghost?" Mahilan winced as Ava lifted his leg onto her lap.

"There's a logical explanation," Ava said.

"Which is what, exactly?" Mahilan asked. "I'm all ears."

"Just because we haven't figured it out yet," I said, "doesn't mean there isn't one." I turned on the heat and put the car into gear.

We'd parked the bright orange SUV off the road, hidden under a thicket of trees. I was thankful Mahilan had gone for the four-wheel drive model. The engine revved as I eased the Fiat out of the mud.

We drove in silence for a few minutes as I found my way back to the main road.

"How you doing, Fish?" I asked.

"The rental car company is going to charge me for all this mud."

"Glad to see you're back to your old self."

"His ankle isn't swelling much," Ava said. "And I'm sure we can find a car wash where we can get the car cleaned. It's only mud."

I glanced at them in the rearview mirror. In the blasting heat, the mud on their skin and clothing was drying. Except for their expressions of fear, they looked as if they'd stepped out of a mud bath at the villa's spa.

We arrived, bedraggled, at close to one o'clock in the morning. I realized it had been exactly midnight when we heard the ghostly wail.

The next morning, we were exhausted. Mahilan and I were also starving, so Ava put a pillow over her head while I slipped on my heels and my brother and I went to breakfast.

"If this is what your research is usually like," Mahilan said as he piled his plate with an assortment of warm breads and soft cheeses from the bountiful buffet, "I should have Sanjay keep you tied up with his Houdini handcuffs."

"The whole idea is that you can get out of them," I pointed out.

"Dammit, this isn't a joke!" A pat of butter molded in the shape of a bouquet of flowers flew off the knife in his hand.

I led us to an empty corner of the arched stone cellar that housed the smaller of the two restaurants where breakfast was served. Medieval sconces with modern electric lights shaped like candles illuminated the space.

"It's not a ghost," I said.

"Just because none of us are possessed like that actor—"

"Fish." I started laughing and couldn't stop. "You really think as Americans who heard the ghostly wail that she's calling us with her siren song?"

"The evidence—"

"Tells us that someone wants to scare us. Someone wants us to believe it's a ghost."

"That would mean they've known for decades, or even centuries, that we'd be coming for Lazzaro's hidden paintings in the present day. I don't buy it, JJ. That hypothesis doesn't make sense. It only makes sense if it's an actual ghost. She could be protecting her cousin's paintings. Did you think of that?"

I tried not to roll my eyes as I dipped a chunk of cheese into a bowl of thick European yogurt.

"Your food habits could be one of the reasons you don't have a boyfriend, JJ."

"Why should anyone care that I like unique combinations of food? And why do I need a boyfriend?"

"Tell me, is there anything in your fridge at home besides jars of spicy Indian pickle?"

"As a matter of fact there is. I—" I took another bite of food to stop myself from talking. I was about to say there was food in my fridge because Lane had gone grocery shopping for me.

Mahilan wasn't paying attention anyway. He was looking around underneath the table. "Is that your phone?"

By the time I found it buried at the bottom of my messenger bag, it had stopped ringing. I'd missed a call from Tamarind. Not Lane. And not Stefano Gopal. It was seven o'clock in the morning in Italy, so it would be ten o'clock in San Francisco. I took my coffee with me and went back to the room to call her back, leaving

Mahilan to get a second helping. I thought longingly of the succulent bacon and freshly baked croissants I was leaving behind.

The villa doors used old-fashioned keys, so between the coffee in one hand and the clunky key in the other, it took me a few seconds to unlatch the door.

When I stepped inside, I saw immediately that something wasn't right. My suitcase sat askew on my unmade bed. The maid wouldn't have unzipped the suitcase, nor would she have left the bed unmade.

My coffee cup clattering to the floor, I ran to Ava and Mahilan's private room, dreading what I might find. *We'd left Ava alone in the suite.*

As I stepped into the room, I heard her singing in the shower through the bathroom door. Relief flooded through me. She was here. Safe.

"Ava?" I called.

The singing stopped but the shower kept running. "You two back already? Give me a second."

I sat down on the edge of the bed to steady my nerves as I waited for Ava. But what I saw next made my relief evaporate: resting on the bed next to me was a calling card. ^V^.

The thief who'd killed Lane's old girlfriend Mia.

He was *here.*

This wasn't a gentleman thief trying to harmlessly scare us off with a ghost. The calling card thief had killed Lilith Vine, followed me to Lazzaro Allegri's treasure, and—I felt a lump in my throat. Lane was missing. I now had a good sense of why his phone was disconnected.

^V^ could have found Lane. The only other time he'd been completely unreachable was when he'd been coerced into helping with a theft in the recent past. Was the calling card thief asking Lane to help with yet another theft?

Or worse. The thief had killed before. What was to stop him from killing again?

CHAPTER 31

I couldn't help crying out as I imagined scenarios too horrible to think about. Would I lose Lane like he'd lost Mia?

I heard the shower stop and the shower curtain pull open. "I'm feeling so much better after getting a little more sleep," Ava said through the bathroom door.

A few seconds later, she opened the door. A towel was wrapped around her head and a robe pulled around her body. Ava was smiling—until she saw my face. I'm sure my face was a mask of horror. I was still reeling from the realization that a master thief was here in Italy with us and my conclusion that Lane had been kidnapped—or worse.

"What's happened?" she asked. "Is it Mahilan's ankle? Jaya? Talk to me. Did he fall? Is he hurt?"

I didn't know how to explain what I'd found. When I failed to dispute her assumption, Ava rushed toward the closet. "I shouldn't have let you two go without both of us to support him. Especially not before I looked at his ankle again. Is it bad?"

I put my arm on her shoulder as she frantically pulled a black camisole from a hanger. "It's not Mahilan. Look around your room. Are things how you left them?"

"What are you asking?" She pulled her robe more tightly around her. "Has someone besides the maid been in the suite?"

"This," I said, holding up the ^V^ calling card, "is the calling card of a thief. A dangerous one."

Ava looked at me incredulously. "Something was stolen? And a calling card was left in its place?"

"No. At least I don't think so. Not some*thing*. But some*one*."

"Mahil—"

"My brother is fine. He's safe and sound, and eating well enough that his ankle should be better in no time."

"Then what are you talking about? This thief stole a person—kidnapped them—and dropped off their card to let us know?"

"I think so." I closed my eyes and thought about when I'd last spoken with Lane. He didn't know I was coming to Italy. And nobody knew about the two of us. Had my being here triggered his disappearance? But how—and why? It was too big a coincidence to think it was unrelated.

"You're not making any sense." Ava took the now-wrinkled card from my fingers. "And this is a strange business card. There's no contact information on it."

"I'm not kidding. It's the calling card of a thief."

"How do you know about thief calling cards?"

I sat on the edge of her bed and put my head in my hands. "It's a long story. You'd better get dressed. I'll go get Mahilan."

I collected a very confused Mahilan from the breakfast room. He'd moved tables and was now sitting with a young couple who were talking about being on their honeymoon trip. He was telling them about the museums in Florence they absolutely had to visit when they moved on to the city later that week. "Michelangelo's *David* is so much more impressive in person," he said.

When he saw me gesturing frantically, he said his farewells and followed me outside.

"It's not raining today," he said, looking nervously up at the sky. "But your expression...Did you hear that ghostly voice again?"

"I'm afraid it's even worse than that."

We found Ava waiting for us impatiently in jeans and a tank top, with bare feet and wet hair. She sat on the couch with her arms crossed, tapping her feet against the plush rug with nervous energy.

"It's time," I said, "for a council of war."

*   *   *

I came clean and told Mahilan I was seeing the guy I met while looking into the ruby bracelet from India, and that because of the things we looked into in Scotland, India, and France, we'd encountered some bad people.

I left out the bit about Lane being an ex-thief. There was no reason for Mahilan and Ava to know how we'd come into contact with that circle, only that we had.

"And now," I concluded, "he's missing."

Mahilan's jaw was set so tightly it was pulsing with tension. I was glad he didn't seem to be able to open his mouth, or I'm sure he would have yelled at me.

"Why," he said finally, "didn't you tell me you were still seeing him?" I'd never seen my brother's face this shade of purple.

"Because I knew you'd worry. Either about the fact that it was a long-distance relationship that would never work, or because of exactly this—that some bad people might come after me."

"We don't keep secrets from each other, JJ. We don't."

"I found a calling card in our suite this morning," I said, "after I saw that someone had been searching through my bags."

Ava handed Mahilan the card. "I believe Jaya when she says he's a professional," she said. "It happened while I was taking a shower to wash off the rest of the mud. I didn't hear a thing."

Mahilan's breath caught and he grabbed her hand protectively.

"I locked the bathroom door," she said. "Force of habit, but it looks like it came in handy."

I didn't point out the lock of a hotel's bathroom door would be no match for ^V^.

"And you know who this person is?" Mahilan whirled to face me. "He's someone you and Lane encountered before? God, I can't believe you kept all of this from me."

"I don't know who it is," I said. "Not exactly. Lane's phone is disconnected. With the timing, and this calling card, I'm pretty sure it's because this thief has him."

On my phone, I pulled up newspaper articles that showed photos of the calling card left behind after high profile museum thefts.

"So," Mahilan said, finding his voice after spending a few seconds scrolling through the photos, "if I'm understanding you properly, you think this Triangle Man kidnapped your boyfriend and then popped over to Bomarzo to leave his calling card in your room? Why?"

"Triangle Man?" Ava repeated.

Mahilan tapped the illustrated marks. "Or Mountain-and-Valley Man. Whatever. These markings look like two-sided triangles or two mountain peaks surrounding a valley. The point is, this is a guy who has a big enough ego to have a graphic artist design him thief calling cards."

"Interesting..." Ava said, studying the card.

"Call him what you will," Mahilan said, "but your evidence is lacking, JJ. It's much more likely this Lane fellow wasn't happy with a long-distance relationship and moved on. Breakups are difficult conversations to have, so he's not calling you back. I'm sorry to be harsh, but there it is. Your theory makes no sense."

"You think I'm imagining that this card means something?" I wasn't going crazy, was I?

Ava cleared her throat. "I hate to say this, but there's a simpler explanation. No, it's too crazy. Forget I said anything."

"What were you going to say?" Mahilan asked.

"Jaya's disappearing boyfriend," Ava said, not meeting my gaze, "who doesn't tell you when he's going off the grid...Is it possible he could be Triple Triangle?"

I nearly choked. "No."

"You said your boyfriend has been around at the same times this mysterious person has been places, but that the thief has never been seen."

Mahilan swore. Repeatedly.

"It's not him," I snapped. *It's not*, I repeated to myself.

"How do you know?" Mahilan asked. "From everything you've

said about how his academic plans were derailed and how he helped you locate missing art in the past, it fits."

"No," I said again, trying my best to stay calm. "It doesn't."

"It's clear that none of us know anything," Mahilan said. "That's why we're all leaving. Today."

Everyone spoke at once. Mahilan won out with the commanding presence he'd developed from several years of courtroom law.

"Only one thing is clear," he said, pausing and holding up his index finger for dramatic effect. "An unknown person—" he paced the length of the suite's living room, wincing as his ankle pained him, "—is following Jaya's movements. The most logical assumption, the theory that's supported by facts, is that this individual wishes to learn what she knows about Lazzaro Allegri's paintings."

"Lane already knows about them," I said.

"You're not helping yourself, JJ."

"There's no *reason* for him to break in here. He knows I would tell him everything I know."

I feared my brother might have an aneurysm. "May I continue?" He held up his index finger again. "I don't know how Triangle Man, whoever he is, is controlling the ghost."

"There's no ghost," I said.

"You saw it," he said. His confident stance shifted to that of the scared little boy, a look I remembered from when we got on an airplane for the first time. "And you *heard* it, Jaya. How can you have heard that *thing* and think that howl was made by a living person?"

"You gave yourself the answer in your choice of words," I said. "A howl. It could have been a wild animal. Everyone says the ghost only returns when it rains, so it's an animal who doesn't like the rain."

"It didn't sound like an animal to me," Ava whispered. Her normally confident attitude was nowhere to be seen.

It hadn't sounded like an animal to me either, but I wasn't

going to admit it. There had to be a logical explanation. There had to be. I was going to find it. And get Lane back while I was at it.

"The only thing we're doing here," Mahilan said, "is looking into a meaningless set of paintings that most likely don't exist. Otherwise we could have gone on vacation anywhere on earth. Yet here in Bomarzo, Italy, there's some sort of danger. A danger that may or may not involve Jaya's boyfriend, who may or may not really be her boyfriend, whom she kept a secret from the one person she promised she'd never lie to."

The look of disappointment on his face was too much for me.

"I don't know what's going on," he continued, "but I don't intend to stay here bringing danger upon the two women I love."

As soon as he said the words, he realized what he'd said out loud. His face turned scarlet.

Ava's hands flew to her mouth. She stepped across the room and kissed him.

Chapter 32

I excused myself—not that Mahilan and Ava were paying any attention to me—grabbed my messenger bag, and left the two of them alone in the suite. I stopped in the breakfast room to grab a *cornetto*, a croissant-like pastry filled with chocolate, and took the snack outside to figure out what I was going to do.

I walked the lush grounds until I found a secluded spot overlooking the beautiful vista of valleys, hills, and vineyards. I must have been standing on the highest spot on the grounds, yet I couldn't enjoy the view. I enjoyed the pastry though. I'm human.

Though the harsh rains of the night before had given way to a cloudless blue sky, the outdoor bench was too damp to sit on. It was probably for the best, since I had too much nervous energy. I checked my phone for messages. There was still no word from Lane.

I had to do something, but every idea I had was a bad one. The least bad idea I had was Henry North.

I'd met North when he used me as bait in a plan to obtain an object hidden at the Louvre. After what I'd learned of the man, what we'd gone through together, and the promises we made when we parted ways, I wouldn't say I felt confident he would help me. But I was certain he wouldn't harm me simply because I reached out to him. I had nothing to lose by trying. Especially now. The only problem was that I didn't know how to find him. Lane Peters would know, except it was Lane I was trying to find.

High atop the hill with the medieval village that had been

turned into a luxury resort, the wind hadn't received the message that it was supposed to leave high-paying guests alone. My hair whipped ferociously around my face, jabbing at my eyes.

The strong warm winds were similar to winds I knew: the Santa Ana winds of southern California and the *Paekaathu* winds of south India. I shivered as I remembered what the Tamil name for these swirling winds meant: *ghost winds*.

I didn't want to stay outside, but I also couldn't face the suite with Mahilan and Ava. I had the rental car key in my messenger bag. That would do. I found the muddy Fiat 4x4 in the villa's parking lot, tossed my bag on the passenger seat, and made a phone call.

Henry North had once lured me to a Parisian hotel under false pretenses. He knew the hotel well, and I had wondered if it served as a home base. I called the hotel. As expected, the desk clerk told me they had no such guest staying there. The polite Frenchman agreed to write down my message and phone number in case the guest checked in at a future date. His bored tone made me wonder how many hopeless messages he'd written down over the course of his employment. I imagined a sad stack of unread messages piled high behind the front desk of the hotel.

I laughed at the irony of me trying to contact North, rather than the pains he'd taken to find me before. The laugh died on my lips. One of the things North had done was listen to my conversations with an ingeniously placed bug.

I spent the next twenty minutes inspecting each item in my messenger bag, from the magnifying glass (for reading historical documents) to the squished granola bar (I hated being hungry). Once I was sure everything was as it should be, I traced the seams of the bag. For good measure, I also looked at the soles of my shoes.

Perhaps I was being paranoid. All right, I was definitely being paranoid. But now that I knew this treasure had attracted a more accomplished thief, I wasn't taking any chances that I hadn't been bugged. As far as I could tell, I hadn't. I would have loved to say I felt better, but I didn't.

I looked out the car windows at the tree branches swaying in the wind. I had to do something to convince my brother we shouldn't leave Bomarzo. And, more importantly, to win back his trust. It hadn't felt like a betrayal, but it was. What kind of life was I leading if I couldn't talk to the person who'd pretty much raised me and who I'd promised I would never lie to? We couldn't count on our dad, but we were supposed to be able to count on each other. I was good at many things, but apparently being a sister wasn't one of them.

It was my natural inclination to go it alone. Alone and all in. North had been right. I'd enjoyed the adrenaline rush of being involved in a criminal enterprise. It was similar to the rush of endorphins I experienced on long runs, but much more intense. That didn't mean I wanted to become a criminal or take unnecessary risks. But taking calculated risks against criminals to save historic discoveries, and bring to justice thieves who'd evaded the law for years and who'd upgraded from larceny to kidnapping or worse? That was something I could get behind. That was a good thing for the world, wasn't it? If it meant keeping my family out of the loop to keep them safe, it was worth it. Unless it wasn't.

I wanted everything, and as a result I had nothing. Was this how Lilith Vine had begun? Full of ideas and energy and wanting to make a difference to both her students and the world? I was a great teacher and put my students first when I was at home, but I was lured away all too frequently. That meant I would probably never have the stable professorial life I wanted, because Naveen would be the one to be granted tenure. I had people in my life I cared about, but I lied to all of them. My motivations were good, but I was no longer sure the ends justified the means.

There was nothing more I could do at that moment to find Lane Peters and the unknown thief or make things right with the people I cared about. But I could realize Lilith's last wishes and bring to light a cross-cultural connection nobody knew existed by finding Lazzaro Allegri's hidden masterpieces.

CHAPTER 33

It was only mid-morning, but the sculpture garden had opened at eight thirty, so the parking lot was already rather crowded. The wind wasn't as strong in the flatlands, so it was a lovely day for a family picnic and stroll in the shadow of macabre monsters.

My quest of the morning was to find Francesco. I didn't know where he'd be on his rounds of the park, so I decided to begin with the stone creature at the center of everything. Making sure there were no green-shirted men in sight, I stepped off the path near the battling giants that towered above me. I cut through the overgrowth and took what I hoped was a shortcut to the Ogre, that guardian of Hell who might hold Lazzaro's secrets.

Tree branches slapped my face. I didn't care. The abrasive touch of the ancient trees grounded me. In the midst of history, I was so close to bringing together the stories of unknown painter Lazzaro Allegri, the Sultan of Gujarat, and Italy's artistic royalty: Michelangelo. I stepped over a rock and emerged from my shortcut near a mermaid and two lions. Almost there.

As my eyes fell on the frozen scream of the Ogre's doorway mouth, I saw that the young mother had been right. The morning sun filtering through the trees cast a celestial light on the beast. In the halo of warm yellow light, he looked almost peaceful. Almost. Like me. Standing in the sacred gardens that had stood for nearly five centuries, I felt both contented and confused, both alone and alive.

The thief ^V^ had to be the person who'd killed Lilith and followed me to Italy to find Lazzaro Allegri's paintings.

But how had he found out about them?

I found Francesco hiding behind his favorite rock, on the lower end of the maze-like park near the outdoor theater, waiting to startle a group of approaching children.

At least I was pretty sure it was him. Today, instead of a pirate hat he wore a full cape with a hood hiding his face.

Francesco had the knowledge that could help me find Lazzaro Allegri's paintings before ^V^. If I asked the right questions, I might be able to glean more relevant pieces of history.

"Ah!" Francesco straightened up from his crouched position and threw back the hood, revealing his full head of white hair. "My friend, *signora* Jaya. It is magnificent to see you today. Though I am sorry for what you must have heard last night." He kissed my cheeks in greeting.

"I'm not sure I follow," I said slowly. Every inch of my skin prickled at the memory of that soulful wail.

"I warned you, did I not, that if you heard the story, you would hear the ghost."

"How did you—"

"I live not far from here. I believe you are staying nearby as well, no?"

I studied his face. His relaxed eyes matched the lips that smiled beneath his Roman nose. Did he know I'd been at the Park of Monsters the night before? If he did, he didn't show it. Francisco couldn't be the thief's source of information, could he? Is that why he'd tried to scare me off with the full ghost story? I groaned inwardly. And who better than an actor to impersonate a ghost? Especially an actor who worked at the place where we saw the ghost.

"I heard it," I said. "And it has me intrigued."

"You must not follow the sound, *signora*. Please. As a foreigner, this is especially dangerous. I told you what happened to the American actor." His eyes were pleading. But he was an actor, I reminded myself.

"Let us go behind the sleeping Nymph. We can talk there

without the *principales* seeing me." He winked and led me to a giant stone woman three times the size of a person. She was lounging on a correspondingly massive stone plank, and from my line of sight she looked more dead than sleeping.

I hesitated before following Francesco behind the giant Nymph. He wasn't kidding that the statue was large enough to shield us from view. The question was whether he was hiding himself from his boss—or if he wanted to get me out of sight.

Even if Francesco was working with a thief and impersonating the ghost, that didn't mean he knew about any violence or would perpetrate any himself. But I knew better than to think I understood what a person was capable of. I kept a safe amount of space between us, but I did follow. With Lane missing and a brazen thief arriving, I was desperate. I was going to find out what Francesco knew. Did he believe what he was telling me, or was he trying to lead me astray?

"I was wondering if you would tell me more about your past life as Vicino Orsini," I said. "Back in the 1500s when you knew Lazzaro Allegri."

"My name was Pier *Francesco* 'Vicino' Orsini," he corrected me. "I even share one of his names. What can I tell you about my sacred gardens? I employed Pirro Ligorio to realize my vision to honor my wife. I—"

"I didn't ask about the gardens. I asked about Lazzaro."

"Ah, yes. He was much older. A strange man. Yet I liked him. We were both misunderstood by our families. This is why my gardens were not maintained by my family after my death. Lazzaro liked to walk in my gardens. They gave him inspiration. I am glad for my friend that he died before his cousin Marguerite and never had to hear her tortured cries."

He was using the same techniques as a fake medium. He seemed to say a lot, but in truth said very little. Everything he told me was vague generalities based on the few facts he knew. He tried to steer things in the direction he wanted, always returning to the gardens of the Park of Monsters, which he knew about from written history. Much less was known of Lazzaro, so Francesco shifted his answers away from facts about the artist to universal human emotions.

Be it through ignorance or purposeful misdirection, Francesco didn't have the historical missing pieces I needed. I didn't have to humor him any longer.

"I know the true history, Francesco," I said. "In the original ghost story, it's Antonio Allegri, Marguerite's husband, who's supposed to be the ghost."

Francesco's easy smile faltered. "The memories, they are veiled, you understand? Not so clear."

"I thought as much."

"You understand, *signora*."

"I understand that you don't actually believe you're the reincarnation of Vicino Orsini."

He peeked over the hip of the sleeping Nymph. When he returned his attention to me, he gave an overly dramatic shrug. "You know I am an *attore*. An actor."

"So it's an act? Why?"

"It is difficult to stand out. It always has been. I was what they call a 'character actor' for many years." He tapped his prominent nose. "After I acted in the doomed film of Bomarzo, I went to Rome. I acted in many films. Never the leading man, but good roles. It was part of my persona that I believed I had lived many past lives. The directors, they believed it helped me get into character."

"But I'm not a filmmaker. And neither are your coworkers. You don't have to fool us."

He grinned. "It became a part of me." He peeked over the Nymph again. "My family is from Bomarzo. Many generations. I was born here. I began acting in local theatrical productions. This is where I was discovered. The director, he loved my story. And now..." He pointed at the green shirt uniform he wore under his cape. "I am too old for most parts, but not yet old enough to play the 'old man' roles. I must find the theatrical wherever I can. These stones and the children who visit them are my audience. For their parents I recite soliloquies."

"So you don't know about the true history of these parts? You were serious when you said the ghost in the story was Marguerite Allegri, not Antonio?"

"You are mistaken. I do know very much about local history. The ghost is Marguerite. Of this I am certain. You heard her cries yourself."

"Wait. You *do* believe in the ghost?"

"I am not so crazy to think that I have the memories of a long-dead man. But is it not also crazy to ignore that sorrowful siren song that calls to us when it rains?"

"Have you ever pretended to be the ghost?"

"*Sei pazza?*" He tapped his forehead. "Are you crazy? This would be bad luck."

I balled my fists in frustration. I must have tensed my whole body, because I felt my heels sinking into the damp ground. Without my boots, I should have stayed on the paved path. What was I doing hiding behind a statue with a man I thought might have been hired to help scare me away from Lazzaro's treasure?

"You are frustrated," Francesco said. "I can see this. I know it is difficult for some people to believe in the ghost. But how could a person imitate that sound?" He cleared his throat and attempted to mimic a woman's moan. It came across more like an injured goose. He tried again. This time it sounded like a rabid sheep.

I agreed it would have been difficult for a person to mimic the sound we heard. Someone with technical knowledge could have generated the sound with electronics. But the ghostly figure we'd seen at the Park of Monsters had to have been a person.

"What about these games you play with the kids at the park?" I said. "Do you ever come back at night to do the same thing?"

He looked as me as if I'd made a rude comment about his mother. "The park is closed during the night. It is not illuminated. Stupid tourists who sneak in after dark have injured themselves many times."

"Yes, well." I cleared my throat. "So nobody has paid you to pretend to be a ghost here at the park?"

"No, *signora*. And if I may be so bold, I must say that these questions are very odd for a historian."

"Triple Triangle doesn't like to work with others, so he won't hesitate to break ties with you. In the most final way possible." I cringed at my clumsy interrogation. I wasn't at my best. North hadn't responded to my message. I was desperate.

"Triple Triangle? Breaking ties? And people think *I'm* an odd fellow." In the shadow of the giant Nymph, Francesco inched away from me.

I sighed. His reactions seemed genuine. I was the foolish person here, not Francesco.

"Could you tell me the truth about something?" I asked. "No acting."

"If I know the answer."

"What do you know about Lazzaro Allegri? Real facts. I'm trying to piece together his travels to India, his friendship with Vicino Orsini, and his connection to Michelangelo. I had hoped Enzo and Brunella Allegri would have more information, but they didn't. They found some dusty old sketchbooks of Lazzaro's in their attic, but that's it."

"Noble families," Francesco said, flicking his hand under his chin. "They only care about their history when it is convenient. Lazzaro was not famous enough to matter. I know only a little more of him than Enzo and Brunella. Lazzaro was the outcast of the family. A friend of Michelangelo, but never famous himself."

I gasped. "There's really a connection between the artists?"

"This is what people say."

"Who says it?"

"My friend tells me this. And he only says this when he is very drunk."

"Is your friend a historian?" I asked hopefully. Even a drunken historian might have good information.

"His family owns the quarry."

"Oh."

"*Mi dispiace*." He raised his thumb and index fingers and twisted both his hands in the air. "I'm sorry it seems I cannot help you. It is the truth that I know more about our local history than anyone. I studied when I prepared for my role. But there is not much to know of Lazzaro Allegri. I have told you all I know. You are on your own, *signora*."

CHAPTER 34

When I got back to the suite at the villa, Mahilan was waiting for me with his arms crossed. "I'm not even going to ask this time. But it's my car rental, so I'd like you to give me the keys."

I handed them over. "I thought you two would be packed already."

"It's not my fault," Ava said. "I couldn't talk him out of it."

"Talk him out of what?"

"If you'll recall," Mahilan said in a clipped voice, crossing his arms, "I arranged for a gourmet chef to give you two a private cooking lesson for lunch today. We leave later today. Before dark. Definitely before dark."

"I don't know if now is the best time—"

"The cooking class is pre-paid. And I know you, Jaya. You have to eat. The lesson is an hour, and then you eat the food you've prepared. Even though you don't appreciate me and what I'm doing, I'll look up options while you two cook. You're going to be late if you don't hurry."

This wasn't about a cooking class. Mahilan still felt betrayed that I hadn't told him about Lane.

"It might be a good distraction," Ava said as we followed a map of the villa to the kitchen where we were to have our class. Ava's pixie hairstyle reacted elegantly to the unrelenting wind. My own bob didn't fare as well.

"I don't have time for a cooking class. I should be doing something."

Ava raised an eyebrow at me and ran her fingers along the smooth stone fence that separated the gravel path from a hilly outgrowth of trees filled with colorful berries. "What exactly should you be doing?"

"I don't know." I picked up a twig and snapped it in my hands. An earthy aroma filled my nostrils. "But something."

"One of the most frustrating things about being a mom is when Carey is upset and I can't help him. All I want to do is *something, anything* that will make him feel better. But these things run their course. I can be there for him, paying attention to the situation. But in the end, the best thing to do is often to wait it out."

"A tantrum isn't exactly the same thing as a murderous thief stalking us."

"Murderous?" She glanced around nervously. "You still think that?"

"Possibly an accidental murderer, because they didn't know she was an alcoholic. But it still worries me."

"This whole trip is surreal."

"I'm sorry Mahilan convinced you to take this trip."

"I'm not. Spending time with Mahilan under stressful conditions has let me get to know him better, in ways I never would have known without it."

"And you're still here. That's a good sign."

We turned a corner and found ourselves standing in front of a kitchen garden with a dozen rows of herbs and vegetables, flanked on each side by fruit trees lined up next to a high stone fence. There was just enough space saved for a winding path. It led to a stone building that reminded me of a medieval church. Several gargoyles looked down from the rooftop.

"I'm surprised I haven't seen this section of the villa yet," Ava said. "This would be beautiful to sketch."

"I bet they don't want guests grazing on the fruits and vegetables. The fence is probably here so we can't easily see in."

"Speak for yourself," Ava said, patting the top of the fence with her hand. On her tiptoes she could have seen over it. Me? Not so much.

I looked around at the colorful surroundings of the boxed-in garden, feeling uneasy in spite of the natural beauty that surrounded me. I felt like I had walked into a landscape painting. Idyllic yet so confining I couldn't breathe. I was tempted to follow the winding stone path that led out of the secret garden.

Ava plucked a miniature apple from the tree nearest us. She gave me a close-lipped grin and pressed her index finger to her lips before taking a bite.

"Don't," she said through a mouthful of juicy apple.

"Bitter?"

"No. It's so sweet I'd swear I was eating a caramel apple empanada like my grandmother used to make. I'm talking about you. I can see you making a move to turn around and run off on your own. Don't do it."

"It's just—"

"Between the ghost and those stone monstrosities, everything feels sinister here, even when it's not. It's affecting your judgment. You can't do anything right now. You're stuck with me and our mystery chef. You ready to go inside?"

Ava was right that there was nothing I could do at that moment. I also hadn't eaten much for breakfast. Being so hungry meant I wasn't thinking straight. This distraction would be good for me, but not for the reason Ava thought. I didn't want to relax. I wanted to give my subconscious time to work out the facts swirling around my mind like pieces of a jigsaw puzzle that I hadn't yet pieced together.

"*Ladies!*" A sturdy man with a bald head opened a set of modern French doors set into the medieval building. "I am Chef Raffaele. Please, come inside." He ushered us through the darkened doorway into a room full of luxury and light. "Welcome to my humble kitchen."

It was perhaps the least humble room I'd seen at the lavish villa, and the opposite of its medieval exterior. The chef began his tour, smiling gleefully. We stepped into a modern kitchen equipped with two stainless steel refrigerators, at least a mile of marble countertop, an island with eight burners and a second sink, and in the corner, a wood-burning oven with a fire blazing. The opposite wall was made almost entirely of glass and overlooked a valley with a vineyard. It was as if someone had imagined the anti-Jaya kitchen. This kitchen would have looked down its shiny nose at my scrappy kitchenette.

Ava raised an eyebrow. "I can imagine Carey's reaction."

"A budding chef?"

She shook her head. "I'm imagining the lecture he'd be giving me right about now. He'd hate all of this fuss over food. He takes after me. An expert microwaver. I don't mean just to heat up food. He got in trouble for taking apart a microwave before. He wanted to see how it worked. He's into robotics. He loves building mechanical devices. That's one thing that school of his is great for; they have all the resources you could want. I only wish I got to see him more. If I had family who—I'm sorry, I don't mean to be melancholy. You're lucky to have your brother."

"I'm not sure he feels the same way right now."

"He'll forgive you. It's because he loves you that he's so hurt."

"The *signoras* like to cook?" Raffaele asked as he handed us aprons.

Ava and I looked at each other and began to giggle.

"No problem," Raffaele said. "But you like to eat, yes?"

"Most definitely," Ava said. "If I didn't, both the Spanish half and Japanese half of my family would disinherit me."

"The spicier the better," I said.

"*Bene.* Then we will all be friends today."

As he pulled bowls, pans, and knives from cabinets, Chef Raffaele told us he was from a family of chefs and sommeliers. He'd traveled throughout Italy and twice been to France, but his wife was pressuring him to take the family to New York. As for himself, he had no desire for more than the simplest pleasures in life: food, wine, and his wife. In that order, he joked.

"I was planning on including *fettuccini al burro* as one of the dishes today," he said, scratching his chin, "but now I must think of a more simple menu."

"I thought that was an easy recipe." My mouth watered as I remembered the pasta with a creamy sauce of butter, parmesan, and spices.

Raffaele clicked his tongue. "Having few ingredients does not make for an 'easy' recipe. We will keep our lunch menu simple. Bruschetta antipasto, zucchini flan, pasta al pesce, and a chocolate tart."

That was a simple meal? Italy was my kind of place.

Raffaele's hands were as large as loaves of bread. If I'd seen him outside of the kitchen, I would have guessed he was a construction worker. But those bulky hands and arms held surprising dexterity. He showed us how to properly hold a knife to chop onions and garlic, and his pieces were minced at least half as small as ours.

To get started, we chopped onions and zucchini for the flan, which would slow cook in olive oil, cream, and parmesan cheese while we cooked the other dishes.

Ava studied Raffaele's onion technique with attentive eyes but unmoving hands, taking it all in. Once she was ready, she began chopping in earnest. Ten seconds later, her pungent onion had been reduced to a professionally diced pile.

"I thought you said you didn't cook," I said.

"I don't. I pay attention to details. That's why I'm so good at business deals. I read body language. It's surprisingly universal around the world, with a few exceptions. It's an essential skill for a woman in a man's world."

"That's why you nearly broke the bones of my hand when we first met."

She grimaced. "I'm sorry about that. I was nervous, so my defenses kicked in. I'm used to having to prove myself, showing I'm not weak. It's amazing the power that lies in a strong handshake."

Next up was an even more precise task: mincing garlic. After her onion success, Ava got cocky. The razor-sharp knife slipped from her control and sliced her hand. A swath of bright red formed across her knuckles. She cried out in pain.

Before I could react, Chef Raffaele had swept Ava to the sink and was running cold water over her hand.

A second later, a man burst through the glass doors of the kitchen, brandishing a hefty stick above his head.

CHAPTER 35

Ava screamed again. So did everyone else. Me, Raffaele, and the newcomer.

"Fish," I said, catching my breath. "What are you—"

"Ava screamed. Is he hurting you?" He kept the large stick raised in his right hand. It had a curved handle. The stick was a cane.

The chef jumped back, getting far from Ava. He raised his hands with palms facing upward toward my brother. "I mean the *signoras* no harm."

"We're fine, Fish," I said. "Where on earth did you get a cane?"

"You were spying on us?" Ava asked. She wrapped a kitchen towel around her hand.

He lowered the cane and eyed the three of us. "With everything that's going on, I didn't want to leave you alone. My new friend Frederick loaned me his cane."

"The elderly gentleman staying two suites down from us with his wife?" I asked. "I'm pretty sure he needs his cane to walk. Especially on these gravely paths."

Mahilan glared at me, then his face softened. "You're not hurt, Ava?"

Ava wriggled her fingers at him. "Garlic-chopping incident."

"Oh."

Raffaele looked at us and scratched his bald head. I didn't blame him. He'd probably tell the story of the three crazy Americans for years to come. "I think," he said, "it is time for *vino*."

Raffaele retrieved a first aid kit from one of the numerous cabinets before uncorking a bottle of Sangiovese wine. He disappeared again into the pantry, and when he emerged opera was playing on the overhead speakers. He handed Mahilan an apron and steered him to the sink, then put him to work taking Ava's place chopping vegetables.

"You could have joined us for the whole class, *signore*," Raffaele said to him. "There was no need to wait outside."

Mahilan looked warily at me before decapitating a zucchini. I knew I was the reason he hadn't wanted to be with us. I should have told him about Lane.

"I'm sorry, Fish," I said.

He answered with a glare and a large gulp of wine.

"What's the music?" peacemaker Ava asked.

"Bomarzo," Raffaele said proudly. "The story of Vicino Orsini."

"His story was made into an opera?" I asked, the gears of my mind spinning at the idea of the historical gems that might be hidden in the musical saga.

Raffaele held up his index finger and thumb. "Tiny bit fact. Very much fiction. But very good. Is a tragedy. Hunchback Duke Vicino Orsini wishes to obtain immortality, but his advisor tricks him. He is instead given poison. The opera is his memories as his life passes before his eyes, before he dies. *Prego!*" He sang along with the recording, his booming tenor voice echoing through the stainless steel corners of the kitchen.

"Your voice." Mahilan gaped at him. "You're a true opera singer."

"Only two years," Raffaele said with a humble shrug. "Not enough time for cooking, so I return home."

Raffaele poured more wine and continued to sing. By the time the second bottle of Sangiovese red wine was flowing, everyone had relaxed. Before I realized what was happening, Mahilan had put down his knife and began dancing with me and Ava. The last time I'd danced like this was high atop the ramparts of Mont Saint-Michel with Lane Peters.

I told myself I didn't have any evidence that ^V^ had hurt Lane just because Lane had known the thief a decade ago before turning his life around. And Lane surely couldn't be the calling card thief, even in his past. Was it possible the master thief wasn't one person, but multiple people? Is that why Lane hadn't wanted to tell me more?

"JJ?" Fish said. "Are you alright?"

"Fine. Just light-headed from all the wine I drank before eating."

"Is time to eat," Raffaele said, turning down the music.

He insisted we enjoy the view from the table on the veranda while he plated the food we'd cooked.

The first course he brought out was the bruschetta. The mix of finely chopped garlic, ribbons of basil, plus salt, pepper, and olive oil, had melded to perfection in the hour in which we'd let it sit. It was served on an azure blue platter on top of oven-crisped bread with an added drizzle of olive oil.

I took my first bite of the crispy flavorful bruschetta as I heard my phone buzz. It was an incoming call, but no number showed. Trying not to get my hopes up, I popped a slice into my mouth and answered the call.

"To what do I owe the pleasure of the cryptic message you left for me?" a posh English voice said. North.

I nearly choked on my appetizer. I stood up from the table so quickly I nearly knocked over my chair.

"I'll be right back," I said to Ava and my brother. "Hang on one second," I said into the phone.

"JJ?" Mahilan said as soon as he'd swallowed a bite of food. "Who's on the phone? What's going on?"

I pretended not to hear him, as I was already halfway through the kitchen as I hurried to the secluded vegetable garden.

"Are you quite ready?" North's voice said. "I haven't got all day."

I glanced over my shoulder to make sure nobody had followed me through the kitchen. Luckily it looked like nobody wanted to abandon their hard-won food to satisfy their curiosity. Yet I didn't quite feel alone. Had the wine gone to my head?

"I'm here," I said. "And I need your help."

"It's nice to hear your voice too, my dear."

"Skip the pleasantries. The last time we saw each other, I believe you said you hoped you'd never see me again."

"At the time, I imagined that if I were to ever see you again, it would be in a court of law, with you testifying against me."

"I didn't. So you owe me. I need—" I broke off and whipped my head around. A movement in my peripheral vision had caught my eye. Someone was peeking over the side of the stone fence. Someone whose face was invisible, shrouded in darkness.

I rushed to the gate. My heel caught on a stone and I stumbled, but caught myself before I fell. I reached the gate. There was nobody on the outside path. Could I have imagined the figure? My mind must have been playing tricks on me.

"I think you're breaking up," North said. "I didn't catch that."

"I need a favor." I scanned the area for another moment, then walked back into the garden.

The voice on the other end of the line gave a sigh. "Everyone needs a favor these days. I believed us to be square, having balanced the scales."

"It's not a big favor. I need you to tell me what you know about Triple Triangle. And, um, how to find the thief."

"Triple Triangle?" North repeated, pronouncing "triple" as "treble."

"I'll text you a photo of the calling card. Give me your number." North grumbled but obliged.

"Ah," he said a moment later. "You know."

"Yes. The calling card was left in my room. It's not only about a theft this time. I think this thief is taking things to a whole other level—"

"I can't win," North grumbled. "And I think I might be more frightened of *you* than of her."

"*Her?*"

"I'd better put him on the line."

"Wait? Her? Him?"

No answer. What was he talking about?

"North?" I said into the silence. I desperately hoped I hadn't lost the connection, since there was no way to call back the unlisted number. "Are you still there?"

"Jones?" The voice on the line was different. It was the last person I expected North to put on the line: Lane Peters.

CHAPTER 36

"You're safe," I said, relief flooding through me.

"It's so good to hear your voice, Jones. You have no idea."

"You could have heard it a lot sooner." Now that I knew he was safe, my relief quickly shifted to outrage. "You're with *North*? I've been worried about you, and not only have you been ignoring my calls, but you're with a man you swore you'd never work with again."

"Where are you? You're all right?"

"I'm fine." There was time to tell him my own story after I'd heard his.

"I have no idea how you found me, but—hang on one second."

I heard muffled voices. Lane and North were speaking, but I couldn't tell if anyone else was there.

"Hello?" I said after a minute. "Lane? North?"

In the silence, I looked around the isolated garden. The only sound was the ghost winds, but I had the strongest sensation I wasn't alone. A swirl of black fabric floated through the air above the stone fence. This time there was no mistaking it.

I was about to leave the garden again, but I was startled by Lane coming back on the line.

"I'm going to kill him," Lane said. I could hear the rage boiling up in his voice. "I was set up. But now he says he doesn't want you on his bad side, so I can tell you what's going on."

"Which is what, exactly?" I regained my senses and rushed back to the only way out of the garden.

"An unbelievable mess, apparently. Are you running?"

"Not exactly." I reached the gate. Again, the outer path was secluded. "Go on with your story."

"Three days ago, North came to me with a last-minute bit of news. He'd had a tip. But we had to act fast."

"Lazzaro Allegri's paintings."

"What? No. This has nothing to do with that wild goose chase." He swore. "Are you saying it's *not* a wild goose chase?"

"I'd better let you finish your story."

"You're going after Lazzaro's paintings?" He groaned. "The timing. I should have seen it. This was a diversion to stop me from helping you. But those paintings don't exist. They can't."

"If you knew what's been happening here in Italy, you'd see that I'm not the only one who thinks the paintings exist. But we can get to that in a minute. What are you doing with North?"

"North had a tip that a Caravaggio painting looted by the Nazis during World War II was being moved from a private collection. There was a limited amount of time to act to get the painting back. And based on the people involved, North thought it advisable to avoid communicating with the outside world while we pulled off the job in case we were being monitored. Part of the deal was disconnecting my phone. It was only going to be for a short time, three days at most."

I groaned. It had only been three days since we'd arrived in Italy. We'd packed in so much into that time that it had felt like much longer.

"North joked that he called me because it was my namesake; he hated to admit he had a soft spot for repatriating paintings stolen for war crimes. I should have known it was a lie, because he wouldn't get paid for this job. All we'd be doing was stealing back a piece of valuable art history that had been stolen."

Not many people knew that Lane Peters' full name was Lancelot Caravaggio Peters.

"And it was far too convenient," Lane continued. "He knew how to push my buttons. He knew I wouldn't feel enthusiastic about returning a painting to the wealthy descendant of a rich family, but that I *would* want to see a lost masterpiece that's been kept hidden returned to the world. So he made up a history for this painting where there was no family claim on the painting, so we'd be turning it over to a museum."

"But it wasn't a real job at all?"

"Until five minutes ago, I would have sworn it was." The anger in Lane's voice came through loud and clear on the phone line. "I fell for it because it was an offer. I wasn't being forced. It was too perfect an opportunity to pass up, so I should have known it was a trick. North's M.O. is to come up with enough contingency plans so he can always get the results he wants."

"So much so that you'll start to believe it was your idea all along," I whispered. I remembered the feeling from my own experience with North.

"That's why he was always so good at his job."

"He made up a fake job to get you out of the way."

"It appears that way."

"So North is Triple Triangle." I squeezed the apple tree I was standing next to, imagining I was strangling North.

"Triple what?"

"Have North show you the photo I sent him."

"Hang on," Lane said.

I tapped my foot impatiently while I waited. My stomach rumbled. My hair was becoming a rat's nest in this wind. And my brother wouldn't wait too much longer before coming to find me.

The flapping wings of a bird landing on the medieval building that housed the kitchen caught my attention. Only it wasn't a bird. It was something I'd seen at the Park of Monsters. Perched in between the gargoyles, a faceless figure stood in billowing black robes.

The ghost.

CHAPTER 37

It wasn't a ghost.

It. Was. Not. A. Ghost.

Of course it wasn't. But the few seconds it took for me to convince my brain of that fact was long enough for the ghost impersonator to disappear.

The figure didn't actually disappear. At least I hoped not. The person must have seen me spot them and decided to slip away. I ran toward the building. The person hadn't gotten down on this side of the building or I would have seen them.

Holding the still-silent phone to my ear, I ran down the twisting garden path, cursing the inappropriateness of my heels for a chase. I followed the outer section of the stone fence along the side of the building. After a few seconds, I heard the sound of Mahilan and Raffaele laughing on the other side of the fence. If a ghost had dropped down onto the picnic table, they wouldn't have been laughing. Where had the ghost gone?

And what did it want? No, not "it." He. She. They. But definitely not "it." I would not let my subconscious get the better of me. I walked back to the garden, keeping my senses alert.

Was the ghost impersonator spying on me for information? Or did the person want to scare me? Why? What did I know?

On the phone line, I heard Lane cursing at North, followed by scuffling. North's muted voice could be heard faintly in the background. I turned up the volume on the phone in an attempt to eavesdrop. "I swear she didn't tell me why she needed the favor," North was saying.

"How could you not tell me?" Lane shouted in the distance. His voice was trembling at the same time.

"What's going on?" I raised my voice loudly enough that I hoped he'd hear me.

"I can't believe you kept this from me, North." Lane's voice still trembled, but there was a raw anger behind it.

"Lane," I shouted. "What's going on? Please come back on the line."

"Jones," he whispered. "Where did you find that calling card?"

"In my hotel suite here in Bomarzo."

"I didn't even know she was alive."

"Who?"

"I can't believe she and North kept it a secret all these years. She must be after those paintings. Though I don't know why she'd leave the card before—"

"Who are you talking about? Who does this calling card belong to?"

"Mia."

"Your ex? Your *dead* ex?"

"Who's not so dead, after all." His voice shook with fury.

"The ghost," I whispered.

"The what?"

"Someone has been spying on me, in search of Lazzaro's paintings. That's why I was trying to get hold of you. They broke into my office to look through the sketchbooks, and they've been following me in Italy, pretending to be a ghost. But Lane, there's more. She killed someone. Lilith Vine is dead."

"Mia wouldn't—"

"It was probably an accident. An organized thief who didn't know Lilith was an alcoholic, not a cold-blooded killer who meant for Lilith to die."

"Trust me, she would never—"

"You're *defending* her?"

"No. I'm simply telling you the truth."

"Can you send me a picture of her?" I thought back on all of the women I'd seen recently. My breath caught. The woman who'd spoken to me at the Park of Monsters. Would she really be so brazen to approach me like that?

"Mia always hated having her photo taken."

"Oh no...No, no, no." My mind raced. Mia was even more brazen than that. The timing of when she appeared. The questions she asked about me. The fact that she would never let Mahilan take her picture. "Amaia Veronique Alba."

"I told you her full name once, and you remembered."

"The *initials*, Lane. The initials. AVA. The symbol ^V^ on her calling card is a stylistic version of those letter. It's my brother's new girlfriend. *Ava*."

CHAPTER 38

Lane said he'd hop on a flight from Germany to Italy that afternoon. He swore Mia—or Ava, as I knew her—wouldn't have a hand in killing anyone, but he was biased.

It was nearly fifteen years since they'd been involved, but those relationships from our late teens and early twenties could leave a big impression.

"Is everything all right?" Mahilan asked when he spotted me.

"A friend having love life troubles," I said as I sat down at the open-air table. I kept my gaze focused on my brother and avoided making eye contact with Ava. If I did, I knew I'd give myself away.

Mahilan tousled my hair like he used to do when I was a kid. "Still helping everyone except yourself."

"I also booked Ava and myself a spa treatment this afternoon," I said. "Hey, where did all the food go?"

"I told you she was coming back," Ava said.

"Sorry, JJ. You know I eat a lot when I'm stressed. Today has been a bit much for me."

"Me too," I said. "That's why I wanted to keep relaxing. Ava and I have been having such a good time getting to know each other, I thought this spa treatment would be a great way to complete the day."

"You're not still worried about your boyfriend?" my passive-aggressive brother asked.

"There's nothing I can do, and I thought the relaxing session would help me work out what's been going on. Remember to return the cane to our neighbor."

I winced as Mahilan kissed Ava's forehead. He left a generous tip for the chef, collected my messenger bag and Ava's designer purse to take back with him to the suite, and told us to have a good time.

"I need to talk to my brother for a second," I told Ava. "I'll be back in a second. Don't go anywhere." I left Ava in the enclosed vegetable garden and chased after Mahilan.

"I can manage to get your purses back to the suite on my own," he said as the straps twisted around his helpless arms. "But seriously, what do women keep in their purses? Bricks? Gold Bars? Marble from that nearby quarry?"

"Did Ava come after me while I was gone?" I helped him untangle the straps. "Fish, how was it possible for you to get our bags tangled in less than ten seconds? And my bag isn't a purse."

"Ava? No. Why would she have gone after you?"

"Oh." Damn. Then she couldn't have been the ghost. "You're sure she was with you the whole time I was gone?"

"I mean, she went to powder her nose for a couple of minutes. But I don't see why that matters—"

"See you in a little while." I gave my brother a quick hug and kissed his cheek. He'd need a lot of taking care of after Ava broke his heart, so it didn't hurt to get started.

Ava was waiting for me underneath the apple tree with an unreadable expression. "We're not going to a spa treatment, are we?"

"Whoops." I held my hand to my mouth and hoped my dripping sarcasm came through loud and clear. "I'm not as good a liar as some people."

Ava pressed her lips together but didn't speak. She followed me out of the garden.

"I thought we could talk on the terrace at the end of that path."

I pointed to the one I meant. "It's far enough away that we won't be overheard, and there's a church in the valley beneath it. Maybe that will help you figure out you should clear your conscience."

"I'm not sure what you mean. My conscience is clear."

"Interesting." I kept walking, and Ava kept up with me. "I just got off the phone with Lane."

A flash of surprise and annoyance crossed her face for a fraction of a second before her serene mask was back in place.

"North gave you up," I said. "He didn't know he was agreeing to help a murderer when he agreed to this favor."

"A murderer?" Ava came to a halt. "Whoa. I don't know what you think you know, Jaya, but whatever it is, murder is not involved."

Her chest heaved. She was clearly nervous. Was she freaked out at the idea of murder, or because I'd discovered her secret?

"We're still too close to the suites," I said. "Come on."

Ava nodded, and we walked the remainder of the distance in silence. The terrace overlooked a sprawling forest. It seemed almost sacrilegious to spoil the majesty of the natural beauty that surrounded us with an airing of lies.

A small stone chapel was barely visible through the trees below, a simple cross poking out atop the tiled roof. It was a secluded spot, but I wasn't innocent enough to think the presence of a church would stop a killer from hurting me. I'd suggested a spa treatment as my excuse so Ava and I would have to leave our bags behind with Mahilan. It was only the two of us out there. My father had insisted I learn martial arts once he realized I wasn't getting any taller than five feet. My jiu jitsu might not have had the best form, but I could hold my own against an unarmed woman.

"I know it's irrational," I said, breaking the silence, "but I'm most pissed off that you're going to break Mahilan's heart. He wasn't acting when he said he loved you."

"And I wasn't acting when I said the same thing to him."

I snorted.

"I'm serious, Jaya." Her voice was pleading. "I'm grateful you brought me here to talk, instead of bringing this up in front of Mahilan."

She paused and pulled something from the back pocket of her jeans. The metal shone in the sunlight.

Perhaps I'd miscalculated. A lot of damage could be done with something small enough to fit in a pocket.

CHAPTER 39

I automatically shifted into a fighting stance before realizing it was only her phone that she held in her hands. The phone case had a shiny metal border that had caught the light of the sun.

"There are two men in the world I love," Ava said. "My son Carey, and your brother." She tapped a password into her phone, then held up the screen to show me a photograph of her with a smiling thirteen-year-old boy. "This is why I do what I do. For him."

"So your image does appear in photographs. You're not the ghost of a dead woman."

That got a sad smile from her. And there was genuine warmth on her face as she looked at the image of her son. She put the phone back in her pocket. "It's not easy pretending to be dead. It's not easy at all."

"I'm so stupid for falling for this figment of your imagination. Who's the kid who posed for this photo with you? Is it North you've been calling this whole time?"

"Carey is real, and he's my son." The force of her words made me wonder if she was telling the truth. She thrust her phone in front of me and scrolled through a dozen photos of her with a growing boy.

"He's real," I murmured. "You really do have a son." A lump stuck in my throat. Carey's age...

"And I'm not working with North."

Her bitter words snapped me back to more pressing matters than whether Lane had fathered a child with Ava. Besides, I couldn't imagine it was true. It was too big a secret for Lane to keep from me.

"North knew you were alive," I said. "He's the one who helped you with a favor this week."

"It's complicated."

"Why don't you tell me your side?" I wondered how quickly she could spin things. She hadn't intended to be found out, but did she have a cover story in place?

She appraised me for a few moments. "I didn't mean for any of this to happen. I never meant to hurt anyone. Emotionally, I mean. I've never physically harmed anyone, even by accident. Ever. I'm not lying about that."

Lane had loved her. I knew that much, though I wasn't going to tell her that. I was doing enough by hearing her out.

"From a young age," she continued, "I realized I could blend in anywhere I went. With my mixed features, people always assumed I was whatever they were. I'm sure you've experienced that."

"Our ethnically ambiguous looks." It was true, but I didn't want to bond with Ava right then. Even though one particularly extreme example popped into my head. When I was in graduate school, one of my Turkish colleagues had been positive I was of Turkish descent. That wasn't an uncommon experience for me, except that in this case my colleague insisted even after I'd shown him photos of me as a small child with my Anglo father and south Indian mother. It's human nature to want people to be like ourselves.

Lane had once said there was another thief who was more of a chameleon than he was. It was Ava he'd been thinking about. Lane was good at blending in not because of his natural features, which were so striking they were difficult to disguise, but because he'd lived in so many countries over the course of his life. He picked up the mannerisms and languages, so with only the smallest of alterations to his physical appearance, such as wearing contact lenses, slicking his hair back, and slouching, he could seem like a completely different person.

"Some of my family in Spain joined the Basque separatist movement, so I left for university in England to escape becoming embroiled in that mess. I did gymnastics, but I was too tall to be competitive. At least in legitimate circles. But that's why I got tapped by someone you know."

"Henry North."

Ava nodded. "He thought I could be an asset. I met Lane through him. I was only nineteen at the time, and Lane was a few years older, just finishing his degree."

"I thought—"

"You're right that Lane was never officially part of the organization. He preferred to stay a lone wolf. That way he could choose to steal things only from rich people's private collections." She rolled her eyes. "But he moved in the same circles."

I tensed as she so easily dismissed Lane's morals.

"He and I went our separate ways after he graduated," she continued.

"It wasn't your 'death' that broke you up?"

"No. He left me because he disagreed with my principles." She bit her lip. "If only I'd let him talk me out of it, I never would have been framed for murder."

"Framed," I repeated.

"Yes, framed," she snapped. "A less scrupulous thief I was working with accidentally killed a security guard. He made it look like I was the culprit, since my calling card was there. I know it was stupid to use one at all, but I was young and arrogant. It was a rush to see my calling card in newspapers around the world, with the authorities baffled. But that poor guard...I never would have hurt him if I'd been working on my own. That's when I faked my death. I stopped using my calling cards. Everything I do now is on a much smaller scale and without recognition. Only enough to get by."

"But your calling card in our room—"

"It fell out of my old black bag that held the rope ladder we used to break into the Park of Monsters. I brought the bag with me because I did reconnaissance ahead of time and knew we might need to use it. I hadn't used it in years, and it ripped that night when Mahilan fell on the stairs. It must have torn open the secret pocket where I kept an extra card."

"How could you do all this, with Carey?"

She choked back a sob. "I did it all for him. It was the hardest thing I've ever done. He was a toddler when I faked my death. He doesn't know...He thinks his mother is dead. He believes I'm his aunt who adopted him." She wiped a tear from her eye. "My family in Japan doesn't know I exist, so I didn't have many choices. I left him with relatives in Spain until he was old enough to go to boarding school. They loved him but weren't a good influence. Even though I haven't been able to be physically present, I've written and talked to him every day of his life. He knows I love him more than anything in the world."

I didn't know what to believe.

"You think I wanted this life?" she shouted into the trees.

"Why are you here, Ava? What's your game?"

"It's not a game. I'm so tired of running. Carey is old enough and clever enough that he's begun asking questions. And I missed Lane. You know what a wonderful man he is. When he appeared in the news last year, I looked him up. I didn't reveal myself to him, because I didn't know if I could trust him not to reveal that I was alive. North was the only person from my old life who knew. He keeps secrets, for a price. Lane, however, doesn't have a price. I had to know if there might be a chance for us."

"You wanted to get back together with him."

"I did. But I wasn't sure if he was seeing anyone. It wasn't difficult to find out about you. Once I did, I had to find out if you were a real threat. I had to find out how Lane felt about you."

I was now so tense I was sure my neck would snap if I moved too quickly. "So you found a way to get to me. Through my brother."

CHAPTER 40

"You're right," she said, blinking back tears. "That's what I did. I arranged to 'accidentally' meet Mahilan. I do a lot of business around the world—just not the kind of business I tell people. It was easy. He's a really sociable guy. He goes to lots of young lawyer mixers in Los Angeles. I thought he'd be a shallow playboy, since that's what he seems to be on the surface. But he's not."

"And you got him to propose a weekend trip to San Francisco where you'd get to meet me."

"I did. And by the time I'd realized what was happening, it was too late to back out."

"What was happening?"

She braced her shoulders and met my gaze. "I was falling in love with Mahilan."

"You don't seriously expect me to believe—"

"Do you want to hear the whole story or not?"

I remained silent.

"When we met at dinner, I thought it was obvious that you weren't seeing Lane. It was only after I heard you saying his name while looking at your phone that I knew I'd need to call in a favor from North to make sure you didn't talk to him while we were here. That photograph of the raven on your phone, it's from him, isn't it?"

"How did you know?" If she told me she had an identical one, I didn't think I'd be able to stop myself from pushing her into the hillside brambles.

"It's worth a fortune, Jaya. I have a trained eye. Even in a picture, I can tell."

"That little bird is only a trinket." But as I said the words, I knew they weren't true. I'd known it was special as soon as I'd seen it.

"No need to get defensive. It's not enough of a fortune to make thieves like Lane and me go after it, so don't worry, I don't think he stole it for you. But it's clear it's an original work of art by a master craftsman. Probably worth thousands of dollars. And what's even clearer is that the person who gave it to you loves you very much."

"The symbol of the Raven of Lisbon. The protector."

She nodded. "You really fooled me, Jaya. Not only because you said you weren't in a relationship, but because of how your face lit up when you talked about Sanjay. I know I interpreted that wrong, but at the same time, I don't think I really did. I think you're in love with both of them."

"I'm not—"

"I'm getting off track. Your love life is your concern. Now that I've met your brother, I truly mean that. I'm not trying to get in between you and Lane. That's why I'm going to tell you the truth." She paused and took a deep breath. "I'm the one who searched your office, looking through Lazzaro's notebooks."

"I knew it," I whispered. Granted, I'd only suspected it for the last hour, since speaking with Lane. But still.

"You'd told Mahilan about the treasure earlier that day, and I knew you were going to see the woman who'd given them to you who was at the hospital. So I thought there would be time to slip into your office while you were gone."

"And you have the skills to do so quickly, without being detected."

She nodded. "Because of Carey, I don't take big risks. But that also means I don't have big payoffs. That school of his is so expensive. I don't spend any money on myself, but I'm still drowning. That's why when I heard about this find you were on to, I thought I could tag along…"

"And steal it out from under me."

"It sounds so crass when you put it like that."

"It *is* crass. You broke into my office to look at Lazzaro Allegri's sketchbooks."

"I already admitted that."

"And this morning you pretended to sleep in so you could look at the research I found at the library yesterday. You hadn't expected me to come back early, so when you heard the key you had no choice but to leave things as they were and hop quickly into the shower, unintentionally moving your own bag so the card fell out."

"Very good."

"That sketchbook of yours," I said. "That's how you case places. Nobody would think twice about a beautiful artist sketching in her notebook."

Ava tilted her head in admiration. "Astute observation, Jaya. Guilty as charged."

I could barely get the next words out of my mouth. "You made Lilith Vine overdose."

"*Definitely* not guilty." She trembled. "If what you say is true, and someone really did kill her, I'm as confused—and scared—as you."

We stared at each other for a few seconds. I didn't know what to believe.

"Think about the timing," she continued. "I only learned of these paintings when you told Mahilan about them in San Francisco. Wasn't Lilith Vine already on the way to the hospital?"

I opened my mouth and then closed it. She had a point.

"Then why are you pretending to be the ghost?"

"That's ridiculous. I'm not guilty of being our friendly neighborhood ghost. I was with you and Mahilan when we saw it, remember?"

"I'm not only talking about the Park of Monsters. I mean this afternoon."

Ava's mouth fell open. "You saw it? You saw it again?"

"Him. Her. The person. Not an 'it.' But yes. I saw the ghost impersonator on the roof of the kitchen." I thought back to the figure in flowing black robes. I imagined both the mourning dress of a devastated widow and the billowing hooded cape of a soldier. No way to tell if it was a woman, a man, or anything else.

Ava hugged her arms to her chest. "The ghost was above us when we were cooking?"

"It's creepy, isn't it? Or it would be if I didn't know it was you. Mahilan admitted you got up from the table for a few minutes."

"That's what you were asking him," she murmured. "I went to the bathroom for two minutes. Maybe three. You said the ghost was on that high roof? And presumably not dressed in jeans and a floral print blouse. How am I supposed to have changed clothes and shimmied up to the roof in that amount of time?"

Even Sanjay's quick-change magician friends wouldn't have been able to pull it off. "Fine. But at the Park—"

"Mahilan had hold of both of our hands," Ava said. "The three of us ran away from it together."

"It was dark," I said weakly. "You could have slipped away." But the more I thought about our encounter with the ghost, the more I kept coming back to how genuinely worried Ava was when Mahilan had fallen down the mudslide. And I hated to admit it, but her explanations weren't hollow excuses. Ava as the culprit didn't fit.

"If you asked Mahilan," she said, "I'm sure he'd tell you the same thing about being together when we saw that thing at the Park. However, I don't advise you tell him anything about our conversation."

"Why not? It's better to have his heart broken sooner rather than later."

"I'm not going to break his heart." Her stone-cold words brought home her conviction.

"How can I believe you?"

"Even if you don't believe me, I'll give you a better reason to keep your mouth shut: mutually assured destruction. If you try to bring me down, I'm bringing you and Lane Peters down with me."

CHAPTER 41

"I don't mean to threaten you," Ava said hastily.

"Mutually assured destruction certainly sounds like a threat."

"It's not. Really." She clasped her hands together. Not exactly a pleading gesture, but close. "Okay. Maybe it is. But it doesn't have to be. What I mean is that I really do want to put my old life behind me and start a new one with Mahilan and Carey. You gave Lane a second chance. Why not me?"

"You can't seriously think I'd let you start a life with my brother—"

"How is it different from what you've got with Lane?"

"He told me the truth about what he did. It was difficult for him, I know, but he did it. He trusted me."

"It's not that simple. I have Carey to think about."

"Your logic doesn't hold. Mahilan makes an obscene amount of money. If you're truly after financial security, trusting that he'll take you as you are seems like a much less risky endeavor than pinning your hopes on a treasure that even Lane Peters doesn't think exists."

"And rely on a man? No thank you. I love him, but I'm not going to be dependent. Hold on. Lane doesn't think Lazzaro's paintings exist?"

I shook my head. "And he's pretty convincing. He gave two reasons. First, we have very little evidence the paintings were saved: only Lazzaro's notes that hint he left the artwork in his studio at the Park of Monsters and his cousin Felix Rossi's letter saying his wife wanted to save Lazzaro's art. You saw the materials. You know there aren't additional facts to support the idea."

Ava swore. "But you seemed so sure."

"I've been known to throw myself wholeheartedly into everything I do, regardless. I'm not so great at moderation. Anything less than a 5K run isn't worth it, the spicier the food the better, and I go all in when I'm following a lead. Shouldn't you have figured that out, since you're 'so great at reading people'?"

"What," Ava said coldly, "is the other reason Lane doesn't think the paintings exist?"

"It's been nearly five centuries. They might technically exist, but even if they do, there's no way they won't have been destroyed by nature."

Ava spun around and cursed at the trees. "Then why are we even here?"

"I thought we were having a lovely family holiday."

"Don't be cute."

"Lazzaro believed his art would survive. He must have had a reason to do so."

"Faith?" Ava's lip curled. "That's why you follow a lead? Blind faith?"

"What's wrong with a little faith? Especially when it's not blind. Even if the paintings have mostly disintegrated, I'm hopeful they'll still have some value to scholars. His work could link Italy and India in ways never before seen during the Renaissance. And before the Mughal Empire took hold in India. Mughal art is what the world is most familiar with. It's a big deal. But only to academics, not to the private underworld art market."

"You're wrong. I know collectors who've paid millions for fragments of old parchments just because of who once touched them."

"You might be right, but I thought you weren't big on taking risks."

She fidgeted. "I need to think."

"You don't have long. Lane will be here this afternoon. If you want to pack up your bags, I can find a way to keep Mahilan occupied for a little while."

"I'm not leaving him."

I groaned. We were going around in circles. "Why shouldn't I turn you in right now?" I asked. "Lane can disappear, so whatever you have on him won't matter. And you don't have anything on me. I know I'd be risking my relationship with Lane, but I don't know what kind of relationship it is anyway."

"I wouldn't be so sure Lane would stay off the grid entirely. I know he wouldn't be able to resist seeing someone."

"If I ended it, he wouldn't contact me."

"I'm not talking about you. I mean Carey."

The creeping suspicion pushed its way back to the forefront of my mind. I tried to reject it yet again. Ava was an expert liar. She was messing with my head.

"Lane knows your son?" I asked as casually as I could.

"Lancelot Caravaggio Peters more than knows him. Carey is short for Caravaggio. He's named after his father."

Carey's name. Ava wasn't lying.

CHAPTER 42

I was glad I wasn't standing too close to the edge of the high terrace, because all of a sudden my legs didn't feel so steady.

"What's the matter, Jaya?" Ava said. "I thought you two were completely honest with each other in every regard."

"I don't believe you." The trees spun. The scent of pine was suddenly too much for me. I must have been missing something. Lane wouldn't have withheld something like this from me.

"You know when Lane and I were involved. Fourteen years ago. Carey is thirteen."

I thought about the photograph of brown-haired Carey that Ava had showed me. He looked a cross between Ava and Lane's coloring. But that didn't prove anything.

"We were too young," Ava continued. "We broke up before I knew I was pregnant, but once he learned I'd given birth to his son, he always kept an eye on us and made sure Carey was provided for. Especially after he thought I'd died and Carey was adopted by an aunt. Who do you think is paying for Carey to be at that expensive Swiss boarding school?"

"You said—"

"I told you I was scraping by. I'm not as successful as you might think. I present myself that way, but it's for show. Because I can't reveal I'm not dead and because I have more scruples than most people in my profession, I don't get as much work as I'd like."

"But he wouldn't..." The last of my sentence fizzled out. I trusted Lane completely, but that wasn't the same as knowing everything about him. He'd purposefully withheld certain information from me because he thought it would hurt me. Had this been the reason he'd never revealed this secret? Why would Ava have named her son after Lane if he wasn't the father?

"Why don't I give you some time to think," Ava said. She gave me a closed-mouth smile, turned her back, and walked down the path toward the suite.

Long after Ava disappeared down the path, I stayed on the terrace, thinking about my options. My mind was filled with so many confusing pieces of information that it was difficult to see through the fog.

A different kind of fog was also rolling in. The blue sky from the morning had begun to turn gray without my noticing. I wondered if another brief summer storm was on its way.

I lay down on the smooth stone tiles underfoot and looked up at the clouds blowing by overhead. So far they were wispy, but darker clouds loomed on the horizon. Closing my eyes and feeling the warm breeze against my face did nothing to calm me. I needed to work off some of this tension.

I slipped into the room to get my running shoes. I'd hoped to avoid detection, but Mahilan and Ava were sitting on the couch together in the shared lounge, laughing and holding hands as they talked. Only Ava's expression changed when I walked in.

She gave me a sharp look and pulled her hand out of my brother's. "We didn't expect you so soon. You said you were taking a walk. To think."

"I don't do walks," I said. "But don't mind me. I'm just here for a second to grab my running shoes." Going for a run meant leaving Ava alone with Mahilan, but for some reason—faith?—I truly believed she loved him and would never hurt him. At least not on purpose.

I ran. And ran and ran.

A text message from Lane popped up on my phone: *At the airport waiting to board. See you soon. xox*

I wanted to scream. How could Lane have kept such a big secret from me about having fathered a child with Ava? Why hadn't he adopted Carey when he thought Ava was dead? What Ava told me didn't fit with what I knew of Lane. She had to be lying about Carey's paternity. He'd have done the right thing. Unless he knew staying away was the right thing. Living off the grid, not knowing if his past would catch up with him, what kind of father would he be?

I stopped to catch my breath at the top of a hill with a sweeping view of cypress trees, wildflowers, and olive groves. Neither running nor the dazzling view was helping me feel better. I texted Sanjay: *Want to cheer me up?*

A few minutes later, he texted me back a photo of Sébastien's rabbit Dèmon inside Sanjay's bowler hat. In the background, Sébastien was working on fixing what looked like a new automaton, and for the photo he held up rabbit ears behind the rabbit. The cranky bunny looked as if he'd curse at Sanjay if he had words. But then again, that rabbit always looked like that. He'd bitten a hole through the toe of one of my favorite high-heeled shoes earlier in the year.

Cheered up by the malicious bunny, I smiled at the thought of how quickly Lane had gotten to the airport to get here when I needed him. And also at the fact that Sanjay had known exactly what to send to cheer me up.

I knew, then, that as infuriating as Ava was, she was completely right about one thing: I did love both of them.

Besides my brother, Lane and Sanjay were the two men I would have done anything in this world for, no questions asked.

The only question was: *How* did I love each of them? For that, I had no answer.

Five kilometers later, I dragged myself back to the hotel room. I hadn't brought a key with me, so I knocked on the door.

"You guys, it's me. Hello?"

No answer. I walked to the villa's bar. It was only midafternoon, but they were probably having a glass of wine. This was Italy, after all. And even though she'd played it cool, I suspected Ava needed a strong drink.

They weren't in the main bar, so I tried the café. They weren't there either. I told myself they'd probably gone for a walk, or a swim, but an alarm went off in my head. I tried to silence it, but as I walked around the grounds, the alarm grew louder.

I went to the front desk and told them I was locked out. It was the woman who'd checked us into the hotel, so she remembered me and let me into the room.

The *empty* room.

Ava and Mahilan had cleared out all of their belongings.

CHAPTER 43

I was drenched in sweat and starving after my 5K run. I didn't need anger and fear on top of that.

Ava and Mahilan had left me a note saying they had taken the rental car and were looking forward to seeing me at the next hotel, far from Bomarzo, later that evening. But Ava had seen to it that the bottom half of the note with the hotel address was missing.

What had Ava said to convince my brother to leave without me? The note was in her handwriting, but I didn't think it was a ploy to cover up kidnapping my brother. I didn't believe she'd hurt him. I surprised myself by my continued belief that she was truly in love with Mahilan. She wanted to get him away from me because she didn't want to give him an opportunity to talk to me alone.

I tried to do what they do in the movies and look for pencil indentations on the sheet of paper underneath the top sheet of the notepad. Either Ava had been careful enough to remove the sheet of paper underneath, or the villa's fancy paper was too thick for the trick.

Mahilan would call me when I didn't appear, but I'm sure Ava would have a solution to that too. Accidentally dropping his phone in the bathtub? Faking an email from me that I was delayed but safe? She was masterful enough at manipulation that I didn't doubt she'd come up with a plausible lie.

After taking a long shower, I ordered food at the villa's bar. More of my new favorite dish, fried Roman artichokes with chocolate sauce, and bread dipped in olive oil and balsamic vinegar.

Lane had gotten me in the habit of sitting in the corner of a room with my back to the wall, providing a view of the various exits and of the people who came in, so I'd selected a seat at the far corner of the bar's counter. I didn't know what good it would do me here, because I didn't know who I was looking for. Ava fit some of the facts, but not others. And I doubted the ghost would walk through the door in costume.

Even though I had the strongest desire to punch Lane, I wanted him there. In addition to the fact that I missed him, he was a helpful sounding board. We made a great team. Where was he? He should have been here by now.

The barista took pity on me, the only person by myself in the room, and brought me a sample of fried zucchini flowers stuffed with ricotta cheese. He said the chef had found the first early-blooming zucchini flowers of the season in the garden and was experimenting with a new recipe.

A text message popped up on my phone. *Flight was rerouted due to a mechanical issue. Be there as soon as I can.*

I groaned and rested my head on the counter.

"This is what happens when I leave you alone for three days?" a familiar voice said. I raised my head and saw a figure in a bowler hat standing in the doorway.

"Sanjay?"

He grinned. He removed his bowler hat as he strode across the bar. In his other hand he carried his 1960s-style suitcase. The bag reminded me of one that my dad had given me that had set off a chain of unexpected events.

"I didn't think I'd had enough of this Sambuca to drink to start hallucinating," I said. "What are you doing here?"

"You said you could use some cheering up," he said, dropping the suitcase to the floor and scooping me from the bar stool into a hug. "It was a short flight from Nantes."

"Thank you," I said into his hair.

He let me go.

"Are you doing all right?" I asked. "And Sébastien?"

"He's doing better. I don't even want to know what this is you've been eating." He eyed the small plates on the counter. "No, I lied. I'm curious about this one." He lifted a piece of artichoke into his mouth.

"Wait, you won't like—"

Sanjay began coughing.

"—the red pepper flakes I added to it," I finished.

I summoned the barista for a glass of water and bread for Sanjay. It took a few minutes for him to recover, but he remained in surprisingly good spirits for having accidentally eaten spicy food.

"I can't tell you how nice it is to be in a country where people speak English," he said.

"Um, Sanjay. You do realize we're in Italy, don't you?"

He batted away the question with his hand. "Hardly anyone in Nantes speaks English as a second language. I was getting homesick." Before resting his hands back on the bar, he pulled a bright orange poppy out of thin air. He handed me the flower.

"You can't help yourself," I said, "can you?"

"Not really."

I gave Sanjay another hug. "Thanks for coming. I didn't expect it, but it feels like home to see you."

"I read minds, you know." It looked for a moment like he was blushing, but I must have imagined it.

"I wish that were true. Then I wouldn't have to organize my thoughts to explain to you how much of a mess my life is right now."

"Is it something we should talk about in private?"

I looked around the half-full bar. Everyone looked like tourists to me. But..."That would probably be a good idea."

Sanjay whistled as we walked into the suite. With a nearly imperceptible twist of his wrist, he tossed his hat onto a coat hook several feet away.

"Where's the Fish-man?" he asked.

"He'd kill you if he heard you call him that, so it's a good thing he's not here."

The reason my bag was so heavy was because I'd brought spiral-bound photocopies of Lazzaro's sketchbooks with me. I lay the copies on the table in the main room of the suite, and told Sanjay the 16th-century story of Lazzaro Allegri and 21st-century story of Lilith Vine.

Sanjay wasn't a history buff, and he had a short attention span when it came to anything besides stage magic, so I focused on the people and their personalities. I made the decision not to tell him about Lane and Ava's pasts. Things were complicated enough.

When I was done with explaining the situation, Sanjay pressed his fingers into a steeple under his chin and closed his eyes.

"I know it's a lot to take in," I said.

Silence.

"Did I break your brain?" I asked.

His eyes popped open. They were bright silver. I couldn't help thinking it was like he was possessed. A shriek escaped my lips. Sanjay closed his eyes again. This time, it was only for a second. When he opened them, they were back to their usual brown.

"That is one freaky illusion," I said.

"Good. I take it you were focused on my eyes and nothing else?"

"What else would I have been focused on?"

Sanjay tilted his head toward the sketchbook photocopies. They'd been rearranged from how I'd left them during my explanation.

"How did you—"

"Haven't you known me long enough to stop asking?"

"This is serious, Sanjay," I snapped. "Someone killed my professor and now they're toying with me."

"I know. I'm not making light of this. I was trying to make a point about how easy it is to miss what's right in front of your face." He picked up my running shoes from the floor and swung them in the air by their laces.

"Watch out for the vase," I said.

"What vase? Oh." Sanjay's eyes widened and he pulled the swinging shoes close to his chest so they wouldn't knock over the vase of flowers. When he straightened his hand, only one sneaker rested in his palm. The other was gone.

"Point made," I said. "I followed your gaze to the vase because I was worried, so I missed whatever you did to my other shoe."

"You're doing the same thing here."

"The ghost is distracting me, I know."

"That's not who I mean. You're forgetting Lilith herself."

"I didn't forget her. She's at the center of everything. She's the professor I betrayed in graduate school, who made this connection about Lazzaro's Renaissance artwork featuring India, and who was killed over it. I know she could have been playing me by withholding that fourth notebook. Using me to get close and then taking all the credit herself. But someone still drugged her, which led to her death."

"No," Sanjay said slowly. "I don't think they did. You only thought that because of your office break-in, since your office was searched right after Lilith died. But you said you later learned that it wasn't actually a break-in by a thief, but simply a miscommunication that your brother's girlfriend forgot to tell you she looked at them. If it hadn't been for the timing, you wouldn't have latched onto the idea of Lilith being drugged."

"You think it's a coincidence that she accidentally overdosed right after handing these notebooks over to me?"

"It wasn't a coincidence. It was purposeful misdirection."

CHAPTER 44

I stared at Sanjay, who was now twirling his bowler hat in his hands in spite of the fact that I hadn't seen him get up to get it.

Ava's actions had obscured everything I thought I knew. She'd admitted she broke into my office—which I'd told Sanjay was innocent snooping, which in the scheme of things turned out to be true. That meant there didn't have to be a secret villain who drugged Lilith to get her to admit that I had the sketchbooks.

"You're following?" Sanjay asked.

I nodded. "There was a *different* reason for someone to have drugged Lilith."

Sanjay groaned. "No. The opposite. There was no drugging."

"There was. She's dead from a drug interaction overdose."

"Which the police think was self-inflicted."

"But why would she—"

"Misdirection. From everything you've told me, Lilith was the person pulling all the strings from the beginning. You weren't a willing participant right away, right?"

"That's right. I wasn't fully convinced until the attack on her."

"It was a trick," Sanjay said. "It would have been a good one if she got the dose right. She probably never meant to kill herself. She simply wanted a dramatic way to entice you."

"She wouldn't do that to herself. And she wouldn't do that to me." But did I know that? I hadn't seen her in years. And she was a desperate woman.

"It's the only thing that fits the facts."

"What about the ghost?"

"Unrelated. A crime of opportunity. You've been running around Italy telling people what you're doing. I'm a master of misdirection, Jaya. I know what I'm talking about. Lilith set this whole thing up."

"Wilson Meeks," I whispered.

"Who?"

"The scholar who died of a heart attack right after Lilith found this clue in his research."

Sanjay looked shaken for the first time since arriving. "If I were you, I'd find out if there was anything suspicious about his death."

I didn't want to believe what Sanjay was saying. Lilith Vine wasn't a murderer. And the Lilith I knew would never have risked her own life to make a point.

Sanjay put his hand on my shoulder. "I'm sorry, Jaya."

"This is surreal. I can't believe this. I need to think." I paced the room with my head in my hands. I couldn't breathe. "I need some fresh air."

I opened the door and crashed into the man whose appearance never ceased to make my heart beat faster and my world feel right. His leather rucksack fell from his hand and landed on my foot.

"Sorry, Jones," Lane Peters said. "I—"

"Lane?" Sanjay asked from directly behind me.

Finding the two men I loved standing next to each other, I was too stunned to speak. Apparently so were they. The two men sized each other up silently for a moment, while I rubbed my sore foot, before they spoke at the same time.

"I didn't realize—" Lane began.

"I should go," Sanjay said. "I never meant to stay. Like I said, it was a short jaunt over."

"There's plenty of room," I tried to say, but Sanjay had already grabbed his suitcase. By the time I could slip my heels back on and follow him, he had disappeared. Knowing Sanjay, that meant I'd never find him.

CHAPTER 45

"I didn't know Sanjay was coming to Italy," I said. I pushed Lane inside and closed the suite door behind us, wondering what had just happened. "He's impulsive like that. As for you, I can't decide whether to kiss you or kick you."

"People in glass houses shouldn't throw stones. I heard about what you've been up to."

"I already told you I was in Italy. How else would you have known to meet me at this place?"

"I know the rest. Ava called."

At the mention of her name, my hazy divided focus snapped back to Lane. If I'd been in front of a mirror, I wouldn't have been surprised to see smoke coming out of my ears.

"She told me the lie she told you," Lane continued. "It was to throw you off balance for long enough that she and your brother could get away."

"The *lie*?"

A look of anguish passed across his face. "You believed her story that Carey was my son? And you thought I wouldn't look after him, or talk about him, or even tell you about it? I thought we knew each other. I thought you trusted me."

"You're turning the tables and acting like *you're* the one who's been wronged?" My throat felt constricted. I needed fresh air. I pushed open the sliding door to the balcony and stepped through to a view of sprawling vineyards.

"She let me believe she was *dead*, Jaya. For all these years."

"Does it matter to you?" Wind blew my hair around face. The *Paekaathu* ghost winds were picking up. Between my expression and my swirling hair, I must have looked like Medusa. "Do you still love her?"

"Of course not. That doesn't mean it's a pleasant sensation to think that someone you used to be close to has been murdered."

I did know the feeling. "It's easier to love a memory," I whispered. "A ghost. They can be anything you want them to be. You're the one who told me that once, Lane."

"I remember. On a train heading from London to Aberdeen."

"A memory won't lie to you. Or act foolish because of jealousy."

"Or run off to Italy without you." The corners of his lips turned up.

"Or let them be fooled by a charming Englishman."

The smile reached his eyes. "You think North is charming?"

I jumped into Lane's arms. He caught me and held onto me. He smelled of sandalwood and..."Have you been eating pickled herring?"

He laughed and let me go. "Guy in the seat next to me on the flight. You don't really believe Ava, do you?"

"I didn't believe her. But I didn't *not* believe her either."

"I'm sorry."

"For what? I thought you said it wasn't true."

"If I'd told you more about Mia in the first place, she wouldn't have been able to pull off this con."

"Can you please call her Ava?"

"With pleasure." The wind whipped his jacket collar up around his neck and tousled his hair. "Mia is dead. It's Ava we have to figure out."

"Why did she name Carey after you?"

"His name isn't Caravaggio. Carey is his full name. In Gaelic, it means 'love.'"

I groaned. Had she played me yet again? I wanted to believe that. I looked into Lane's eyes, no longer hidden by the long hair he'd worn when I met him, but partly obscured by the thick frames of his glasses. I pulled the glasses off.

"If I have pickled herring on my face, I'm going to be terribly displeased with that gentleman on the flight."

"No herring. Just you."

"You're wondering if you can believe me. I get it. This is all so much to take in." He took his glasses from my hand. "You need time. But you can believe me when I tell you Ava wouldn't have killed anyone. She's a good person. If you don't count the larceny. And deceit. Oh, and grand theft auto."

I may have groaned again.

"But as I understand it," Lane continued, "we have more important things to deal with than us."

"We do."

I sat in the stone cutout window inside my abandoned suite looking out at the *Paekaathu* ghost winds blowing the olive trees below. Lane twirled a pencil in his hands as he leaned against the back arm of the couch and watched the wind with me.

"Do you need a cigarette?" I asked.

"I'm fine." He tossed the pencil onto the pad of paper where Ava had left her note. "But I'll be better if I understand what's going on here."

"Sanjay had the craziest theory," I said, wondering how I could look into the supposed heart attack of Wilson Meeks. Could Sanjay be right about Lilith? Not only did it not ring true, but Sanjay didn't have all the facts.

"Don't tell me his theory," Lane said. "You'll bias what I think. Tell me the facts."

"Here's what I know," I said, hopping down from the window. "You already know a lot of this from when you saw the sketchbooks in San Francisco. Lilith Vine, a scholar thought to be crazy, or at the very least obsessive, found a letter from a cousin of Lazzaro Allegri, written in 1570, that suggested a set of 'blasphemous masterpieces' were left behind by the artist after his death. This information was buried in a paper by Wilson Meeks, an elderly scholar who recently died of a heart attack. Lilith's research into Lazzaro indicated he was a protégé of Michelangelo."

"Have you substantiated that?" Lane asked.

"No. It was one of the things I wanted to ask Lilith, but then she died. A local scholar had heard that the men were friends, but again, there's nothing to back it up. What we do know is that Lazzaro traveled to India in 1528, where he made paintings of Indian royalty in the Renaissance style. Upon his return to his home of Italy in 1550, he was ostracized by his family for embracing Indian culture, but found a kindred spirit, or at least someone who didn't judge him, in Vicino Orsini, the Bomarzo nobleman who envisioned the Park of Monsters."

"And we think Vicino gave Lazzaro a space on his land to do his art," Lane said.

"That's another speculation, if we're sticking to facts. At this point, after looking at the Park of Monsters, I think there might be a clue there, but not the studio itself. What we know for certain is that after Lilith saw the letter from Lazzaro's cousin Felix Rossi, she found more evidence that supported the idea that Felix's wife insisted on saving Lazzaro's artwork after his death. Lilith traveled to Italy to follow this line of research. She located Enzo and Brunella Allegri, descendants of the Allegri clan, living in their ancestral home."

"They sold her three sketchbooks they found in their attic." The spinning pencil was back in Lane's hand. "Which she gave you and you showed me."

"It turns out she lied about buying them. She paid to borrow them. And there were four sketchbooks. Not three."

"But you only had—"

"Lilith lied to me about that too." Was it really a stretch to think she'd tried to fake an attack as well? "She kept one of them from me. My guess is that there's a key piece of evidence in that fourth sketchbook."

"Why enlist your help if she wasn't going to give you everything?"

"Presumably so she could make the discovery herself, after I got her the rest of the way there. That's why I think there's something in these three sketchbooks I do have. She saw the same clues we do. Pointing her to the Park of Monsters, where it looks like Lazzaro has an art studio in a covered grotto. She mistranslated some of the Italian, because she thought she knew it well enough to not enlist help. It pointed her toward the Proteus sea monster, but she wasn't able to locate a hidden cave nearby. She returned home empty-handed and reached out to me. Unfortunately, I get a lot of email because of that reporter who made the public think I wanted their treasure-hunting ideas. So Lilith's email was buried in my junk mail, and I didn't see it until weeks after she wrote to me. In the meantime, she contacted my colleague Naveen Krishnan."

"You don't think he's following you again—"

"I don't. It looks like all he did was fail to tell me Lilith Vine had contacted him in search of me. I spotted Lilith's email without him. She entrusted the sketchbooks to me, asking me to pick up the search where she left off, because her health no longer made it easy for her to traipse through overgrown forests. She asked me to go back to Italy and give her some of the credit when I located Lazzaro's paintings."

"Which you both believe survived for nearly five hundred years." Lane shook his head. "Even though there's no way hidden paintings would have survived the test of time, untended out there in the woods, even inside a sheltered grotto."

"Which is exactly what you told me when I showed you the sketchbooks. Ye of little faith. Someone out there believes the paintings survived. We know that because—" I stopped myself. I was going to say because someone was willing to kill for them, but did I really know that someone had drugged Lilith? Ava was the one who searched my office, and it was impossible for her to have gone to see Lilith. Was it really a coincidence?

"Because what?" Lane prompted.

"Right after Lilith gave me the sketchbooks, she died of a drug interaction. Once the drugs were already taking effect, she called me to tell me about the fourth notebook. Oh, and the guy whose research turned her on to this discovery died of a heart attack."

"You're here in the lion's den with someone who doesn't think twice about killing people." Lane snapped the pencil in half.

I'd tried to select my words carefully so as not to bias his impression, but he'd jumped to the same conclusion I had. Not the same one as Sanjay. "Sanjay had a different interpretation of the facts."

Lane took off his glasses and rubbed his hands across his face. "He thinks it was a hoax?"

"How did you—"

"He's a magician. It's the type of thing that would be great to confuse things in a stage show. But in real life, it doesn't make sense. Nobody rational would put themselves in danger like that."

I grabbed my phone and looked up something online, just to be sure.

"The date of this obituary," I said. "Wilson Meeks didn't die of his heart attack until after Lilith emailed me. I didn't see the email until later, but she really did hope I would be able to talk with him. That means Lilith didn't do anything to him." Sanjay's theory didn't work. My shoulders relaxed and I let out a sigh of relief. "But you realize that brings us back to Ava."

"Who wouldn't hurt anyone."

My shoulders tensed again. "Ava is the one who planted the seed of an idea in Mahilan's mind that the three of us should come to Italy together, under the pretense of spending time together as a family."

"Who else knew what you were up to?"

I swore. "Stefano Gopal." My old advisor who was nowhere to be found.

CHAPTER 46

I paced through the suite, watching the wild wind through the windows and scrunching a water bottle in my hands.

"Before I left for Italy," I said, "I met with my old advisor, Stefano Gopal. But I trust him. Plus I didn't talk to him until after Lilith died." But where was he now?

"If Lilith's death was an accidental overdose, the person who's following you here in Italy isn't connected to her death. It could still be Stefano."

"All right. Let's take the ghost impersonator as a separate question. Stefano is too old to climb on boulders and rooftops and impersonate a ghost. I think." I thought of ninety-year-old Sébastien, who could have done it. I tugged at the ends of my hair. There was no way to rule out anyone.

"We're getting off track. You're a historian, not a detective."

"You're right. History is the thread we need to follow. It's impossible to figure out what's going on right now without understanding the history. That's what we've got to get back to."

"The missing history of Lazzaro Allegri."

"Exactly. I met with Stefano because he has an interest in cross-cultural Indian history and speaks fluent Italian, so I wanted to get his opinion. He pointed out Lilith's mistranslation of Lazzaro's notes and told me I needed to be looking for running water, such as the fountain not far from the Ogre hellmouth carving, not the Proteus sea monster statue. Once I arrived in Italy and visited the Park of Monsters, I learned his translation might not be right either. There was no running water near the Ogre. The Pegasus statue is a fountain, but there's no secret grotto there either."

"I wonder how he kept it so secret."

"Once you see the land here, you'll understand how the forest reigns supreme. Everything is surreal. The wind, the forests, the stone monsters. One of the first things I did here, after visiting the Park of Monsters, was meet with Enzo and Brunella Allegri, Lazzaro's descendants who loaned Lilith the sketchbooks. The Allegris told me they gave Lilith four notebooks, not three, and that's when I realized that's what Lilith had been trying to tell me before she died."

"What did you think of them?"

"Are you asking if it's possible the Allegris are after Lazzaro's treasure and could be the culprits? They're less likely suspects than anyone. They'd own any art left by their ancestor, and Lilith had explained to them her interest was in making the discovery to study the art. They have no motive. If anything, they're worse off if I can't find Lazzaro's paintings."

"And they'd have no reason to tell you about the fourth sketchbook if they were the ones hiding it."

"Exactly. Plus, they were helpful. They pointed me in the direction of a local historian, Francesco. He told us the famous local ghost story from the 16th century involving Marguerite and Antonio Allegri."

"You can skip the ghost story and get back to relevant history," Lane said.

"The ghost story is relevant."

Lane laughed. He stopped after I didn't join in. "You're serious?"

"The person following us is impersonating a ghost."

Lane's eyes flicked to the windows. "To try to scare you?"

"I haven't figured out if they're trying to scare me off or if they're spying on me. But the creepiest thing about the ghost is what it did long before I arrived. Someone has been impersonating a ghost for centuries—and in the 1960s, they killed someone."

"I take back my objection. I think you'd better tell me the ghost story."

"In the ghost story the locals know, Marguerite Allegri is a ghost who haunts an area of the woods when it rains. She died of grief in the 1500s, upon news of her husband Antonio's death, which she learned of during a fierce rainstorm. He was killed at war, by the hands of foreigners, so in the 1960s it's said she exacted her revenge on a foreign actor who was filming a movie at the Park of Monsters."

"How did he die?"

"After hearing her wail during a storm, he was curious and went in search of her. When he emerged from the woods, he was possessed. He died about a week later with his body frozen in terror."

"You don't really believe—"

"I don't. But there's something going on. Lazzaro's notes about his hidden art studio and this ghost story are both related to the rain. And a local librarian, Orazio, found me a 16th-century account of the ghost story, in which Antonio is the ghost, not his wife. The story changed over time."

"That's not unexpected. Why do you think it matters?"

"It's the incongruities of history that can reveal what really happened. I'm so close to seeing it, Lane. I can't quite grasp it, but I have to believe there's a rational explanation."

"How can you even question that?"

"The locals told us about the superstition that only once a person has heard the ghost story will they hear the ghost when it rains." My throat felt dry. I took a swig from a water bottle on the side table. "We saw a ghostly figure, and heard an inhuman ghostly wail. All of us."

"The atmosphere. It has to have been the atmosphere. And it was only because you'd heard the ghost story that you equated a sound with being a ghost."

"But we saw it too."

"Where?"

"Mahilan, Ava, and I snuck into the Park of Monsters in the middle of the night so we could look for Lazzaro's hidden studio. I can't believe I thought I bonded with her that night." I cleared my throat and told myself to focus. "We didn't find a secret hiding place, because the ghost chased us off."

"The Park of Monsters around midnight? It's enough to make normally sensible people imagine animal sounds and shadows are ghosts."

"It wasn't an animal. And it was terrifying. I don't believe it was a ghost. But that sound...It was difficult for me to believe it was fake." I shivered at the memory. "After that, I wanted answers even more than before. I wondered if Francesco, the actor who works at the park and who knows about local history, could be the ghost. Unlike the Allegris, he could do with the money. But he doesn't fit the evidence. Neither do the other locals I've met. If you insist Ava is innocent—"

"She is."

"As much as I hate to admit it, I know you're right. She has an alibi for both ghost appearances. What am I missing?"

"Ava's involvement complicated what would otherwise have been more straightforward. She seized the opportunity to get Lazzaro Allegri's paintings for herself, but she didn't hurt anyone."

"Except my brother."

"She's not going to hurt him."

"Emotionally. She's going to break his heart. He doesn't deserve that. But I'll accept she's not playing the ghost. Which I know isn't a ghost."

"Then what are you so afraid of?"

I stopped pacing and faced Lane. "I'm not afraid."

"You are, Jones. I know you."

I let his words sink in. "I'm not frightened of this. Not exactly."

"Then what?"

"I'm going to become her, Lane." I whispered the words, not

quite ready to admit the truth out loud. "I'm afraid I'm going to become just like Lilith Vine. Giving her the benefit of the doubt and assuming she didn't harm Wilson Meeks or try to hurt herself to trick me, I mean the rest of it. What she did with her life."

"You enjoy a good scotch. That hardly means you're going to become an alcoholic."

"Not that. Her career. She made a big discovery in her twenties. After that, her whole life was spent trying to recapture that former glory. She chased one thing after another. Never focusing. Never contributing to historical knowledge as she otherwise might have."

"Ah. You think her fate awaits you, because you have been known to follow a lead. I believe you were *thirty* when you found—"

I threw a pillow at him. "Ouch."

"That didn't hurt."

"I'm weakened because I haven't had anything to eat all day. I've been stuck in transit."

I tossed him a granola bar from my bag.

"Really? You've been eating Tuscan delicacies and I get a squished granola bar?"

"We're in the region of Lazio, not Tuscany. And you're trying to distract me." I smiled in spite of my frustration. "Thank you."

"You're welcome. And you're not going to become Lilith Vine. You've made real discoveries that have not only furthered historical knowledge but helped a lot of people. Unlike her, you're not chasing phantoms."

"Speaking of phantoms—"

"I know. We should get back to your ghost."

"The ghost doesn't fit into the timeline. Not even the revised one with Ava. The locals couldn't all be in on a conspiracy to invent a false ghost story and then convince me it had been invented during Lazzaro Allegri's lifetime. Even if we were conspiracy theorists, it's simply not possible to get a whole province of Italy to go along with such a charade. Besides, I'd swear that the 16th-century book from the library that contained the ghost story was authentic. How does the ghost story fit into the puzzle? I should take you to the Park of Monsters so you can see the setting for yourself."

"That's not what I was thinking should be our next step."

"How can you say that?"

"I trust that you didn't miss anything at the park. In broad daylight while the park is open to visitors, I'm not sure what I would catch that the rest of you missed. I'm not an expert on topography, rock formations, or hidden meanings in Latin inscriptions. But there was a glaring omission in the steps you've taken: Lazzaro's paintings."

"Haven't you been listening to me? That's all I've been talking about."

"Not his missing masterpieces. The two paintings he sent home from India. The ones that are accounted for."

I squeezed my eyes shut. How could I have overlooked that?

"Don't worry, Jaya. We each approach things from what we can bring to the table. Since I know art history, it's those paintings I thought of. While I was on my way here, I looked on the internet to see where they're located. They're in a museum not far from here. If we hurry, we can make it before the museum closes."

CHAPTER 47

Before we headed out the door, I found the rope ladder and scoured the suite for my sneakers, since I still planned on bringing Lane to the Park of Monsters.

"I can't believe it," I said, holding a solitary running shoe in my hand. "Sanjay truly made my second sneaker disappear."

I fumed about Ava as Lane drove us to the museum in his rental car. I was going to kill her for leading Mahilan on and breaking his heart, even if she had eventually fallen for him too. Not to mention for trying to steal Lazzaro Allegri's paintings out from under me. And for making me realize that I loved both Lane and Sanjay.

"If you're right that Ava is in love with your brother," Lane said, "she's on borrowed time, trying to figure out her next move so she can both find her treasure and keep her man."

"Are you okay with that?"

"The fact that she's moved on? It was a shock to find out she was alive, but I've been over her for fifteen years, Jaya."

"Why are we pulling over? We're not there yet."

Off the side of the narrow road, Lane put the Opel Mokka, a small SUV similar to the Fiat Panda, into park. With one hand he undid my seatbelt, and with the other he pulled me across the car into his arms. When I came up for air from his kiss, his glasses were fogged up.

"Sorry," he said. "I couldn't wait a moment longer to do that."

*   *   *

I turned my head to one side. Then the other. Wasn't that what people did when trying to appreciate art? I stepped closer. Then I stepped back, making sure to do so carefully. The floor sloped in the small museum housed in a 15th-century home.

"Lazzaro's paintings are awful," I said. The building itself captured my imagination more than the paintings filled with a cacophony of colors. I could imagine the generations of families who'd lived under this roof. Even if the floor had been leveled, the low roof would have been a reminder of how old the building was. Lane had to stoop to walk through the doorways.

"I wouldn't go quite that far," Lane said. "There's a certain raw talent you can see in his artwork."

"I don't see it."

"He was young when he made these. It looks like he was still finding his form. The museum and its scholars saw the value—"

"It's a small museum. Are you sure it's not because the Allegris are a noble family?"

"Nobility doesn't mean much in Italy."

"I thought there were tons of noble families here."

"That's the problem," Lane said. "There are too many, so it's nothing special. Influential families were granted titles through promotions within the Catholic church, judicial appointments, or simply buying them. I'd guess that nearly half of Italy can claim noble blood."

"Okay, so he didn't get in this museum because of his ties to nobility."

"I'm wondering if he got in because of his ties to Michelangelo," Lane said, looking around. The small room was filled with 16th-century paintings. "This placard says Lazzaro worked with him, but doesn't back it up."

"Lilith mentioned that too, but I didn't find anything to back up that assertion either. Maybe she saw this same placard when she visited Bomarzo. I wonder if everyone got that wrong, thinking there was a connection because Lazzaro was once heralded as 'the next Michelangelo.' Which doesn't necessarily mean they knew each other or had any connection."

"But it was a small community in many ways," Lane murmured.

"Stefano also told me about a theory that Michelangelo designed the Park of Monsters with Vicino Orsini."

"The gardens were designed by Pirro Ligorio. Not Michelangelo."

"Stefano wouldn't entertain a theory that didn't have supporting evidence."

"Is he an art historian?"

"No, of course not."

"This is my specialty, Jaya. Whatever connection Michelangelo might have had to Lazzaro Allegri, it wasn't through the Park of Monsters."

He must have seen the look of disappointment on my face.

"Maybe Lazzaro knew Michelangelo around the Florentine art scene and got so sick of him that an offer from that Sultan of Gujarat was welcome. There's your answer about how he got to India." Lane made a mock bow.

"Was Michelangelo really that bad?"

Lane shrugged. "There's no way to know. Most experts think he was a jerk, but you know that history is written by people with their own biases. Art history is no different. Does it really matter?"

"Of course it matters."

"Michelangelo left us beautiful art that speaks to our souls. The Renaissance is about rebirth. Bringing classical ideas of truth and beauty into the lives of everyday people, using new techniques like perspective. That contribution to the world lasts longer than whatever slights he inflicted on people during his life. That beauty and truth last for eternity."

I brought Lane's lips down onto mine, not caring if anyone saw. As it happened, not many people appeared to appreciate Lazzaro Allegri's early paintings. We were alone in the room.

"Am I forgiven, then?" Lane asked, adjusting his glasses.

"That was for bringing truth and beauty into my life. I'm not sure about the forgiveness part."

"I shouldn't have kept things from you. Anything. I was trying to protect you by not telling you more about the circumstances of Mia's—I guess I should try harder to call her Ava now—about the circumstances of what I thought was Ava's death. I even have an old photograph of her I took without her knowing. She was always careful."

I wondered how careful she was being right now, on the run with my brother. Lane didn't believe she was a killer. Did I believe that too?

"You look worried again," Lane said. "Look, this possible Michelangelo connection doesn't matter. It isn't going to help us find Lazzaro's art."

"No, you were right to bring us here to the museum. I've been so focused on the location of his art studio that I haven't been doing what I do best—analyzing things through history."

"You've done that without even realizing it, Jones. You've found Lazzaro's history: the Allegri ghost that bridges past and present. There's got to be a reason why someone is pretending to be the ghost."

"You can ask the ghost the next time we see him. Are you ready to go?"

"First let me see if I can find someone who works here. They should know more than these general descriptions they've placed next to Lazzaro's artwork."

We found the museum curator. She only spoke Italian, but Lane spoke well enough to communicate our interest. As she spoke, her face grew animated and Lane gripped my arm.

"What's she saying?" I asked. "Is she telling you about the Michelangelo connection?"

"Not exactly. She says it exists, but that's not what she's saying right now. Someone else was asking her about the history of Lazzaro's paintings. Today. He's still here in the museum."

CHAPTER 48

The man at the museum could be our ghost.

We found him in the reading room, which in this rustic museum meant a windowless closet in which two bookshelves, a desk, and a temperature-control thermostat had been installed.

"Stefano?"

He stood up from the desk and kissed my cheeks. I was glad that was his preferred mode of greeting, because my hands had suddenly become clammy and my whole body tensed. *Stefano was in Italy.*

"Lane Peters," I said, "meet my grad school advisor, Dr. Stefano Gopal."

"A pleasure," Stefano said, extending his hand.

Lane glanced sharply at me as he took Stefano's hand.

As the two men began shaking hands, my tense shoulder relaxed. I beamed at the two of them. Stefano was taller than Lane. Far taller than the ghost. I hadn't thought about it before, but the ghost was a smaller man. Or a woman.

Stefano couldn't be the ghost.

"Be nice," I said softly to Lane. "It's not him."

"I must be becoming an old man," Stefano said. "I didn't catch what you said."

"It was nothing," I said.

"Not only that," Stefano said. "I missed your call while I was in the air, but I didn't think I'd called you back yet to tell you I'd be here." He frowned. "And you're blurry."

"It's not your vision. Your glasses are on top of your head. And your memory isn't going either. We're here looking into Lazzaro Allegri."

"Great minds. I wasn't able to stop thinking about those sketches you showed me."

Stefano hadn't been able to resist the lure of Lazzaro's treasure either. It was a long trip from San Francisco to Bomarzo, which explained why he hadn't called me back right away.

"Have you been to the Park of Monsters yet?" I asked. "You got the translation wrong."

He shook his head. "I only arrived yesterday. But I did *not* mistranslate. Italian is my mother tongue."

Lane, who'd been silent as he sized up Stefano, picked up a book from the shelf and spoke a phrase of rapid Italian.

"He's a clever one," Stefano said, leaning back on his heels and grinning at me before taking the book from Lane's hands. "Testing my Italian, eh? You picked up a copy of a book on pagan traditions in Renaissance gardens, not an essay about witchcraft in classical architecture."

Lane acknowledged the successful test with a nod.

"Then either Lazzaro purposefully misled us," I said, "or more likely, the answer is in his missing fourth sketchbook."

"There's another sketchbook?" Stefano asked.

"Jaya," Lane said sharply, speaking over Stefano.

"He's not our ghost," I said. "I'm sure. He's too tall and broad-shouldered."

"A ghost?" Stefano said.

"We have a lot to catch up on," I said. "Can we take you to dinner?"

"I would love to, but I'm afraid I have a date."

"You work fast, Gopal."

"It's the full head of hair." He smoothed his think white waves. "Not so common when you get to be my age. But it's not a problem for us to stay here a while to catch up."

"I thought the museum was closing soon," Lane said.

"It is. But the staff will be here for another hour. And Dafne, the curator, is my date." He winked. "What have you kids discovered?"

"No hidden grotto," I said. "There's no water near the Ogre. And I checked—there wasn't a stream near there in the past either. That's why we're here, to see where following Lazzaro's art will take us."

"Who's your friend?" Stefano asked. "You introduced him, yes, but why bring him?"

"He's an art historian," I said before Lane could reply.

"One who's missing the connection between Lazzaro and Michelangelo that you all seem to be making," Lane said. "And that's probably taking us down the wrong rabbit hole. I don't see how it helps us find Lazzaro's artwork."

"It might not," Stefano said. "And I'm more interested in Lazzaro's connection to Bahadur Shah's court in India. And it gives us our answer about how his paintings survived after all this time."

"You have the answer?" Lane asked.

Stefano held up a sheet of faded paper inside a protective clear cover. "A letter Lazzaro wrote to a relative."

"He tells them the location of his studio?"

"No. In this letter he speaks of the humid climate of Gujarat and how he was impressed with local artists who adapted to the conditions of heat and moisture."

Lane nodded with awe. "He learned their techniques."

"How does that help us?" I asked.

"It tells us," Lane said, "that when we find his paintings, there might be something left of them after all."

CHAPTER 49

We left Stefano to his date and drove back to Bomarzo. We both tried calling Ava and Mahilan, but neither was answering their phone. Lane agreed with my assumption that Ava wouldn't hurt Mahilan.

Then why did I feel so nervous?

"We're not going to make it back to the Park of Monsters in time," I said, pointing at the setting sun. "It closes at sunset."

Instead of another visit to the stone monsters, we found a hole-in-the-wall restaurant. Nobody there appeared to speak English. That meant we were in for great local food, and also that we could speak freely. As usual, Lane asked for the table in the back corner and took the seat facing the door.

"I'm ravenous," I said.

"I've never known you to not be ravenous. It's one of my favorite things about you."

"Just how good is your Italian?"

"Definitely good enough to ask for the daily special. Extra spicy."

I smiled, but immediately felt guilty about letting myself enjoy a romantic dinner. "What am I going to do about Mahilan?"

"I promise we'll figure it out. I'm more concerned that there's an unknown actor out there. The ghost isn't Ava and it isn't your professor."

"Please don't tell me you're starting to believe it's a real ghost."

"I don't think it's a real ghost. Obviously."

"Obviously," I joined in far too quickly. If he'd heard that sound, and seen that shadow...My skin prickled as I recalled that night. The sound of thunder rumbling in the distance made me jump.

"You okay, Jones?"

"Fine. I just felt a little chill. I think there's a draft."

A waiter swooped in with a plate of salt cod with raisins, pine nuts, and tomatoes, cooked in olive oil and onions. I had no idea what the dish was called, but it was delectable.

"What I don't understand," Lane said, "is why someone wanted to use that old ghost story to stir up fear."

"It's becoming more obvious to me that the ghost impersonator wants to keep us away from something. Isn't that always the point in those old *Scooby-Doo* episodes?"

Lane grinned at me and raised his glass of Chianti. "To Scooby-Doo."

After clinking glasses, I turned to look out the window. A light rain was falling against the front windows of the restaurant. "It's raining," I whispered.

"You can have my jacket if you need it for the walk to the car."

"That's not what I meant. The ghost only cries out when it rains. I have a feeling you're going to meet it tonight."

"This is much more sensible than your idea," Lane said twenty minutes later as we sat in the warm dry car on the side of the road at the highest hilltop we could find.

"My idea of waiting inside the Ogre's mouth was spookier though."

"I need all the comfort I can get right now. I thought the waiter was going to have a stroke when I asked him if they could speed up our dinners so we could leave quickly. Either that or kick us out of the restaurant."

"We got out of there in time. It's not raining heavily yet. That's when we heard the ghost the last time."

Lane glanced at his phone.

"Looking at the time, or for a message from Ava?" I asked.

"Both. She can't ignore us forever. She has to either come clean to your brother or find a way to convince you not to tell him what's going on. How's she going to do that?"

"What would you do in that situation?"

"You already know what I did in a similar situation. I told you everything. Maybe they're having a heart-to-heart conversation as we speak."

"Somehow I doubt it. Are you sure we shouldn't be outside?" I made a move for the car door, but Lane took my hand to stop me. I said, "We've only seen one car go by the whole time we've been up here. It's not like anyone will see us."

"How will getting soaked to the bone help us?"

"I don't know. But I feel like we should be closer to the action."

"I thought we didn't know where the action was," Lane pointed out.

"There are two spots related to the ghost. The Park of Monsters and the nearby unclaimed forest where nobody wants to go."

"I wish you'd stop calling it 'the ghost.'"

"Do you have a better name for it?"

A ghostly wail pierced the air.

Lane's grip on my hand tightened. With his other hand, he locked the car door.

"That is one freaky sound," he whispered.

"It sounds different tonight."

"Like it's another person impersonating the ghost?"

"No, that's not it. It's like...tonight the sound is less intense. When it was pouring two nights ago, I'm sure the shriek carried for miles. Tonight, her cry is weaker, but we can still hear it. It's nearby."

"Thanks for that cheery thought." Lane let go of my hand and twisted around in the car to look out the car windows in every direction.

"The scream isn't just softer. There's something different about it. But still only sounding once."

I could barely see the rocky hillside forest that surrounded the car. Raindrops tapped faintly on the windshield. The water fell so gently that I could barely hear it.

"The strength of the rain," I whispered. "*Mi trovate quando diluvia.* 'You'll find me here when it's pouring rain.' Why not just say when it's raining? I know it could just have been an overly dramatic statement since he was an artist, but I feel like I'm missing something."

"You're talking about the quote from Lazzaro's sketchbook?"

"Stop squirming. You're making me nervous. Yes, his note next to the Orcus drawing that said we'd find him there when it was pouring rain."

"You're missing or adding a word."

"What?"

"The Italian and English don't match up."

"I'll never forget that quote. I memorized the original because Lilith and Stefano had translated it differently. Here." I scrolled through the photos on my phone until I found the picture I'd taken of that page of the sketchbook.

"*Mi trovate quando diluvia,*" Lane read. "I'm fairly certain that translates to 'You'll find me when it's pouring rain' or 'you'll find me when it's flooding'—but not 'you'll find me *here.*'"

"You're right. That's what Stefano said." I groaned. "I've been filling in an extra word in my mind because it's what made sense..."

"Why do you suddenly look like you're a million miles away?"

"Because I know where Lazzaro Allegri's treasure is."

CHAPTER 50

"Okay," I said, "I don't know the exact location of Lazzaro's paintings, but I've figured out what's going on."

"Because of a word you inadvertently added to a translation?" Lane asked.

"It was the piece I was missing. The text didn't mean he was seeking shelter when it rained. It meant exactly what it said: that people would be able to find him when it was pouring rain."

"What am I missing, Jones? I don't see what that has to do with his studio, the ghost, and the rain."

"The scream only sounds during the rain *because it's the sound of a 16th-century machine*. The reason the wail is heard only once is because the rain pushes open a lever."

Comprehension lit up Lane's face.

"The clue was in the ghost story," I continued. "The original ghost story holds that Antonio Allegri is the ghost, but the modern version has it as his wife. That's because when the machine wasn't so old, its rusty gears had a lower pitch. But over the centuries of not being maintained, the sound became more and more of a high-pitched screech."

"That's brilliant, Jones."

"That's why the ghost is only heard when it rains. And tonight, the rain is lighter but has been going on for longer, so the water must have built up more slowly. That's why tonight's ghost scream was softer and I don't expect it could be heard from a long distance. It has to be nearby."

I reached for the door handle.

"Hang on," Lane said. "Where are you going?"

"To find Lazzaro Allegri's hiding place before the rain stops and the opening closes back up."

"You sure this machine is in Lazzaro's hidden spot?"

"Positive. Well, nearly positive. The theory fits. So many Renaissance gardens were once filled with automata that were operated by hydraulics."

Lane groaned. "I should have thought of it as soon as I heard that sound. It was the prerogative of bored noblemen to create wild sculpture gardens. Amusement parks for the wealthy during the Renaissance, powered with hydraulics."

"The clue was in the translation the whole time. Stefano Gopal thought Lilith Vine had misinterpreted *mi trovate quando diluvia*. Lilith believed it referred to a biblical flood and Stefano believed it meant a shelter from the pouring rain. That's why Lilith suspected Lazzaro's artwork was near one of the Park of Monsters' creatures that looked like it was rising from the ocean, whereas Stefano was sure it meant Lazzaro could hide from the rain inside Orcus, the Ogre king of the Underworld. They were both wrong. Lazzaro meant exactly what he wrote, that the pouring rain was one way to open the door to his hiding spot. 'You'll find me when it's pouring rain.'"

Lane shook his head. "I should have seen it. You showed me the sketchbooks."

"We all missed it. And nearly all of those Renaissance gardens with moving sculptures have fallen into complete disrepair, so I didn't think about it as a possibility. In this modern age of computerized machines, most people don't care about such inventions. Sanjay was telling me about a hydraulic sculpture garden in Germany that's still operational. The gardens at Hellbrunn Palace. When he talked about his visit there, he sounded like a kid meeting Santa Claus."

"Art historians love to debate each other about whether things like that count as art or not."

"Why wouldn't a Renaissance sculpture garden count as art?" I asked.

"Because those sculptures are primarily rude jokes. Bored noblemen used their hydraulic toys to spray water on unsuspecting visitors. There were even water holes on stone benches that sprayed guests' seats when the host was ready for them to leave. But in the case of Hellbrunn, the four-hundred-year-old automata are still in working order because they've been kept up. I'm not sure in this case—"

"Lots of creations have survived without being tended to. Just look at our Park of Monsters, which is only a little worse for wear. In the 1950s all people had to do was cut away the overgrowth. I know it's not powered by hydraulics like Lazzaro's hidden garden, but that's why Lazzaro's deteriorating machine makes that horrid screeching sound."

Now that I'd figured out the secret of our false ghost, the sound really did sound much more like gears squealing than the moan of a ghost. Human imagination was a funny thing. I laughed ruefully.

"What is it?"

"Human imagination. I know how the poor actor in the 1960s must have died. Francesco said that after he went in search of the ghost, he came back injured, started having fits like he was possessed, then died with a look of horror on his face. He wasn't possessed. But if he found a rusty old lever—"

"Tetanus."

I nodded. "Which causes muscles to contract, causing fits. And it especially affects the jaw."

"Making it look like he died of fright."

"We've covered everything. Now can we please get out of here and find this treasure?"

We zipped up our jackets, turned on our flashlights, and headed out into the light rain. I wished again that I had my sneakers, but my heels would have to do.

"I don't know if this is a good idea," Lane whispered as his flashlight bounced against the earth. In the darkness, I couldn't tell whether or not there was a path. "I should have put in my contact lenses."

"I'm sure it's around here somewhere. We're in that no-man's-land between Allegri and Orsini land. The origins of the ghost story are based right here. This has to be it."

"If there's no ghost," Lane said, "then what the hell is that walking toward us?"

CHAPTER 51

I held my finger to Lane's lips. "Ghosts don't use flashlights," I whispered.

We turned off our own flashlights. The "ghost" switched off his as well.

Lane cursed under his breath, but otherwise the dark night was still, with only the sounds of an owl and the softly falling rain hitting the lush greenery that surrounded us. We stood there for several minutes, and I felt myself begin to shiver.

Raindrops gathered at the tip of my nose. I wiped them away, but felt a sneeze coming on. I couldn't stop it, so I buried my nose in the crook of my arm. If our ghost was close, he would hear it and know where we were. But we still didn't know where he was.

"My eyes are adjusting," Lane whispered. He took my hand and pulled me slowly up the hill.

"We're going the wrong way," I whispered back.

"No, we're not. We're not going to find anything without our flashlights. And we're not using our flashlights when a dangerous unknown person is out there tracking us."

"But who—"

"We already know of more than one person with bad intentions."

He had a point. I didn't object as we made our way back to the car.

Lane unlocked the door for me, but before getting inside

himself, he walked a few dozen yards in each direction. I turned up the heat and eased out of my wet jacket. Even though I could see him, I locked the doors, only unlocking them once I could make out Lane's face at the window.

"What were you doing?" I asked.

"Looking for the car of whoever is following us."

"Did you find it?"

He shook his head and started the engine. "No. They're clever. I almost wish it had been a ghost."

"I wish we had that fourth sketchbook," I said. "Neither scholarly research nor pretending we're in the Scooby Gang is working."

We were back at the villa. Since Ava and Mahilan were gone, Lane was sharing the master bedroom with me. "I bet that sketchbook has the information about where this hydraulic hidden room is located. Do you think room service runs this late?"

"At a place this posh, I'm sure it does." He tossed me the menu.

"If only Lilith hadn't tried to be so clever by feeding me only portions of information because she wanted me hooked before she arrived and saved the day, then I'd have that fourth sketchbook. She has to be the one who had it. Maybe I should call Tamarind and have her break into Lilith's house after all."

"Jaya."

"Hmm?" I said, studying the room service menu. Sneaking through the rainy Italian countryside expends a lot of calories.

"Do you even know what you're saying?"

"Not really. I'm starving. I'm confused. And my brother has been kidnapped by your not-dead ex-girlfriend. Of course I don't know what I'm saying. I don't even know what I'm thinking anymore." I threw the menu across the room.

"It's late. We should get some sleep."

"I can't believe I got all the timing about Lilith wrong because of Ava," I grumbled.

"Not all of it," Lane said. "The only thing she obscured is the break-in at your office."

"Meaning the ghost could be someone who's been here in Italy this whole time." I thought about everyone I'd met here who could possibly know about Lazzaro's paintings. "We've got Francesco, the elderly actor with a flair for the dramatic. He knows more about the history of this region than most people."

"He could have known about Lazzaro's artwork, but not how to find it."

"Then there's Niccolò, the kid who works at the Park of Monsters. He knows I'm looking into this because he translated materials for me at a local library. I met him by chance, and when he found out I was American he wanted my help practicing his English. And at the library, he got help from the librarian too. Orazio. He doesn't speak English but worked hard to help me. Neither of them seems likely."

"I doubt it, but it's good to consider all possibilities. What about your 'chance' meeting with Niccolò? Was it truly chance?"

"I got lost while on a run, and he passed by on his scooter. I was running on paths until I sought out a main road to find help. There's no way he was following me, if that's what you're thinking."

"And the librarian?"

"Orazio was far more interested in the wine I brought him than this particular history. That leaves Enzo and Brunella Allegri, the distant relations of Lazzaro who live in the ancestral castle. But they're the ones who loaned Lazzaro's four sketchbooks to Lilith. They told me about it themselves. And they're the only ones with no possible motive, because they'd own whatever Lilith discovered."

"Who else did Lilith meet with here?"

"You know, I never thought about that." It was a stupid omission, but I'd been so distracted by other things I hadn't asked that specific question. "Does it even matter at this point? Who cares if there's someone who feels like dressing up as a ghost? If they weren't in California to hurt Lilith—"

"You're forgetting something important, Jones."

"Of course I'm forgetting something important," I snapped. "I'm tired and starving. So, um, what am I forgetting?"

"Lilith was drugged. Not stabbed or shot. There are ways of making someone take something even if you're not physically there with them."

"How? Like threatening them on the phone, saying that something bad will happen if they don't do as told?"

Lane shrugged. "It's a possibility."

"She wasn't being forced. Her beloved husband was dead. They had no children. There was no one she loved who could be used against her." Poor Lilith. "All we know for sure is that Ava and my brother are missing. We have the solution to where Lazzaro's paintings might be if they survived, but we don't know how to find it until the next time it rains. And, if our unknown 'ghost' killed Lilith Vine, he did it in a way so ingenious we can't fathom it. Either by transporting himself from Italy to California, or by forcing her to drug herself."

My phone rang, startling both of us.

"Your brother is on his way back to you," Ava's clipped voice said. "He'll be there soon."

I let out a sigh. I wasn't sure if it was relief or sadness. "You told him?"

"Not exactly."

"Then why is he—"

"I'm out of the game, Jaya. All I ask is that you think about what's best for Mahilan."

"You want me to put in a good word for you?" I asked, staring incredulously at the phone.

"If Mahilan loves me as much as I love him," Ava said, "don't you think we'll both be happier together?"

I was speechless.

"Let me talk to her," Lane said.

When I handed over the phone, she'd already disconnected.

Just then I heard the sound of a key turning in the lock.

CHAPTER 52

"Fish," I said, relief flooding through all five feet of me as I embraced my brother. I looked behind him. "Where's Ava?"

"Her son is sick, so she had to go see him. I offered to go with her, but I guess she wasn't ready for that level of commitment—having me meet her kid. On my own, I thought it made more sense for me to come back here to get you." He gave a start, noticing Lane's presence for the first time.

Lane stood and extended his hand. I introduced them.

"Reports of your disappearance have been greatly exaggerated, I take it," Mahilan said with a chuckle.

"You were right, Fish. He hadn't been kidnapped. I blew things way out of proportion."

"I've known you since birth, JJ. I know you go all in when you have an idea."

"She's been like this forever?" Lane asked.

"Afraid so."

"JJ and Fish," Lane said with a smile on his lips.

"So you've been keeping my sister safe while I went on ahead to the new hotel with my girlfriend," Mahilan said. He'd been subtly taking in Lane's appearance since he'd noticed his presence.

"Why did you two take off without me?" I asked.

"Ava told me your boyfriend was coming and you went to get him at the airport," Mahilan said. "I wish you'd waited for me to get out of the shower to tell me, but I understand." He looked from me to Lane. "Is something wrong? Did you mean for us to wait for you?

Oh, God. It's not the ghost, is it? JJ, this is exactly why I wanted us to get out of here."

If I hadn't known Lane so well, I wouldn't have detected the awkward emotion that passed across his face.

"Mahilan, you'd better sit down. We need to get you up to speed."

Lane and I were on the same page: We weren't ready to reveal Ava's secret to Mahilan. Aside from pursuing a crime of opportunity, we didn't think Ava was involved. Instead, we told him how I'd figured out the ghost's secret, which would point to the hidden location of Lazzaro's paintings the next time it rained. My brother was visibly relieved to learn that there was no ghost.

"What's the plan?" he asked.

"We draw out the ghost," I said.

"How do we do that?"

"By publicly searching for Lazzaro's hidden mechanical stone garden."

Mahilan frowned.

"We're not going to find it without more information," I said, "at least until the next time it rains. This area is so overgrown. That's why the Park of Monsters was lost for so many centuries. Even searching a few square miles will take forever. We looked up weather reports, and that storm front has passed. Since it's summer, there's not going to be another rainstorm for quite some time. Without more information, there's too much ground to cover to find the spot. We need to find out what our ghost knows."

"And we can't wait that long," Lane said.

"Why not?" Mahilan asked. "Why can't we just leave right now, and come back when it's rainy season?"

"The person following us in the Park of Monsters may have killed Lilith Vine. If we leave them here, justice won't be served, plus they might be methodical enough to find Lazzaro's grotto. Who knows what they'll do with his paintings."

"This plan is our best hope," Lane added.

"I don't like it, JJ," Mahilan said.

"Without at least a few hours' sleep," Lane said, "we're not going to be any good at figuring this out."

"You're staying here?" Mahilan asked him.

"He can stay in my room," I said. "What? I'm thirty, not thirteen."

In the morning, we were awoken by the shrill sound of the hotel room's phone. I was the first to reach it.

"I'm sorry to disturb you," an Italian-accented voice said. "This is the front desk calling. There's a man here to see you. Normally we would never think to disturb a guest before eight o'clock, but this man...he is quite insistent."

"Who is it?" I asked.

"He did not give his name, but he says you will want to see him. He says he has a 16th-century sketchbook."

CHAPTER 53

I roused Lane and my brother. We quickly dressed and went to the front desk.

Francesco, the white-haired actor, was waiting impatiently, pacing the length of the small lobby while the desk clerk kept a veiled eye on him. He clutched a worn notebook in his hands.

"Is that—?" I began.

"I did give my name," Francesco insisted, shooting a look of disdain at the desk clerk.

The clerk clicked his tongue. "I do apologize if it was wrong to wake you. The villa will provide you a discount voucher for a future visit—"

"It's fine," I said.

"We'll take the discount," Mahilan said.

I elbowed my brother. "Let's all go outside."

I introduced Lane to a distracted Francesco and led us to one of the many secluded tables perched throughout the grounds. Nobody sat, but it gave us the privacy we desired.

"You found Lazzaro's notebook?" I asked. "How did you—"

"All these years," Francesco said, shaking his head. "All these years I thought I was simply a character actor, playing a role."

Lane and I exchanged a look. His expression told me I should let Francesco continue at his own pace. It was difficult not to interrupt. Seeing that notebook in his hands and not being able to look at it was killing me.

"I admitted to you," Francesco continued, "that I did not truly believe I was the reincarnation of Pier Francesco 'Vicino' Orsini, the creator of the Park of Monsters. I learned this morning that I was wrong."

The three of us stared at him. Mahilan gave a hesitant laugh.

"Yesterday," Francesco said, "I would have laughed too. But not today." He waved the worn leather-bound notebook in his hand. "The only way I could have found this notebook is that I, as Lazzaro Allegri's friend Vicino Orsini, knew where to find it."

He must have given the desk clerk the unbelievable name of Vicino Orsini. Everyone in these parts knew the famous man.

"Where did you find it?" Lane asked.

"I had the most vivid dreams last night," Francesco said. "I believed at the time they were simply dreams, but now I know the truth. They were a vision. The vision led me to sleepwalk through the forest. When I awoke, my shoes at the foot of my bed were coated in mud, and Lazzaro Allegri's missing sketchbook was on my nightstand."

He was a great actor, I'll give him that. I couldn't tell that he was lying. But it was far too convenient.

"It was you," I said. "With what you knew about local history, you knew Lazzaro Allegri's paintings would be an incredible find. So when you learned that Enzo and Brunella had Lazzaro's old sketchbooks, and that they sold them to Lilith Vine, you teamed up with her."

"No, *signora*, I am not acting now. You must believe—"

"But there's not enough information in there to find Lazzaro's hiding spot, is there? His sketches, even in this notebook, must not explain the hydraulic mechanics, probably because it was an engineer who built it for him. He was an artist and possibly an architect, but that's it."

"Yes, this is true," Francesco said. "But what do you speak of hydraulic mechanics?"

"You needed someone who could correctly interpret the sketchbook," Lane said. "That's why you started following Jaya around when she got here."

Francesco looked furtively between us. Was he gauging how difficult it would be to run, since we hadn't believed his ploy?

I groaned. "And you're an *actor*. You must know lots of people in California. You could have offered to split the profits of the paintings with a confederate who drugged Lilith Vine, accidentally leading to her death."

Francesco's face turned bright red. I knew we'd discovered how he'd done it.

We all stood stock still for a few seconds. Then Francesco bolted. He crashed into Mahilan's shoulder as he rushed past us, and his steps faltered. Mahilan cursed and grabbed Francesco's collar. The elderly actor took a swing at my brother, clipping his nose. Lane pulled Francesco off of Mahilan, who grabbed his injured nose with his left hand and balled his right hand into a fist, connecting with the side of Francesco's head. The actor crumpled to the ground.

I lifted Lazzaro Allegri's sketchbook from the dewy grass.

"Well," I said, standing over Francesco's prone form, "I guess that answers the question about who was playing our ghost."

CHAPTER 54

"This is it," I whispered, turning the pages of the sketchbook. "This sketchbook has a map that shows where Lazzaro's hidden grotto workshop was located. That's where he left his paintings."

"Why didn't the ghost use this to find them, then?" Lane asked. "If this is what he needed, why did Francesco show it to us?"

Mahilan moaned and clutched his injured nose. I handed him a packet of tissues from my bag.

"Look at the map," I said, turning back to Lane. "It's not clear where it starts. The missing clue was the ghost wail. The nearby section of woods on Allegri land where everybody was scared to go because of the mechanism that squealed in the rain and sounded like a ghost. Lazzaro's studio isn't inside the Park of Monsters."

"Anyone following the map would have assumed it started in the Park of Monsters because of Lazzaro's drawings of the park's sculptures," Lane said. "But now that we have a notion of where the hydraulic device is, we can find the real location of his paintings. If there are any paintings to find. The preservation techniques he learned in India might help things last, but in this overgrown rainy forest, I still have my doubts."

"Spoilsport."

"I think my noth ith broken," Mahilan said, holding a stack of tissues to his nose.

"Let me take a look," I said. He whimpered as I lifted his hand away. "Lane, do you know anything about broken noses?"

"I don't think it's broken," Lane said, "but it's going to give you a black eye."

Mahilan gasped. My brother was vain. A black eye wouldn't be good for his looks.

"And we should clean up your knuckles," Lane added.

Mahilan gasped again, noticing his bloody knuckles for the first time. We all looked from his hand to the crumpled form of Francesco.

"I had no idea you had it in you, Fish," I said.

"He hith me."

"You two stay with Francesco," I said. "And get Mahilan some medical attention."

"Where are you going?" Lane asked.

"To find Lazzaro's paintings, of course. What? Why are you two looking at me like that? We have our ghost. You two can give a statement to the authorities. With Italian bureaucracy, that will take forever. There's no way I'm staying here for that, now that we have the answer."

"She's always been like this?" Lane asked Mahilan.

"Yeth."

I took my brother's rental car, which he'd had washed since I'd last been inside.

To follow the map in the sketchbook, I first had to get back to Enzo and Brunella Allegri's land. All the roads around Bomarzo were small and winding, so I picked the one my phone's GPS suggested, which took me close to the Park of Monsters.

Sirens sounded behind me.

That's all I needed. A speeding ticket. Or worse. I hoped my brother had added my name to the registration on the rental car. I gripped the steering wheel and glanced in the rearview mirror. It wasn't a police car. It was an ambulance. I gripped the wheel even harder. Could Mahilan or Francesco be that badly hurt? Francesco had still been unconscious when I'd left him. Had Mahilan hit him harder than he meant to?

I slowed and pulled over, letting the ambulance pass me. It

wasn't going toward the villa. It was heading toward the Park of Monsters.

I shifted the Fiat into gear and followed the ambulance.

Five minutes later, I pulled into the Park of Monsters parking lot, empty except for two police cars and the ambulance. We'd been woken up early by Francesco, and it wasn't yet eight o'clock, the hour when the park opened. Whatever had happened here, it wasn't a tourist who'd had an accident.

A police officer emerged from the main entrance and began speaking urgently in Italian to me. I couldn't understand him, but his gesticulations made it clear he wished for me to stand back. A moment later, a man and a woman carrying a stretcher came into view. On the stretcher was Orazio, the helpful librarian who'd shared wine and history with me.

My hands flew to my mouth as I saw that Orazio's head was covered in blood. His eyes were wide open, staring upward but not seeing the new morning sky.

CHAPTER 55

The kindly librarian's lifeless body was loaded into the ambulance.

Had he come here on his own in the night in search of Lazzaro's hidden grotto and fallen off a rock in the darkness? He might have pieced something together with his historical knowledge and what Niccolò and I had told him.

But Orazio hadn't seemed like a careless man. Nor was he particularly interested in what I'd been seeking at the library. It seemed more likely that Francesco forced the old librarian here to use his knowledge, thinking Orazio would be able to read the map in the missing notebook.

I called Lane, but his phone went straight to voicemail. So did Mahilan's. They must have already arrived at the police station.

The police officer in the Park of Monsters parking lot continued to gesture at me. This time, I'm fairly certain he wanted me to leave. I was happy to oblige.

My hands shook as I steered the car out of the parking lot, away from the stone monsters that had claimed the librarian's life. Poor Orazio. He'd been so friendly and eager to help. Lazzaro Allegri's treasure had taken another life.

I didn't know where I was heading. I had no idea where Lane and my brother were, and didn't have the Italian to find out. While Lane and Mahilan sorted out Francesco with the police, there was only one thing I knew I could do.

*   *   *

I held up the sketchbook to the landscape in front of me, double-checking that this was the right spot.

Centuries of overgrowth had changed the details of the cypress, pine, and chestnut trees, but a violin-shaped boulder at the edge of a rocky hillside was unmistakable. This was it. Somewhere right here I would find Lazzaro Allegri's art studio, where he painted in secret after returning from India in disgrace.

I traced my hand along the rock. I could see the inlet where centuries of rainwater had smoothed it into the violin shape. As my fingers felt the alternatingly smooth and rough surface that Lazzaro's hands had touched four hundred and fifty years before me, his secret spoke to me.

My breath caught as I found a piece of rock that wasn't connected to the rest. A lever that had been smoothed by centuries of rainwater. The map had also been difficult for Francesco to follow because even if he'd passed this very spot, if he didn't know he was looking for a hidden lever he never would have seen this.

I laughed out loud. "Lazzaro Allegri's ghost!"

Should I go to the main house and get Enzo and Brunella to share the discovery with them? No, I wasn't sure yet that I was right.

There was something else that wasn't right about this whole situation.

A twig snapped behind me. I was suddenly very aware that I was in the middle of an overgrown forest, following a secret path only known in a five-centuries-old notebook.

"Lane?" I called. Had he caught up with me already?

A gaunt figure stepped out of the shadow of a tree.

"Enzo," I said, breathing a sigh of relief. "You startled me. I'm so sorry, I know I'm on your land. I should have come to see you first, but I was going to come see you as soon as I found..." There was something in his face that made my voice falter.

"No need to apologize," Enzo said with a smile. His eyes were bloodshot and dark circles hung under them. "This is *fantastico*. You found it. I thank you for finding Lazarro's studio."

Though the words themselves were friendly, my senses screamed at me. I'd made a grave mistake. I thought I was safe on my own because the ghost, Francesco, was in custody. But Francesco hadn't confessed. He'd gotten scared and tried to run.

"Why don't we go get help before we open the lever that leads to the grotto?" I said to Enzo. "We don't know if it's dangerous inside after all these years."

"I'm sorry," he said. "I wish it had not come to this."

A knife gleamed in his hand.

CHAPTER 56

I stepped backward and stumbled over the overgrown knotted roots of a chestnut tree. I steadied myself on the boulder, wishing I wasn't in my heels.

Enzo gripped the knife tightly in his hand, but he wasn't moving toward me. There were still several yards between us.

He motioned with the knife. "You push the lever."

"Lever?" I rubbed my knee.

"I have been watching you. I know what you have found."

"Don't you want to do the honors yourself?"

"Push." He jabbed the knife in my direction.

I edged my way along the boulder, back to the rock lever. I followed the water-worn crevice with my fingertips, knowing it would lead me to the lever that could be manually operated when it wasn't pressed open by the rain. The barely visible lever was covered in rust that had poisoned the American actor.

I cringed. "I can't—"

"Push," Enzo said again.

I lifted my foot. Slowly, so as not to agitate the knife-wielding aristocrat. I took off one of my high heels. "To reach the lever," I said quickly.

I used the shoe's heel to push through the narrow opening that contained the lever. The cold stone gave way, pushing downward. I braced myself for what might follow. Would the rock crush my hand instead of opening a section of stone?

A high-pitched wail pierced the air. A dozen birds in the vicinity scattered. At a moss-covered juncture that had looked like a natural crack, especially because of the moss, the boulder split apart, revealing a two-foot passageway.

"*Fantastico*," Enzo murmured again. "I am truly sorry, *Professoressa* Jones."

"I don't understand," I said. "This is your fortune. I'm a professor, not a thief. I'm not going to steal the artwork in Lazzaro's studio. It belongs to you. There's no need for you to do this." Or to have done *any of this*, I thought to myself. He had no reason to drug Lilith and kill Orazio.

"You don't understand as much as you think." His tired eyes and thin lips narrowed. "I don't own this land."

"You don't?"

"It belongs to my cousin. Just as Lazzaro Allegri lived on the land as a courtesy of his wealthy cousin, as do I. I have the Allegri name, but not a title, and not any claim on the land."

"But you live in the castle—"

"A crumbling pile of rocks that won't even stay warm in the summer." He spat out the words. "The house is falling apart. I have no money for a cook or housekeeper, so I had to let them go years ago. Brunella has been unhappy every day since then."

I thought about Brunella's suggestive clothing, stretching the seams of her expensive fabric nearly to the breaking point. She wasn't trying to be provocative. She didn't have money to buy newer designer clothes.

"My cousin lives like a king in Rome," Enzo continued with bitterness, "and he takes pity on me so he lets me stay at this house, rather than having it sit empty. The only condition is that I maintain the gardens, which were once much renowned. For this, we receive a small stipend to live on."

I realized my mistake about Francesco. I thought he was lying to me about the "vision" in his dream, which led him to Lazzaro's missing notebook. But there was another explanation. Like Lilith Vine, Francesco had been drugged.

"You're the ghost," I said. "Why impersonate the ghost, if you weren't trying to scare us away?"

"*Stupida.* I did not try. Rain was predicted. This is why I was wearing my hooded cloak in the rain at the *Parco dei Mostri.* It was your brother who call me a ghost. This is what gave me the idea that I could follow you without you seeing it was me. I know the secrets of the old buildings here, so I knew if you saw me following, I could get away."

That first night at the park, my brother had yelled that it was the ghost. We hadn't seen more than the shadow of a man dressed for the rain. But on the roof of the medieval kitchen building, he'd been purposefully disguised in flowing black fabric to create the illusion of being a ghost. And I knew, now, why Lane hadn't found the car of our pursuer. We were on Allegri land. Enzo had been driving the car we saw on the small road that night, so he knew our location. Afterwards, he parked the car at home and came back to spy on us on foot.

"I only wished to find Lazzaro's studio," Enzo said. "It should have been mine. I could not find it, even with the map. You could not either. I had to 'convince' Francesco to give you the map. He did not know this, of course. I fooled you both."

I saw it now. After failing to find this hiding spot with the map in the sketchbook, Enzo had started following me, thinking my knowledge would lead me to it. But when he realized I wasn't going to be able to find Lazzaro's hiding place without the missing notebook, he needed to find a way to get it to me. So he gave Francesco, who was known to be crazy, a drug that would give him hallucinations, put mud on his shoes, and left the notebook for Francesco to find. The dramatic actor filled in the missing pieces in his mind.

I never took my eyes off Enzo, but I had time to think. He wasn't moving. He must be planning his next move too, wondering if he should make me go into the passageway, or if he needed to kill me first.

A scraping noise sounded from the rock opening. It was sliding back into place. It must have been weighted so it would shut automatically, keeping the spot hidden. Both Enzo and I looked to the heavy rock that was sliding shut.

Could I jump Enzo without getting slashed too badly in the process? If he had any training in combat, he would have already acted. There was a chance.

"I see your eyes," Enzo said. "Do not think of running away. If you do, I will kill your friend."

"My friend?"

"The magician."

I gulped. "Sanjay?"

"I find him drowning his sorrow at the *Fantasma* bar."

The bar at the bottom of the hill. Sanjay must have stopped there after he left.

"He is a very loud man, yes?" Enzo said. "He talks much of you."

I groaned.

"He performs *fantastico* magic tricks," Enzo said. "I would hate to see him dead."

"You can't—"

"There are many secret passageways in my old home. Nobody will find him."

"What do you want?" My voice shook. It was my fault Enzo had Sanjay.

"You go," he said, pointing with the knife.

"Into the cave?"

"*Sì, sì.* Where else could I mean? You go."

I pushed the lever a second time and looked into the dark abyss as the ghostly wail sounded. What could I do but go along with Enzo?

CHAPTER 57

I was about to step into the chasm when the sound of snapping branches came from behind us.

"Brunella?" I called, hoping she'd seen her husband follow me to this spot.

"Brunella does not know," Enzo said, whipping his head around.

"She doesn't know what you've done? How do you expect her to not find out?"

"She will be happy when we have money again. You don't know what she used to be like. When I met her, she was the most beautiful woman I had ever seen. Both her body and her mind. She gave up her job to come live here with me. It was good for many years, until the money ran out. She had not worked in so long that she could not get a good job again. She works part-time at a hotel."

"She's the one who found the sketchbooks in your attic," I said. "That's why she knew there were four notebooks."

"I did not wish her to be at home when you called, but it could not be helped."

"It was you who dealt with Lilith Vine directly. And you only sold her *three* notebooks. After Lilith told you about Lazzaro's treasure, you thought you could pocket the money from selling insignificant sketchbooks, but keep the relevant one for yourself, the one that would lead you to the paintings."

"*Sì. Professoressa* Vine also thought I owned this land. She thought it would be a great thing for me when she discovered the artwork. She approached me with a very generous offer for anything of Lazzaro Allegri's that I had. I told Brunella of this, and she climbed to the attic first. There she found four sketchbooks. This is why she believed we sold *Professoressa* Vine all four, as she told you when we met." He shook his head. "After Brunella found my ancestor's drawings, I looked at them. Such nonsense, with monsters as well as people. But one of them had a map. Why would a man draw a map, if not for something of value?"

"Lilith never saw Lazzaro's fourth notebook," I whispered, "but as she was dying she realized the third book ended too abruptly and you'd held something back from her."

"Yes," Enzo said. "It was a mistake. Anyone who studied the other three would come to see there were pieces missing."

"Enzo!" Brunella's voice. "Enzo, are you here? I hear the sound of the ghost, but there is no rain. What is happening?"

"We're over here!" I called. "Brunella! It's Jaya Jones! I'm here with Enzo."

Enzo lunged at me but stumbled.

"What in God's name?" Brunella said as she came into view. "Enzo, are you having an affair with *Professoressa* Jones?" She narrowed her eyes and stomped towards him. "I knew you had been acting strangely since they arrived. This is where you meet? A cave in the forest?"

Enzo tucked the knife into his pocket. He had told me the truth: She didn't know.

"I was just leaving," I said, creeping away. "We're not having an affair, just a misunderstanding. *Arrivederci.* Bye." With Brunella distracting Enzo, I hoped I'd have time to find Sanjay at the Allegri house.

"Stop," Enzo said. His voice wasn't loud, but it was forceful.

When I turned, the knife was back in his hand.

"Enzo?" Brunella gawked at the blade.

"We cannot let her leave," he said. "If you let her leave, you will be left with nothing. Your life will be a disgrace. But if you help me now, you will have all the riches you desire."

"He's killed two people," I said. "And he kidnapped my friend. He won't hesitate to kill us both."

"That's a lie," Enzo roared. "I will not harm you, Brunella."

"You harmed *others*?" she said.

"I did this for you, *mia amore*."

"You killed people for me?"

"Yes, you see how much I love you." Enzo smiled. He was happy he had an opportunity to tell Brunella what he'd done.

"You," Brunella said while Enzo beamed, "are a lunatic man."

Enzo's smile turned into a snarl. I was glad Brunella was on my side, but I wished she'd played along. Now that Enzo knew Brunella wasn't as impressed with his actions as he'd hoped, he had no reason not to kill us both. And Sanjay, as soon as he was done with us.

"Two of us against one of you," I said to Enzo, "but we'll let you go."

"I am the one with the knife, *signora*."

"Why, Enzo?" Brunella's lip trembled.

"My cousin would have taken the paintings *Professoressa* Vine found. We are the ones who live on this land. Why should we not be the ones to benefit?"

"It is true you killed people?" Brunella asked. "Please tell me this is a nightmare."

"*Professoressa* Vine was not going to give up," Enzo said, then he spun to me. "But I did not mean to kill her. When she visited me again before she left Italy, I crushed my anxiety medication into powder and mixed it into the sweet drink mix she liked, and gave it to her as a gift. I believed this would distract her once she was home, making her forget about seeking my ancestor's treasure. I wished her no harm, only to leave me to find the treasure first."

Brunella was crying now. But she was doing something else at the same time. While Enzo was facing me, Brunella locked her eyes on mine and gave me a barely perceptible nod. She inched her way not toward the boulder, but the area of brambles next to it. What was she doing?

"Finding Lazzaro's studio was not as simple as *Professoressa* Vine made me believe," Enzo continued. "I could not find it. I needed more time. More help."

"Which you got when I arrived," I said, taking small steps toward Brunella. "You had no way to get me that fourth notebook without showing your hand. It occurred to you that you could use Francesco. You weren't certain it would work, so you also tried to get Orazio's help, because he'd helped me with research."

"Stop moving," Enzo snapped. "I see what you are doing, trying to escape."

"That's not what I'm doing," I said, taking another slow step. I saw what Brunella was up to. The mess of overgrowth next to the hillside boulder wasn't simply a patch of brambles and weeds. It was decades, if not centuries, of fallen branches that covered an opening below. We were leading him there.

Confusion crossed Enzo's face, right before giving way to another emotion. Fear. He fell through the spot we'd led him to, on top of the insecure overgrowth that had grown over a natural opening on the hillside. He cried out as the moss-covered branches gave way, and he fell into a rocky crevice next to Lazzaro's hidden grotto.

CHAPTER 58

It took three men on a rescue crew to lift Enzo from the narrow opening through which he'd fallen. He had a broken leg, so he couldn't climb out. The police moved a stone into the entrance to keep the rock from sliding back in place. They were waiting for him next to the boulder.

So was Brunella. Before the police pulled her off of him, she gave him a rather large bump on the head.

Enzo yelled at the police. Since he was speaking Italian, I couldn't understand the words. But from the way in which his chest was puffed out as he spoke, I thought it was a good bet he was claiming to be a nobleman they should bow down to. If that was the case, Lane was right: Nobility in Italy didn't carry much weight.

I told an English-speaking police officer that Sanjay was being held hostage somewhere in the Allegri house, possibly in a secret dungeon. He looked skeptical. Perhaps I should have used less dramatic words than "secret dungeon." To prove my point, I called Sanjay. His phone was off. That convinced the police to search the house. I went with them.

I apologized for the confusion with Francesco, but assured them they'd also find evidence that Enzo had killed an American professor, and probably Orazio as well. Since they didn't know what might lie beyond the fissure in the boulder, the police weren't concerned about securing this area of forest. I'd come back and search for Lazzaro's lost masterpieces—just as soon as I found Sanjay.

With the help of the police, I hunted through the Allegri house. "Sanjay?" I called from every room.

No answer.

The police removed paintings from the walls and pushed antique furniture aside as we searched for secret rooms.

Nothing.

"*Qui!*" a young officer called out.

I followed the sound of her voice to a three-foot hole in the wall behind a kitchen cabinet. She grinned and stepped through the wall.

"Sanjay?" I called.

Instead of a voice reply, my phone buzzed. A text message from Sanjay popped on the screen: *Your shoe is in the vase.*

My shoe? The vase? Was he delirious? He could be dying in an airless dungeon and thinking jumbled thoughts of me in his last breath. I choked back a sob.

"Is empty," the police officer said, shaking her head as she crawled back into the kitchen with cobwebs in her hair.

Where are you? I texted Sanjay.

Landed in Nantes. Forgot to tell you where you could find your sneaker. Knew you'd be missing it by now.

I groaned. Sanjay hadn't answered his phone because he was on an airplane. Enzo had been bluffing.

Mahilan and Francesco arrived in a police car. A swath of bandages covered my brother's nose. I wished Lane could have been there too, but whenever police were involved, he disappeared. Stefano Gopal would be arriving soon. He was on his way with his new girlfriend, the museum curator. I explained to everyone what I'd found in the forest.

"If Sanjay's Houdini handcuffs won't hold you," Mahilan said, "I'll have to think of something else."

"She has found the treasure," Francesco said. "You cannot fault her for this."

Mahilan glared at him. I wasn't sure if it was because Francesco had contradicted him or if he was still mad about his nose. I couldn't help laughing. With his overly bandaged nose, the glare had less gravitas. He turned the scowl to me, but I cut it off with a hug.

"I'm glad you're here, Fish," I said. "You can make the discovery with me."

"You haven't gone inside yet?"

I shook my head. "Nobody has. Enzo fell into a natural canyon formed by rainwater along the hillside. It's next to the grotto, but not part of it. We need to go through that doorway in the rock to find whatever Lazzaro Allegri left behind. You up for a little hike?"

Mahilan looked around and shook his head sadly. "Look at all the moisture and moss in the woods, JJ. I hope you're prepared for whatever you'll find. I don't know what will be left of any paintings."

"I've got a theory about that." An idea had been forming in my mind, based on what we'd learned in the museum of Lazzaro's observations of Indian art. Not about technique, as Lane and Stefano thought, but something far simpler. Something that had been in front of us this whole time.

I led the way back to Lazzaro's hidden grotto, wondering if I was right. The tips of my heels sank into the damp soil on the walk, but I didn't mind. My heels had saved me yet again.

"We're here," I said, pointing at the rock holding open the entrance.

I pulled my flashlight from my bag and led the way through the dark doorway that had opened in the rock. Shallow steps, carved from the rock itself, led downward, following the edge of the sloping hillside.

"This was made possible because of my memories of my past life?" Francesco asked, following behind us.

"About that—" I explained how Enzo had drugged him and planted the sketchbook. As we followed the steps down, I also apologized to Francesco for suspecting him, and on behalf of my brother for punching him. Mahilan wouldn't apologize himself, since he was still upset about his sore nose and black eye.

"Why did you run?" I asked, pausing as the ground leveled out.

"When three Americans believe you to be a murderer," Francesco said, "running seems a prudent course of action."

"You've read too many movie scripts," I said.

Francesco grimaced. "This is true."

"JJ," my brother whispered. "Look."

I no longer needed my flashlight. Natural light filtered through an opening from above. Treetops prevented much light from getting inside, but in the past it would have been even brighter.

Lane was probably right: no paintings could have survived in the open for all these centuries, no matter what the technique. But I still felt a tingling anticipation as I stood on the threshold of Lazzaro's hidden workshop. Could my theory be correct?

I took my brother's hand, and we stepped into a cavern cut into the hillside.

CHAPTER 59

Inside Lazzaro's hidden art studio, three stone monsters that rivaled those of the Park of Monsters greeted us. Only these weren't nearly as big, and they weren't made of bedrock from the area where they were carved. These were made of Italian marble.

These creatures explained why Lazzaro's sketches looked like the figures from Vicino Orsini's Park of Monsters, but drawn with creative license. They were Lazzaro's own interpretations of the mythological creatures that were all the rage in late-Renaissance Italy. Lazzaro's sketches were models for these sculptures he'd crafted in stone.

"Sculptures," Mahilan said. "Monster sculptures. I thought you said he made paintings. Not sculptures straight out of a Salvador Dalí painting."

The reason Lazzaro thought his artwork would survive was so simple it had been staring us in the face the whole time. Lazzaro Allegri's masterpieces weren't paintings. They were sculptures.

Michelangelo had thought of himself primarily as a sculptor and had to be convinced to paint the Sistine Chapel. References to Lazzaro being the next Michelangelo weren't based on his mediocre paintings, but on his promise as a sculptor. Because Lazzaro's first works had been paintings, we'd all assumed his "masterpieces" would be paintings too. But none of the original documents we'd studied said the word painting. "Artwork" and "masterpieces," yes, but not "painting."

And I couldn't forget "blasphemous." It was his studies of the

Sultan of Gujarat's court in India that had made his family want to hide his achievements. They relegated him to a far corner of their land. Unable to fully cut ties, they let him continue to create beautiful art through unsightly subjects, unsure of what to do with him.

"We all jumped to the wrong conclusion by thinking he was only a painter," I said. "It was stupid. I didn't question what I was told. But nothing in the original letters or notes says 'paintings.' Only 'art' or 'masterpieces.' Renaissance men worked in many mediums. The idea was that it was the message and the craftsmanship, not the materials, that made a piece of art."

Mahilan nodded and approached a figure that looked similar to the Ogre from the Park of Monsters, with wild eyes and a screaming mouth. The open mouth on the three-foot marble head didn't lead to hell. It led to a cozy square foot in which a bird had made its nest.

"Didn't you think he made art that depicted Bahadur Shah's royal court in India? Sorry, JJ. It turns out he's just another Italian sculptor."

"Just another—?" Francesco sputtered. I'd forgotten he was there.

"If you two punch each other again," I said, "I'm kicking you out of this cave."

Francesco crossed his arms. "You said I had read too many movie scripts. If it were not for my success in film, you would think this room was all there was. But I know there is always—"

"Another secret room!" Mahilan cried. His banged-up nose forgotten, his face transformed into that of an eager toddler. He spun around, searching.

"I already spotted it," I said, pointing. "Lazzaro would have needed somewhere to work when it was raining. It's behind that sphinx."

We stepped through to a covered section of the hillside cavern. In the center of the room, my flashlight bounced off of two tables, a chair, and stone-carving materials, all covered in moss and dust.

Behind the furniture stood a rough slab of marble with only a corner chiseled out. But along the far wall, five finished marble carvings stood in a line.

"*Ada-kadavulae*," a voice said from behind us. "It is like the Ajanta and Ellora caves of India, mixed with the royal court style of Persian miniature paintings, but with the Renaissance treatment of realism in the human body. May I borrow your flashlight, Jaya?"

Stefano Gopal squeezed my shoulder and pointed the flashlight at each of the figures. We stood in awe at a rendering of Bahadur Shah, Sultan of Gujarat, standing in marble in the center of four members of his court, just as he had been drawn in Lazzaro Allegri's sketchbooks. The muscles in the warrior's chest and arms were visible through the sculpted clothing.

There was nothing risqué or blasphemous about these figures. Unlike most Renaissance subjects, these weren't nudes. But the physical realism of the Renaissance was present in the formation of the bodies. At the time, Indian art was symbolic but vibrant in its storytelling. Lazzaro's sculptures captured elements of *both* styles.

Along the base of each of the figures was an army of miniature elephants, one of which held a miniature man in his trunk. I took the flashlight back from Stefano and looked more closely. A raven coat of arms was carved on the man's coat. Of course. The man being strangled by the elephant was Portuguese—the nation that had betrayed and killed Bahadur Shah.

"You've found it, Professor Jones," Stefano said. "You've found a connection never previously known to have existed. This is truly a treasure of art history."

CHAPTER 60

Six weeks later, I sat in my office and put the finishing touches on the paper I'd written about the discovery.

Enzo's cousin, the man who owned the Allegri land, had been horrified to learn of what Enzo had done. He and his wife came from their home in Rome to see their ancestor's hidden sculptures, and quickly understood the importance of Lazzaro's artwork. They loaned the sculptures to a museum for study while they decided on where they would end up. Based on her knowledge of Lazzaro Allegri's paintings in her small museum, Stefano Gopal's new curator girlfriend would be one of the people granted access to study the sculptures.

I was one of the scholars authorized to study the works of art as well. While Lane was in Portugal setting up a museum with his friend, and Sanjay was in France learning from Sébastien and making sure the old magician got back on his feet, I'd stayed on in Italy for another two weeks. It was a good thing I loved to run, because otherwise I would have outgrown all of my clothing due to my indulgence in the local cuisine.

I'd then traveled to India for two weeks to study the Sultan of Gujarat's royal court. What I found there brought my research full circle. In the archives of Bahadur Shah's court were records of Indian artists working with Lazzaro Allegri. They'd taught each other.

Now, sitting in my office and typing the last revisions into my paper, I felt a deep sense of contentment that I'd been able to give

Lilith Vine much of the credit for noticing a small reference in a paper by Wilson Meeks that turned out to be a clue to one of the biggest cross-cultural art history discoveries of the century. It wouldn't bring her back, but it would restore her legacy.

I was also at peace with the fact that I wasn't a scholar like Wilson Meeks, who'd been content to sit in a library and make small connections. But I also wasn't like Lilith Vine, who was pulled in every direction and let her obsession destroy her personal life, her health, and her scholarly integrity. I was my own person, following my intuition in addition to the academic roadmap laid out for me.

While reporters had written about the discovery and news magazines had run pseudo-scholarly articles on Lazzaro Allegri's artwork, I'd taken the time to understand the full context of his life and art, including the last piece of the puzzle: I found Lazzaro's connection to Michelangelo.

I'd gone down some blind alleys the last couple of weeks, while following up with scholars across the world from my home base of San Francisco, but I finally found what I was after. My paper didn't have to appear first. It was the one that revealed Lazzaro's secrets and that would stand the test of time.

"What are you smiling about?" Naveen stood in my office doorway. Even though it was summer break, my cutthroat colleague was dressed formally in one of his usual suits.

"I finished that paper I was working on," I said, closing my laptop. "I should celebrate. Can I buy you a cup of coffee?" With the satisfaction that comes from finishing something you've poured your soul into, I could be generous in my feelings towards Naveen. No sense being snarky and rubbing it in.

"I should buy *you* the coffee," he said.

"Why's that?" I stuffed the laptop into my bag and stood up.

"That interesting discovery Lilith Vine contacted us both about."

In my generous mood, I held my tongue instead of pointing out she'd only contacted him as a way to get in touch with me.

"It was such an interesting idea," he continued, "I did my own research and wrote my own paper on it."

I stared across the desk at him. "You—"

He leaned into the door frame and smiled. "It was published in an online journal this morning. You might like to read it. See what real scholarship is about."

I sat back down in my desk chair harder than I intended.

"Are you feeling all right?" he asked. "Maybe we should take a rain check on that coffee."

He couldn't have, could he? How did he get all the details to write a paper? My arms shook with anger as I opened my laptop. I found his article quickly. It was the front page article in a leading journal. I felt like I was going to be sick.

I was about to slam the computer shut when I saw his opening paragraph. I ran my hands through my hair, which had been tinted a dark brown by a month in the Tuscan and Indian sun, and let out a breath of relief.

Naveen had gotten it wrong. He was asserting that the supposed Michelangelo connection was fake. He'd written his article as if he was exposing a fraud.

I jumped to the citations at the end of the paper. Materials provided by Brunella Allegri were cited as one source. I shook my head. Poor Naveen. Brunella and I had become friends during my extended stay in Italy. She was bitter about Enzo, and was willing to take it out on any man she thought was lying to her. She'd heard me mention Naveen as a man who'd once tried to undermine me, so she must have remembered the name when he contacted her.

Naveen hadn't learned that the marble Lazzaro used for his sculptures was from the same quarry Michelangelo had used, he hadn't uncovered the fact that the two men had been there at the same time, and he hadn't made the final shocking discovery I'd unearthed.

Those old records led me to something far beyond what I expected: It was Michelangelo himself who'd helped Lazzaro set up his studio.

Michelangelo knew what it was like to be prevented from working on what he wanted to. It was his idea to make a secret entrance to Lazzaro's art studio. Michelangelo, who'd once hidden out in a secret room to avoid detection, had been the one with the skills to build the entrance disguised by a hydraulic lever. He wasn't the architect of the Park of Monsters, but because he'd visited, there were enough fragments in historical records to lead scholars to speculate about a connection. Lilith had jumped to the wrong connection, as had others, but her instincts had been right.

I thought about running to catch up with Naveen, but decided against it. He'd find out his error soon enough. As would the rest of the academic world.

Besides, I wanted to fit in a run before my dinner date. My brother was back in San Francisco. Not with Ava, but in town for a job interview at a boutique law firm.

I couldn't bring myself to break my brother's heart by telling him the truth about Ava. She'd told him she was staying with Carey while he recovered from his illness—which I knew to be fake—and would be spending the rest of summer break with him. He wouldn't be seeing her for a while, so I had time to figure out what to do.

I also had time to figure out what it meant to take charge of my own destiny. The summer was only halfway over. I wondered where it would lead me.

Lane had asked if I wanted to come visit him. Now that we knew Ava had faked her own death and there wasn't any looming danger from Lane's past, we no longer had to hide. But I'd declined the invitation to go back to Europe.

Sanjay had told me he'd be heading to England, once another young magician came to stay with Sébastien, to join a music tour with a musician friend of his. I wondered if Sanjay's pal Tjinder knew the true extent of his sitar-playing skills.

I'd declined Sanjay's offer to visit him as well. I didn't know what the future held, but for now, I was happy on my own.

After a run through Golden Gate Park, I met Mahilan at the Tandoori Palace.

"How'd the interview go?" I asked, joining him at the corner table. He'd already been seated and ordered us two Kingfisher beers. I was glad to see his nose had healed completely. "You can take your tie off now that it's just us."

"I *like* wearing a tie." He loosened it infinitesimally. "I fear San Francisco might be too informal for me. After running through Italian forests and being chased by insane noblemen, I feel the need for constancy."

"Don't order off the secret menu," I warned.

"Noted. What's up with you telling me Sanjay couldn't play the sitar? While I was waiting for you, Juan was telling me he plays badly only when you're around."

"That can't be right."

"For a brilliant little sister, you can be surprisingly obtuse."

"Who uses the word 'obtuse' in conversation? It's just me on the tabla for a while anyway." I looked over that week's secret menu. "I'm on my own here at the restaurant, and in every way."

"I take exception to that statement," Mahilan said.

"You're right." I raised my glass and clinked it against my brother's. "It's you and me against the world, Fish."

"Like old times, JJ. So when do I get to read this paper of yours?"

"Soon."

"What's the holdup? I thought you'd finished your research."

"I have. I'm done writing it too. But I haven't come up with a title."

"That's easy," Mahilan said.

"It is?"

"The key piece of history that tied everything together was the hydraulic sculpture that kept Lazzaro's studio secret for centuries. You figured out that Michelangelo designed it, but after he and Lazzaro died it wasn't tended and was mistaken for a ghost. That makes it—"

"Michelangelo's Ghost."

AUTHOR'S NOTE

The modern-day characters in *Michelangelo's Ghost* are fictional, but the historical figures aside from the Allegri family are real, as is the Park of Monsters.

The Park of Monsters is a Renaissance sculpture garden in Italy that exists as I describe it. It's off the beaten path, but it's worth a day trip if you find yourself traveling to Rome or Florence. The surrounding area is similar to what I describe in the book, but I changed the names and details of the villa, restaurants, and wineries.

Pier Francesco "Vicino" Orsini is the true historical figure who conceived of the macabre park, but scholars disagree about his motives. Many historical "facts" contradict each other, but the history Jaya unearths is as accurate as history has recorded—except for Vicino's friendship with the fictional character of Lazzaro Allegri. Lazzaro and his Allegri relatives, including the ghosts, are fictional.

Michelangelo is, of course, real. And yes, there is a theory asserting it was Michelangelo, not Pirro Ligorio, who was the true architect of the Park of Monsters. Is it possible this is true? The dates fit, as does the location. Michelangelo spent time at a nearby marble quarry. However, it's unlikely there wouldn't be more historical evidence if it were the case (and unlikely that Michelangelo wouldn't have taken credit for it). Yet at the same time, the more historical research I undertake for my novels, the more I've come to realize that history is far more complicated than what's presented in school textbooks.

One of the aspects of history that fascinates me most is the world travel that happened long before travel became as easy as it is today. Explorers, missionaries, traders, artists, servants, and slaves have visited and learned from other cultures for millennia. Some of that history has been recorded, but much of it is still being pieced together. There's not much recorded history about what Indian and European artists learned from each other during the Renaissance, but with the other ideas being shared between those cultures at the time, why not art? Bahadur Shah of Gujarat was a patron of the arts before he was killed by the Portuguese.

The rediscovery of the Park of Monsters is nearly as fascinating as the park itself. The park was opened to the public in 1552, but after Vicino Orsini's death in 1585 his labyrinthine sculpture garden fell into disrepair. Before visiting, I couldn't imagine how that had happened, but after seeing the feral forest surrounding it I came to understand how nature could easily take over. It wasn't until a century ago that people again stumbled upon it and thought it worthwhile to clear away centuries of overgrowth. Salvador Dalí was one of the people involved in doing so, and the otherworldly sculpture garden has inspired many artists, poets, and filmmakers. In 1954, four hundred years after it first opened, the park was bought by Giovanni Bettini and restored for the public.

I don't want to say too much about the solution of the mystery at the Park of Monsters in *Michelangelo's Ghost*, in case you're reading this note before finishing the book, but I can say this: The details of the explanation are historically accurate.

Like the treasures in my other novels, this one is fictional but based in very real history, making it possible that something quite similar is out there, waiting to be found...

GIGI PANDIAN

USA Today bestselling author Gigi Pandian is the child of cultural anthropologists from New Mexico and the southern tip of India. She spent her childhood being dragged around the world, and now lives in the San Francisco Bay Area. Gigi writes the Jaya Jones Treasure Hunt mysteries, the Accidental Alchemist mysteries, and locked-room mystery short stories. Gigi's fiction has been awarded the Malice Domestic Grant and Lefty Awards, and been nominated for Macavity and Agatha Awards. Find her online at www.gigipandian.com.

**The Jaya Jones Treasure Hunt Mystery Series
by Gigi Pandian**

Novels

ARTIFACT (#1)
PIRATE VISHNU (#2)
QUICKSAND (#3)
MICHELANGELO'S GHOST (#4)

Novellas

FOOL'S GOLD (prequel to ARTIFACT)
(in OTHER PEOPLE'S BAGGAGE)

Henery Press Mystery Books

And finally, before you go...
Here are a few other mysteries
you might enjoy:

MURDER IN G MAJOR

Alexia Gordon

A Gethsemane Brown Mystery (#1)

With few other options, African-American classical musician Gethsemane Brown accepts a less-than-ideal position turning a group of rowdy schoolboys into an award-winning orchestra. Stranded without luggage or money in the Irish countryside, she figures any job is better than none. The perk? Housesitting a lovely cliffside cottage. The catch? The ghost of the cottage's murdered owner haunts the place. Falsely accused of killing his wife (and himself), he begs Gethsemane to clear his name so he can rest in peace.

Gethsemane's reluctant investigation provokes a dormant killer and she soon finds herself in grave danger. As Gethsemane races to prevent a deadly encore, will she uncover the truth or star in her own farewell performance?

Available at booksellers nationwide and online

Visit www.henerypress.com for details

PRACTICAL SINS
FOR COLD CLIMATES

Shelley Costa

A Val Cameron Mystery (#1)

When Val Cameron, a Senior Editor with a New York publishing company, is sent to the Canadian Northwoods to sign a reclusive bestselling author to a contract, she soon discovers she is definitely out of her element. Val is convinced she can persuade the author of that blockbuster, The Nebula Covenant, to sign with her, but first she has to find him.

Aided by a float plane pilot whose wife was murdered two years ago in a case gone cold, Val's hunt for the recluse takes on new meaning: can she clear him of suspicion in that murder before she links her own professional fortunes to the publication of his new book?

When she finds herself thrown into a wilderness lake community where livelihoods collide, Val wonders whether the prospect of running into a bear might be the least of her problems.

Available at booksellers nationwide and online

Visit www.henerypress.com for details

THE SEMESTER OF OUR DISCONTENT

Cynthia Kuhn

A Lila Maclean Mystery (#1)

English professor Lila Maclean is thrilled about her new job at prestigious Stonedale University, until she finds one of her colleagues dead. She soon learns that everyone, from the chancellor to the detective working the case, believes Lila—or someone she is protecting—may be responsible for the horrific event, so she assigns herself the task of identifying the killer.

More attacks on professors follow, the only connection a curious symbol at each of the crime scenes. Putting her scholarly skills to the test, Lila gathers evidence, but her search is complicated by an unexpected nemesis, a suspicious investigator, and an ominous secret society. Rather than earning an "A" for effort, she receives a threat featuring the mysterious emblem and must act quickly to avoid failing her assignment...and becoming the next victim.

Available at booksellers nationwide and online

Visit www.henerypress.com for details